Learn Me Goodest

Learn Me Goodest is available online at Amazon (print and Kindle), Barnes and Noble (print and Nook), the iPad store, and smashwords.

I invite you to follow me on any or all of the following internet media:

Blog – http://www.learnmegood.com
Facebook – http://www.facebook.com/learnmegood
Twitter – @learnmegood
Email – learnmegood2@yahoo.com

All rights reserved. No part of this book may be reproduced in any form, or by any electronic, or mechanical means, including information storage and retrieval systems, to include, but not exclusive to audio or visual recordings of any description without permission from the copyright owner.

Copyright © 2018 by John Pearson. All rights reserved.

ISBN-13: 978-1719315586
ISBN-10: 1719315582

This one is for my parents, who have always been there for me

Introduction

They say good things come in threes. I'd like to believe that is true as I at long last publish the third Learn Me Good book, the goodest of them all. With any luck, the Jack Woodson saga will now enter the holy pantheon of revered trilogies like The Lord of the Rings, Back to the Future, and Beverly Hills Chihuahua.

There never would have been a second book, much less a third, if people hadn't been interested. So I say to you, the reader, thank you! No, not just for not skipping over the introduction, but thank you for reading my book(s)! It means a tremendous amount to me that anyone would read what I've written, and I am deeply appreciative. I continue to be amazed at the popularity of the first two Learn Me Good books, as people seem to enjoy reading them as much as I've enjoyed writing them.

So let's move on to the recap. Here's the part where you imagine the next few paragraphs scrolling upwards on a big screen, with a thrilling John Williams score playing.

Jack Woodson has left his engineering job and become a grade school math teacher. Overwhelmed at first, he gradually gains his bearings and learns to thrive in the test-heavy, common-sense-light environment. His first year ended on a high note.

Eleven years have passed. Now married to Jill, a fellow teacher, Jack enters the new school year an experienced veteran with proven lessons to call upon, a tried and true system of classroom management, and a trained ear for recognizing bogus homework excuses.

As anyone who personally knows me could tell you, Jack Woodson, by and large, truly is me, only with slightly better self-control. We both went to Duke, we both love ketchup, and we both have a wry, sarcastic sense of humor that sometimes gets us into trouble. This time around, though, there are some pretty major differences between John Pearson the author and Jack Woodson the character. For one thing, Jack does not travel out to Los Angeles to appear on Jeopardy! in this book. I won the 2013 Jeopardy! Teachers Tournament and lost to the eventual champ in the next year's Tournament of Champions. It was an amazing experience, but it would not have fit well into Learn Me Goodest. In that vein of thought, though, I have no doubt that Jack absolutely knows that the state of Alaska celebrates Seward's Day, whereas I, clearly, did not.

The biggest difference between us, of course, is that Jack Woodson will be a teacher until he dies, whereas I myself have left the education field. Money and the needs of a growing family were my chief reasons for changing careers, and while Jack faces those same issues, he doesn't have to suffer the consequences. So though Learn Me Goodest is most probably the last written chapter in Jack Woodson's life, we can safely imagine him instructing youngsters until retirement age. Or at least until the district outlaws jokes about Uranus.

I do want to take just a bit of space to address some comments and reviews I've seen regarding my books on major book-selling websites. Most of the reviews have been very positive, even the ones not written by my mother, so that makes me really happy. I can appreciate most of the not so positive ones as well, because humor is a very subjective thing, and not everybody is going to find everything funny. Case in point, I can't stand the Austin Powers movies, Napoleon Dynamite, or British claymation shorts.

However, there have been a few reviews that claim the books are terrible because I just took a bunch of old emails from the past and slapped them together in a book without any editing at all. I think my response to those claims can best be summed up by a quote from Luke Skywalker in The Last Jedi – "Amazing. Every word of what you just said was wrong."

Just to reiterate, these emails were never written or sent in the past. They are completely made up as a framework for telling the school stories. If I am ever under investigation by the FBI (Heaven forbid!) and they confiscate my computer, they will find an unusually large number of my friends' photoshopped heads on movie monster bodies, but absolutely no emails to Fred Bommerson about Marvin, Esteban, and the rest of the kids.

Furthermore, I take great offense to the suggestion that I didn't do any editing at all. If anything, I have been obsessive in my edits and revisions. This is not to say that the keen-eyed reader won't find a misspelled word, a misplaced comma, or a dangling participle (how embarrassing!), but I have done at least seven revisions on each book in the trilogy, striving for the best storytelling and flow.

But hey, if you're reading this book, it probably means you liked the first two, so I'll stop justifying my writing process! It's unlikely that anyone who hated Learn Me Good would be reading the third in the series – unless they're like me with the television series Smallville, noting it getting progressively worse and worse but continuing to watch with the thought, "It's almost unwatchable, but I've invested this much time in it; I need to see it through to the bitter end."

All right, it's time to wrap it up. As with the others, Learn Me Goodest is based on a true story, which means there really and truly were some kids at a school one time who had a male teacher. I'll do even better than that and say that most of the stories involving kids did happen during my teaching days, though names have been changed, some events have been embellished, and many more mythical creatures were inserted into the narrative.

Major thanks to my friends and family for supporting me and helping me complete this book. Special thanks to Xavier Rodriguez for letting me use his classroom once again for the cover photo and to Carley Barnes for putting the final cover artwork together.

And thank YOU, kind reader! Thanks for reading, thank you for recommending my books to friends and family, thank you for writing genuine reviews, and thank you for corresponding with me through Facebook and email. And a very special thank you to anyone who can get a copy of Learn Me Goodest into the hands of Evangeline Lilly or Jennifer Garner. I would be in your debt for life.

John Pearson   March, 2018

Date: Monday, August 25, 2014
To: Fred Bommerson
From: Jack Woodson
Subject: Grand reopening – All math half off!

Howdy, Fred!

Is it just me, or has it been a really long day? I suppose it was just another Monday for you there at good ol' Heat Pumps University – Go, Fighting Elements! – but today marked the first day of my TWELFTH year of teaching! Can you believe that I'm one-twelfth of the way towards being a gross teacher?

Is it too early in the year for bad math jokes?

For the past two weeks, I've been setting up my classroom, prepping my lesson plans, and attending staff development meetings. It hasn't been easy getting back into the swing of things. I think whoever said, "All good things must come to an end" had to have been a teacher, depressed in late August.

But here we are again, and as the mighty warrior-teachers of yore used to say, I'm ready to grab the bull by the golden eggs. Today was an auspicious beginning, and I am exhausted. As usual, falling asleep last night was about as easy as finding a decent hamburger joint in India, and when I did finally drift off, I dreamt of classroom doors that wouldn't open, textbooks that had blank pages, and faculty meetings that had no point. At least I did get to sleep in a little later than Jill. You'll recall I wanted to modify part of our wedding vows to say, "In good times and in bad, in sickness and in health, in long commutes to school and in short…"

She wouldn't let me add that part then, and just between you and me, she's not too happy about it now either. Her drive to school takes almost 40 minutes while mine is a mere 15 minutes away. I rolled out of bed this morning a few minutes after she left for her school. After she left unnecessarily loudly, I might add.

Our principal, Mrs. Forest, decided about a month ago that Mr. Redd and I should swap spots, so I'll be teaching fourth grade this year. Her reasoning was, "Because you're both excellent math teachers and will be able to really help your new grade level."

Sounds legit. And before you ask, no, I will not have the same kids I had last year, the ones I've gotten to know and who know me. They'll be nearby, in Mr. Utoobay's and Mrs. Karras's homerooms, so I'll see them often enough. But in yet another decision I can't comprehend, Mrs. Forest chose to give me the kids from last year's other sections, because, you know, management.

Before the school day began this morning, Mr. Vann and I held down our usual spots out in front, supervising the carpool drop-offs. There seemed to be an unusual number of near-collisions, rude gestures, and jackrabbit takeoffs, but that's probably just because it was the first day of school. I have no doubt that as we progress a few months into the school year and everyone grows more used to the procedures, that number will rise.

Speaking of rude gestures, the people who live in the house directly across the street from the school decided to turn on their lawn sprinklers at precisely the moment the first cars pulled up to the curb. Kids who were dropped off on their side had the pleasure of walking into school with wet pants, as did I, since I frequently had to go to the other side to help kids cross the street. The whole time we were out there, the owners stood behind their glass storm door, watching. I didn't pay much attention to them, but I'm sure they were rubbing their hands together gleefully and slapping high fives whenever a kid was splashed.

At 7:45, I headed inside to pick up my students. After a battle royale worthy of the Hunger Games took place in the gym, my homeroom was whittled down to 20 kids, and I brought them upstairs to my classroom. The fourth grade hall is directly above the third grade hall, so now I'll be on the giving end of the ceiling-shaking dance parties. The classroom is identical to the one I had last year, and for that matter, identical to all of the other classrooms in this wing. Except that it's not on the ground floor, which apparently makes a huge psychological difference with children.

Two kids immediately ran to the windows and began ecstatically describing the view. My room overlooks the basketball court and beyond that, the faculty parking lot. It's a pretty spartan view, but from the way these kids were acting, you would have thought they were atop the Eiffel Tower. Of course, their jubilation caused most of the other kids to rush to the windows as well. Some joined in on the delight, while some took a peek and then glanced at their classmates to see if something was wrong with them. One girl rolled her eyes and said, "It's the playground. Whoop."

I think I'm going to like Marina.

As in years past, I let the kids choose their own seats on the first day. This always gives me an eerily accurate picture of whom should NOT sit next to whom once I make up the actual seating chart. When Mrs. Bird and I (she moved up to 4th grade with me – YAY!) switched classes a little before noon, two of her girls – Kirstie and Tracy Jane – walked into my room with their arms draped over each others' shoulders. They sat down together and proceeded to chat every opportunity they got. They'll have a great time together during recess, I'm sure, but in a few days, I will be placing them on opposite ends of the classroom.

We didn't do anything academically rigorous today (don't tell anyone), but I gave my standard expectations speech, this time with a Liam Neeson twist:

"What I do have is a very particular set of skills, skills I have acquired over a very long teaching career. Skills that make me a nightmare for people who don't do their homework."

Only time will tell how effective that speech really was. After that was out of the way, we had a fun "Get to know me" icebreaker activity where I gave a pop quiz with questions all about me. When I spoke the words "pop quiz," some kids started to panic, and one kid named Eld'Ridge inexplicably looked towards the window like he was thinking of escaping the room that way. But once I explained that I didn't really expect them to know most (or any) of the answers, they had fun with it.

My first question was, "What is my middle name?"

The best (and wrongest) answers were "Woodson," "Teacher," and "Math."

Fun fact: my father claims he never considered naming me Jack Math Woodson, because he never liked math in school. However, my mom did have to talk him out of "Intro to Circuitry" as my middle name. True story.

For the question, "What job did I have before I was a teacher?" my favorite guesses were "Ice cream truck worker," "Walmart cashier," and "Pizza boy."

Question 5, the final question, was by far the toughest, but I wanted to give the kids a little insight into one of my greatest passions. I asked the kids to spell the complete last name of Duke basketball's Coach K. I'll pose that same question to you, Fred, and see how close you get. The answer will be in my next email, but until then, no Googling!

After the pop quiz about me, I gave the kids a little bit of time to write some questions about themselves then turned them loose to share with their classmates.

Listening in on the kids' conversations gave me a treasure trove of potential questions to ask in next year's pop quiz, including,

"What color is my toothbrush?" "Am I allergic to cheese?" and, "What are the names of my 11 pets?"

For the school as a whole, the really big event from today was that part of the cafeteria roof collapsed! It happened during first grade lunch, around 11:00. A 10' x 10' section of the ceiling fell, narrowly missing a few kids. No one is sure what caused it, though popular theories include gas leak, water buildup, and the devious ghost of the school's namesake.

The school's namesake is actually still alive, but let's not worry about that right now.

Having part of the ceiling fall was a scary event, and I sure am glad it missed those children. Nobody's last meal should be stale pizza rolls and a patty of some potato-like substance.
Talk to you later,

Matt Mattix

Date: Thursday, August 28, 2014
To: Fred Bommerson
From: Jack Woodson
Subject: Over 1 Bajillion Served

Hey bud,

I applaud your effort, but Coach K's name is actually spelled K-R-Z-Y-Z-E-W-S-K-I. Don't feel bad, at least you had the correct first letter. No matter how many times I emphasized his name as Coach "K", my young ward Eld'Ridge insisted on beginning with an X. Good luck in Language Arts this year, Mrs. Bird!

I suppose I can't hold kids too accountable for their spelling when the state of Texas can't even spell the word "star" correctly. Our 4th graders will take three standardized tests this year – math, reading, and writing – and they're all part of the STAAR test system. I'd love to meet the genius who decided the acronym needed one more A in it.

"Hey guys, the extra A is for Awesomesauce!"

The prior test name – TAKS – was pretty easy to say, but I refuse to simply call this new test the "Star." In my mind, there are only two acceptable ways to pronounce STAAR. My pronunciation of choice is to go full Forest Gump and make it two syllables, as in, "I'm not a smart man, Jen-nay, but I gotta take the STA-AR!"

Option two doesn't win a lot of love from my female colleagues, but it never fails to crack up Mr. Redd and Mr. Utoobay. It involves channeling your inner Captain Kirk at his angriest, shaking a fist at the sky, and bellowing, "STAAAAAAAAAAAAA-AAAAAR!!!"

The big tests are in the future, though, as we always begin the year with the relatively simple concept of place value. Fourth grade goes up to the billions place now, so this gives me the opportunity to reaffirm that no one appreciates my Carl Sagan impersonation.

Making place value tables to see where each digit goes is an important skill, but so is being able to read and write a multi-digit number in word form. There are always some kids who (at first) want to read a large number by just calling out the digits one at a time. They read the number 42,719 out loud as four-two-seven-one-nine. No "thousand," or "hundred," or even "forty-two." I always have to remind a few kids we're not reading a phone number. Just to amuse myself today, though, my first example number was

8,675,309. When Carmine inevitably read it one digit at a time, I said, "Jenny, I got your number! For a good time call!"

I may get some phone calls myself.

As is always the case, I'll have my work cut out for me with some of these kids, but I know a gifted student looking for a lesson extension when I see one. Not satisfied with the millions and billions we explored, Akasha proudly told me she knew about trillions and quadrillions but was wondering if there was a gazillions family. "Sure," I told her. "It comes right after the bajillions."

Akasha smiled knowingly and laughed. Hey, someone who gets my humor! This is going to be fun!

Not everyone understands me, though. Take Alvaro, for example. Alvaro is a little muppet in Mrs. Bird's class. Now when I say he's a muppet, I'm not suggesting that he's made of felt or that somebody's hand is up his butt. He just really reminds me of Dr. Bunsen Honeydew with more hair and a slightly more human flesh tone. He has a perfectly round head and a wide mouth that seems to be perpetually open. He also wears an expression of wide-eyed surprise most of the time. Yesterday when I asked the kids to take out their science books, Alvaro very loudly and confusedly said, "Science?"

This afternoon, I didn't realize I had a small hole in my shirt until Alvaro pointed it out to me. I thanked him for bringing it to my attention, and I mentioned that I sometimes wore this shirt to church.

When Alvaro looked at me in surprise, I added, "Because it's my hole-y shirt."

When he continued to look at me in surprise, I thought to myself, Akasha would have appreciated my joke. Fozzy Bear probably would have, as well.

I know it's only the first week of school, but still the kids have been very slow to complete any work these few days. I finally had a little pep talk with them today. I commiserated with them, saying that vacation was great, but it's over now, so it's time to break out of summer mode and get back into school mode. At the end of the day, Rajiv came up to me in tears. When I asked what was wrong, he sobbed, "I think I'm still in summer mode, and I don't know how to snap out of it!"

I assured him that acknowledging the problem was a definite first step on the right path.

I'm worried I have a multitude of kids who are perfectly content to stay locked into summer mode for the foreseeable future.

On the plus side, I'm really getting to see just how good of a math teacher Mrs. Fitzgerald is, since I now have most of her kids from last year, and student performance at the beginning of a new school year is always a direct reflection on the previous teacher.

Just kidding! Jill actually ran in here as I was typing that last sentence to see why I was laughing so maniacally. In reality, student brains are like beach balls with a slow leak, and summer vacation tends to leave them completely deflated. I certainly can't give Mrs. Fitzgerald a hard time about it when Mr. Utoobay, who has my kids from last year across the hall, comes over to ask why ten kids are writing their place value charts backwards. Or why one of my prize pupils is still referring to the "Horrid Thousands Place."

Oh well, this is why we teach, then reteach, then re-reteach. In some of my education classes, I heard that kids need to hear something eight times before they can remember it. With some of these kids it might be closer to a bajillion.

Talk to you later,

Placedo Value Domingo

Date: Wednesday, September 3, 2014
To: Fred Bommerson
From: Jack Woodson
Subject: Wednesday's child is full of glue

Hey man,

I certainly hope your work emails are not monitored, because comparing upper management – particularly Reggie – to a muppet could get you in serious trouble. It doesn't matter how incredibly accurate the comparison to Sam the Eagle may be. Also, before I forget, congratulations on your latest sales achievement. One bajillion heat pumps is quite the accomplishment, and don't let anyone tell you otherwise.

Apparently, Mrs. Forest feels that we all are in sore need of motivation after only one week of school. She's been attaching the starfish story to the bottom of every email, and she even printed an individual copy for each teacher. You know the starfish story, right? A guy on the beach is throwing starfish back into the ocean, and someone asks him why he bothers, since there are a million of them on the beach – far too many for one guy to ever save. The guy solemnly responds that he is having a positive impact on each starfish he actually does put back in the water.

I'm not exactly sure why my principal wants me to start throwing students into the ocean, but I'm game, I guess.

To answer an earlier question, no, I'm going to have to use a different incentive for good behavior this year. The leftover M&Ms from my wedding worked great last year when they were relatively fresh. But now I would feel downright guilty handing out candy with "July 2, 2013" stamped on it. Come to think of it, those M&Ms might come in handy when we get to the elapsed time lesson later in the year.

Speaking of elapsed time, or at least relapse time, I hope you had a nice three-day Labor Day weekend. I had my fantasy football draft Saturday, then Jill and I just relaxed and were lazy the rest of the time. Jill has a pretty rambunctious group of second graders this year, and she keeps asking if I want to trade kids.

Long weekends are always a treat, but the short week that follows always seems extra hectic. Maybe I'm just saying that because I've never witnessed a kid put a glue stick up his nose during a five-day week.

Yes, Cesar somehow inserted a glue stick into his left nostril this morning. I'll leave it to others to express shock at his motive; I'm in awe of the logistics. I don't know that I could fit a Sharpie into my nostril, and that's barely half the diameter of a glue stick. Each of Cesar's nostrils must be wider than my entire nose! I suppose it's possible he's spent much of his life widening them by inserting progressively larger items, much like those guys with hoops in their earlobes, but that would imply he's actually put some concerted effort into something. Ironically, this odd act registers as the most work Cesar has put into anything so far this school year. I know we've only been in class for a little over a week, but Cesar has yet to complete a single morning's warm-up problem, he hasn't done any homework for me or Mrs. Bird, and most days I break a sweat just trying to motivate him to take a pencil out of his bag. He and Ja'Kendrick in Mrs. Bird's class seem to be content to just occupy a desk for the required hours every day without picking up any knowledge.

One thing Cesar absolutely does not skimp on is breakfast, though. The kid has been tardy every day since last Monday, and he walks in every morning carrying a paper bag with a sausage roll or a couple of donut holes. The size of the bags imply he's already eaten much more. According to Mrs. Frisch, during Career Day last year, Cesar told her he wanted to be a heart doctor. With the way he's going, he'll be his own most frequent patient.

At any rate, Cesar didn't seem bothered by this morning's nasal intrusion. He was grinning madly and trying to get everyone to see his special trick. He caught our attention, all right. He also earned a free glue stick, because I sure as heck wasn't going to let him put it back into the community supply!

I suspect Cesar hatched his plan based on yesterday's discussion in science class. We were talking about safe and unsafe practices, debating the merits of wearing safety goggles, covering cuts, and not rollerblading with scissors. One scenario that I presented for discussion was a boy getting some unknown chemicals on his hand then rubbing his nose. Most of the comments from the kids were along the lines of, "His nose could burn," or, "He might lose his sense of smell," or, "His nose might explode."

All very valid comments. But I definitely heard Gavin say, "Or he COULD get superpowers!"

So good luck, Cesar! Maybe you'll come to school next week with the ability to fly or turn invisible. More than likely, though, you've just gained the ability to snort hotdogs.

Other kids have shown a bit more practicality in science-related matters. I had them working in groups to make thought webs illustrating answers to the question, "What do scientists do?" Their webs included thoughts and phrases such as, "Discover dinosaur eggs," "Make experiments," and "Study electricity."

I did have one slightly disturbing response. Olivia wrote "Discover dead bodies."

There's someone who has clearly been watching too much CSI.

Veena's thought web contained the most bizarre answer of the day – "They did the spray that smells good."

I'm guessing she meant perfume, maybe? I'll put Cesar right on it. With his new super powers, I'm sure he'll be able to sniff out the answer in no time.
Talk to you later,

Sugar Spray Leonard

Date: Friday, September 5, 2014
To: Fred Bommerson
From: Jack Woodson
Subject: The Best Little Mathhouse in Texas

What's up, Fred?
    Where on earth are you planning on finding a radioactive tiger? Myself, I've pretty well given up on the dream of ever having super powers. I'm definitely not going to get any by shoving stuff up my nose. Though I'll admit, whenever there's an early morning electrical storm, I do always say a little prayer before stepping into the shower.

"Please, God, let me not get struck by lightning. Unless I'd get super speed like The Flash, and in that case, fry me good!"

    I also want to make a very clear distinction here… Yes, Larry certainly "did the spray," and he did it quite often. But he's no scientist, because Veena clearly stated scientists did the spray that smells GOOD.
    Maybe some scientists can come in and figure out why my room is so darn cold. Seriously, I teach in a meat locker this year. The temperature differential between my room and the rest of the upstairs has got to be at least 15 degrees. Other teachers walk into my room and immediately ask if they're about to experience a ghost sighting.
    Personally, I like it. It's so much better than sweltering in a warm, stuffy room. Plus it allows me to more accurately say, "Math is cool!"
    The kids complain about it every day (the temperature AND my jokes), but many of them have started bringing a sweater or a jacket, knowing what to expect. Not everyone, though. This morning when I saw a few short-sleeved kids shivering, I felt compelled to ask, "You've all been here for nine days now; how long is it going to take before you recognize this is a cold room and come prepared?"
    Eld'Ridge immediately replied, "About 100 days?"
    I'm a little worried about my kids' thinking skills this year.
    There are other causes for concern as well. Through no encouragement from me, my students have ventured out of G-rated territory. You're familiar with a Venn diagram, right? Two overlapping circles, used for comparing things? I had the kids compare

addition and subtraction today, and I learned there is a right way to draw a Venn diagram and a disturbingly wrong way to draw one.

It's hard to go wrong if you just draw two circles (or rectangles) and let them overlap, as long as those two shapes create the intersecting space in the middle. The problem arises when you actually draw a separate central element on the diagram, especially if that third piece of the Venn is a long skinny oval that protrudes from the bottom of the picture.

Beto's Venn diagram looked decidedly X-rated, though to his credit, it did display correct information about plus and minus inscribed on "the junk." Beto seemed blissfully unaware of the nature of his work, but when it came time for partner sharing, I invited him over to share with me instead of one of the other students.

I showed Mr. Utoobay later, and he quipped, "Looks like someone's been taking their Venn-agra!"

If only Beto's Venn diagram was an isolated example. It's not just happening in my class, though. Mrs. Bird told me she had the kids writing summaries of a classic fairytale, and at least four kids left off the ending letters of the main character's name. We can probably chalk this up to laziness or sloppiness, but it changes the whole story when Granny's basket of goodies is being delivered by Little Red Riding Ho.

The Big Bad Wolf's motive does seem a lot clearer in this version, though.

At the risk of having you call the cops on me and my morally depraved classroom, let me share one other related story. My warm-up activity the other day was completing paired pattern tables. I wrote one with "number of pentagons" on the left and "sides" on the right. Another table had "chairs" and "legs" as its labels. The kids needed to find the rule and fill in the missing numbers for each table. When they were finished, the next step was to create their own table.

Some of the student-generated tables were great – "comic books and pages," "quarters and cents," and "loaves of bread and slices." Some were a bit inconsistent or random – "dogs and televisions," "boys and roses," and "cookies and vampires."

Then there was one that was well-intentioned but grossly misspelled. Blanca clearly envisioned a table that showed how many wheels any number of wagons would have, with the assumption that each wagon had four wheels. She spelled wheels correctly. However, "wagons" somehow became "wangs."

Her spelling was atrocious, but her quantitative skills were sound. She chose to use big numbers on her table, and I had to give her credit for saying there would be 104 wheels on 26 wangs.

Needless to say, the Little Red Riding Ho summaries, Blanca's wangs, and Beto's dangling Venn diagram will not be going up on the student work bulletin board this week. We don't need the fourth grade hallway to be the MOMA of the elementary school.
Talk to you later,

Wang Chung

Date: Monday, September 8, 2014
To: Fred Bommerson
From: Jack Woodson
Subject: I like to do drawrings

Hey buddy,

I have to say, it's highly unusual to be barely into the third week of school and already have a full moon. Yet there it was, first thing this morning. A first grader fell down in front of me, and his lack of belt, underwear, and dignity all added up to a big shiny butt sighting. Some things you just can't unsee. Mrs. Bird was nearby at the time, and she and I exchanged a look that said, "It's going to be one of those years."

Something else I'm not going to be able to unsee is the grotesquely bulging Venn diagram Tom Winter emailed where he compared wagons and wangs. Someone clearly had a lot of free time and access to an unmonitored computer over the weekend.

Thanks for your helpful suggestion regarding my cold room situation, but I looked in the phone book and couldn't find any listing for "Little Red Riding Ho Air Conditioning Repair." I'd love to see a picture of her business card, though.

On the topic of pictures, I found a drawing today that one of my students had made in art class. It included the title, "What can we do to make the world a better place?" The number one bullet point, in big block letters, was "RECYCLE."

Ironically, I found this particular piece of artwork in the trashcan, located approximately 1.5 inches from my ginormous, impossible to miss, plastic recycling bucket.

I have always been a big stickler for having kids draw a picture when doing math problems, especially word problems. A picture helps you see what is really happening in the story and can show you which operation you should use to solve it. Convincing the kids to draw a picture is often a major struggle, though. That step tends to fall through the cracks, and while I'll admit it's not mandatory, I highly encourage it.

Some of my kids this year clearly don't yet comprehend the true point of drawing a picture. Jeauxsifeen, for instance, really wants to please me and tries her best to follow directions and use strategies. She always draws a picture when doing word problems. Her pictures are beautifully drawn, fully illustrating every detail mentioned in the story. We're talking art that rivals Michelangelo's

Sistine Chapel ceiling. Unfortunately, her pictures don't illustrate the math of the problem.

Last week, I gave the kids a problem where Matthew had 23 books and Laura had 25, and I asked how many books they had altogether. When we do problems like this together, I draw a circle to represent each child and I put the numbers inside their respective circles. I then draw a big circle around the two smaller circles to show a joining or addition. Nothing outlandish.

That's not the strategy Jeauxsifeen went with, though. She drew two fully articulated kids draped in the finest of raiment, standing in front of bookshelves, with a field of waving grain visible just outside the ornately decorated window. If you looked really closely, you could see titles and detailed pictures on the cover of each of Matthew and Laura's 48 books.

Then there's Lewith, who merely illustrates an equation. We've done many, many examples of mathematical drawings in class, and I know Mrs. Fitzgerald did last year as well. One of the guidelines is that operation signs should not be a part of the drawing. If you have five boxes, and each box has a nine in it, it's clear to see that you've illustrated 5 x 9. Lewith, however, chooses to draw a big bubble five, a wavy times sign, and a big bubble nine. Sometimes there are "action lines" coming off of the times sign, I guess to show how exciting the multiplication is as it's happening.

While it's not yet what I'm looking for, at least Lewith and Jeauxsifeen draw pictures that do relate somehow to the problem at hand. Tracy Jane draws images that have absolutely nothing to do with the problem. Earlier in the year, she drew smiley faces or cute little kittens for most problems. After I spoke with her about making the pictures show what was really happening, she changed her approach. Now, it's not uncommon at all to see a picture of a little girl sitting at a desk (sometimes labeled with the name "Tracy Jane" and an arrow pointing at the girl) working on a piece of paper. There might even be a speech bubble coming from the girl that says, "Math is fun!"

We had a near breakthrough recently. Last week, there was a problem that read, "The city of Austin sends seven trucks to pick up 63 tons of trash every Monday. If each truck picks up an equal amount of trash, how many tons will get picked up by one truck?"

I watched as Tracy Jane drew a picture of seven trash trucks, which I thought was a great start. All that was needed to finish the drawing would be the number 63 up at the top, with arrows showing that this number was being split amongst the seven trucks. Instead, she drew two men in hard hats approaching the trucks – presumably to collect and sort the trash. She finished her masterpiece with the requisite stink lines emanating from the fetid trash trucks. Her drawing featured no numbers at all.

Ah well, back to the drawing board, if you'll pardon the pun. Maybe I'll write a few sample problems to give my kids the chance to showcase their ability to draw a full moon.
Talk to you later,

Word Problo Picasso

Date: Thursday, September 11, 2014
To: Fred Bommerson
From: Jack Woodson
Subject: All I really need to know I learned in horror movies

Howdy pardner!

    I'm saddened to hear you're still having to remind Larry what should be recycled and what should not. You're a true hero for going around after him and moving his Diet Coke cans from the trash to recycling and his grease-stained fast food bags from recycling to the trash.

    If it was me, I'd dump it all back onto his desk until he received the message. If you ever want to threaten him with that, I could have Jeauxsifeen draw a detailed picture of what it might look like.

    It looks like I have quite the cast of characters this year. Regardless of academic ability, it's always fun to see how each kid stands out through a personality trait, skill, or attitude. Apparently, this is not going to be the year that my class roster remains constant, though. Mrs. Bird and I have already each lost one student, and a new one enrolled in my class today.

    Against All Odds, this kid arrived here in my Land of Confusion, and it's just Another Day in Paradise. I hope you can see where I'm going with this, because I'm not going to be able to do justice to the crazy drum riff from In the Air Tonight in an email.

    My student's name is Phil Collins. He didn't talk much today, but he seems nice enough and did well on the little quiz I gave him. When I first met him and learned his name, I asked, "Phil Collins, like the singer?" and he looked a bit embarrassed. I followed up with, "Well my name is Mr. Woodson, like the teacher!"

    Phil looked at me like I was crazy, so he should fit in just fine among all the other kids who don't appreciate my humor.

    Omar, on the other hand; he gets my humor. He has a wicked sense of humor himself, though he apparently likes to walk on the darker side. I've heard him talking with other kids about horror movies that I would never want to see myself, much less let my 10-year-old child see.

    Today, though, he had us in stitches out at recess. Mr. Utoobay and I were sitting at the picnic table at the edge of the playground, watching the kids. Omar and a couple of boys from Utoobay's class came and sat down at the table with us to chat. Out of nowhere, Omar went off on a rant against characters in horror movies, and it was epic.

As best as I can remember it, this is what he said:

"People in horror movies are so stupid! Why do they always go TOWARDS the weird noises in the house? And they never turn any lights on! Did you forget where the light switches are?? Why are they always tripping and falling down when they run away? Listen, the killer is wearing a mask – HE should be tripping! And if you go to explore a dark room, why don't you take a friend? Then when the killer jumps out, you can sacrifice the friend and get away! Sacrifice the friend!"

Luckily for Omar, the other boys still seemed willing to be his friend after hearing that. Here's hoping they're never around him when the lights go out.

Another interesting kid is Andres. He reminds me a little of George from the Steinbeck novel Of Mice and Men. He's a big sweet kid who's not always all there, and I don't think I'd let him anywhere near my puppy. But man, is this kid passionate about pizza! When it came time to label thinking journals and math folders, most of the kids wrote their names on the front covers. Not Andres. Instead, he wrote "Pizza King." He told me the password to his iTouch at home is Pizzaking123 (practically hacker-proof), and I have honest to goodness heard him telling the kids at his table all about a magical place called Pizza Town, of which he is the Mayor.

Last week, I included a couple of pizza-themed problems on the homework, and Andres had tears of joy in his eyes. He didn't do the homework, of course, but he loved the theme.

Gavin is a kid I really enjoyed talking with during recess last year when he was in Mrs. Frisch's homeroom. This year, he's in Mrs. Bird's class, and I absolutely love having him as a student. This is a kid who will sit patiently while other kids are shouting out ridiculously wrong guesses then roll his eyes and give an annoyed grunt before giving the right answer – and then explain WHY it's the right answer.

At recess today, Gavin told me there was a new Walmart that had just opened up near his apartment. He said that he loves to go there to buy chips and soda. He LOVES soda, by the way. When I asked him where the money to buy his chips and soda comes from, he said he does chores and his parents pay him.

"I've been working for money all my life," he proudly told me. You've got to admire a young capitalist like that.

On a side note, I know just how much Gavin loves soda because he told me, and I quote, "It's like crack cocaine to me." I was simultaneously appreciative of his proper use of a simile and deeply disturbed that he knew that particular one.

A little further down the spectrum, Rodrigo is a kid that really just seems happy to be there. Mrs. Fitzgerald had him last year and said he's not high academically, he's not low academically, he's just inherently capable. He's also perpetually happy, which in my book is a good thing. He has already made colorful cards for Mrs. Bird and me. Hers said, "You are the Awesome Reader!" Mine said, "You are the Genius of Math!"

I feel like this class has a lot more personality (and GOOD personality) than others I've had in recent years. Now if they'll just drop the laziness and start doing the steps I am showing them! Still, they're fun to talk to and joke around with.

I don't think I'll be going anywhere alone with Omar, though.
Talk to you later,

Assistant (to the) Mayor of Pizza Town

Date: Tuesday, September 16, 2014
To: Fred Bommerson
From: Jack Woodson
Subject: A Welcome Addition

Dear self-proclaimed "Genius of Prototype Design,"

Jill and I received the most incredible news last night! She is pregnant! I'm going to be a dad!

I just can't bring myself to say, "WE are pregnant," because I don't want to inflict the image of me with a protruding belly on anyone. Though Latya never seemed to mind exposing us all to his engorged tummy in the cubicles of HPU.

Last night, Jill had gone out with some girlfriends, and I was watching Monday Night Football. When Jill got home, she disappeared into the back of the house for awhile (avoiding televised sports is nothing new for her), but then I heard a shout. She came running into the living room, and she shoved something that looked like a blue highlighter in my face. Let no one say I'm not a quick learner, as I rapidly realized she was showing me a pregnancy test, AND I rapidly learned how to read a pregnancy test.

Jill visited her lady doctor today, and she confirmed the good news (maybe with a green highlighter?). This is so exciting! But now we need to get serious about picking a name; we have a May 22 deadline!

Hey, before I forget, I'm very proud of you for working for money all your life. You and Gavin are kindred spirits. Though he spends all his cash on chips and soda, while you blow all your cash on beer and video games.

I'm glad to hear Tiffany agreed with all of Omar's points regarding horror movies when you mentioned it to her at lunch. I'll be sure to pass on her additional observation that anyone who willingly purchases a freaky doll, a cursed animal appendage, or a murder mansion pretty much deserves their fate. Omar will be even better prepared for his next diatribe.

But hey, back to our positive pregnancy test, I have a tale from the classroom for you, and I can easily tie it into the theme of being positive.

Positively wrong, that is.

As a gainfully employed adult engineer, you no doubt check your math carefully on a daily basis, wouldn't you say? I try to instill that value in my students, even if on a much simpler level. Whenever the kids do a subtraction problem, I insist that they check their answer by working backwards. We know 84 - 38 = 46, because 46 + 38 = 84. 231 – 27 does not equal 216, because 216 + 27 does not equal 231.

I tell the kids that the simple act of adding gives them a chance to know immediately whether or not they got the right difference when they subtracted. What a great feeling to be absolutely positive about your answer, especially when the problem involves tricky regrouping! It's not as great a feeling as finding out your wife is pregnant or hearing McDonald's is bringing the McRib back, but it's definitely in the Top 3.

Checking subtraction with addition ("using fact families," in school lingo) reveals so many errors when done correctly. I am amazed at how many kids in the third and fourth grades still forget to regroup when subtracting. When they see 2 - 5, their brains immediately flip the problem into 5 - 2, which is just not the same problem. Strict mathematicians would tell the kids there is no commutative property for subtraction, but I tell the kids, "No Harry Potter magic in my classroom!"

Miss Phelps told a funny story once about trying to show a student why he needed to regroup. He had told her that 3 - 4 = 1. She asked him to hold up three fingers since that was the starting number. She held up three fingers herself to show him what she meant. She then asked him to put down four fingers. The kid folded his three fingers down, one at a time, but then looked uncertain of what to do next. When Miss Phelps reminded him that he needed to put FOUR fingers down, instead of realizing he didn't have enough fingers to do that, this kid slowly reached out and folded one of HER fingers down.

Adding to check subtraction is only valid, of course, if you actually compute the sum, and not if you just copy the original number into the answer spot. I've seen 150 - 25 = 135 (wrong) followed by 135 + 25 = 150 (even more egregiously wrong) on far too many papers throughout the years.

RT is one of the worst offenders when it comes to checking his work because he doesn't just cut and paste the beginning number. He actually DOES add his difference and the number that was subtracted. However, if his addition doesn't give him the starting number like it should, he erases the offending sum and writes in the number he wants it to be.

Just in case you're not as outraged as I am right now, let me put it in very clear terms in all caps... BY HIS ACTIONS, HE

KNOWS WITH ABSOLUTE CERTAINTY THAT HIS SUBTRACTION ANSWER IS WRONG!!!

The whole point of checking a problem like this is to give yourself a chance to make corrections if the numbers don't match up. RT knows that he is positively wrong, and he accepts that.

To me, this is far worse than Susana checking 58 - 17 by subtracting 41 - 17 (conceptual error) or than Kiara checking 40 - 13 by adding 27 + 31 (brain fart).

So RT loses the points on a test for being wrong, and then I hand the test back to him and make him fix the errors anyway. Here's hoping he'll soon realize that he's going to have to make corrections no matter what, and it's far better to make them BEFORE the problems are marked incorrect.

Putting RT's severe minus infection aside for now, Jill and I are going to go celebrate OUR positive results!
Talk to you later,

The Plus One

Date: Thursday, September 18, 2014
To: Fred Bommerson
From: Jack Woodson
Subject: Fruit and Veggie Tales

What's up, Fred?
 Thank you very much, and I will pass on your congratulations to Jill. We were talking last night, and we wanted to ask if you would be our son's godfather. Keep in mind, this entails more than just stroking your chin and doing a bad Marlon Brando impersonation. I know Larry will be crushed, but tell him I'll definitely keep him in mind for our tenth or twelfth child.
 And yes, I did say "son." It's way way way too early to have any kind of definitive blood work or tests or anything, but boys run in my family. My grandfather had a brother, my dad has a brother, MY brother has two sons. We just don't have girls, and haven't for something like seventy generations. Confucius himself once prophesied, "Woman who go to bed with Woodson man wake up with Woodson boy."
 Jill is convinced she will be the one to end what she calls "The Woodson Curse" and bring a little girl into the family. But the chances of that happening are, as Reggie is overly fond of saying, "in the noise."
 Speaking of noise, this year, morning announcements are at 9:00, at which time a group of fifth graders who sound like they are hopped up on 15 cups of coffee come over the PA and race through the pledges. Then either Mrs. Forest or one of the assistant principals says a few things, and they always wrap it up with, "You may now begin your instructional day."
 I'm very intrigued, but I haven't yet directly asked what they consider the 7:55 to 9:00 block of time, if not part of the instructional day. An aperitif for the mind, perhaps? Or did I miss a memo, and we're really supposed to be making quilts during that time?
 Another aspect that doesn't make much sense is our new attendance reporting situation. We learned during the week before school started that the whole district would be using a new computerized attendance system that would make the process easier than ever. We learned minutes later that our school leaders still wanted teachers to send in the good old-fashioned paper attendance sheet every day, just in case our online entries didn't take.

We are to a paperless system what Hummers are to Green vehicles.

I mentioned assistant principals earlier, as in more than one. Mrs. Zapata has been here nearly as long as I have, but this year, we have an additional AP, Ms. Butler. So far, I'm not impressed. Her major contribution to the operation of the school seems to be monitoring the cafeteria during lunchtime. And by "monitoring," I mean "yelling at the kids through a bullhorn to keep quiet."

This is not an exaggeration. The lady literally walks around with a loudspeaker, using it to speak to the kids when the noise levels rise. I wouldn't be surprised if her blaring voice was what brought the cafeteria roof down the first day of school.

I can't blame her for the fruits and vegetables debacle, though.

A couple of years ago, Mrs. Forest started a "Friday Fruits" program at the school in an effort to get the kids to eat healthier. The idea, and not a bad one, was for the kids to have a healthy snack during their day. Sometimes there was watermelon, sometimes there was papaya. Sometimes there were vegetables. Often, it wasn't on Fridays. In theory, everyone would take a five-minute break, munch on some apple slices or pineapple wedges, and then resume learning that day.

In practice, though, it's never quite worked out that way. For one thing, the kids usually don't actually want to eat the snacks. Part of this is a child's natural tendency to avoid anything healthy, but a bigger part of it is the poor choice of offerings. Typically, the kids love it when it's a pineapple wedge or a cluster of grapes, or even orange slices. But often, it's some weird unappetizing-looking fruit, or a vegetable the kids have no interest in eating. At least once every couple of weeks, the snack is a big bag of broccoli. I mean that literally. A bag the size of a backpack, filled with huge florets of broccoli. Or sometimes cauliflower, broccoli's less hip cousin.

Once there was a big bag of carrots. Not baby carrots. Not even medium-sized carrots. No, these were gigantic, grizzled veteran carrots. One was 13.5 inches long. I know this because instead of making the kids eat them, I had the kids use them to practice measurement with rulers to the nearest half inch. Since metric measurement is on the math curriculum as well, I can also tell you the shortest carrot was 16.5 centimeters.

The other problem is the assumption that snacking would only take five minutes. The first few times we did this, it took upwards of half an hour, and that's not counting the time it took to actually BRING the fruit to the classroom.

The kids don't always like to eat the snacks, but they sure do love going to get them. When the announcement comes over the PA system to send a couple of students to the office to pick up the fruits or veggies – and we never really know when it's going to happen; there is no schedule – even the biggest vegetable haters in the class clamor to be chosen as a courier. Meanwhile, the hallway sounds like a horse track as kids from every room take off running to retrieve the goods.

Even once it's in the room, passed out, and ready to be eaten, the kids demonstrate that they would much rather discuss and critique the food than actually consume it. Especially when they send exotic fruit like star fruit (yep, it's in the shape of a star) or pomegranate, which just looks like a blood bomb, waiting to be lobbed at somebody.

At times, the program has seemed to eclipse everything else at the school. There have been calls for fruit time during PE, at recess, and once even during a scheduled practice STAAR (the extra A is for Asparagus!) test. Last year, during one of our staff meetings, Mrs. Forest asked why it might be beneficial to give classroom tests on days other than Friday. I offered, "Because Friday tests are likely to be interrupted for a call to come and get the fruit of the week?"

That actually earned me a standing ovation from several of the teachers. And to her credit, Mrs. Forest even cracked a grin at that one.

One other thing, the stuff can't be distributed during lunch time, because that would make too much sense. Fruits and vegetables have no place in a school cafeteria, I guess.

My solution? I pass out the stuff while the kids are working. They know they have half an hour to eat it, otherwise it will be thrown away. They also know they have to continue to work during that time, and deadlines don't change.

This year, the Random Fruits and Vegetables program has been upped to TWO days a week, due to its popularity with non-students and non-teachers.

I think we may need to look into starting a sister program where someone collects all of the uneaten fruit and vegetables – and there is a LOT – and takes the leftovers to a food bank or homeless shelter. At least then someone would benefit from the healthy foods.

For the most part, the kids are pretty blasé about the whole program. Except for Rodrigo, who always shouts, "Oh boy! I hope it's a big bag of broccoli!"

He's totally sincere, by the way.
Talk to you later,

Kiwi Herman

Date: Wednesday, September 24, 2014
To: Fred Bommerson
From: Jack Woodson
Subject: Another sum body done sum body wrong song

Hey buddy,

Jill was somewhat perturbed, but I was very amused to see Tom Winter's latest masterpiece. Did he show you? I opened the attachment on his email to find my head photoshopped onto a ridiculously ginormous pregnant body.

Must be triplets!

Sorry to tell you, but I doubt you'll be able to start a Friday Fruits program at HPU. Believe me, you should be happy. It's way more trouble than it's worth. I can certainly understand your desire to give Latya more limes to stave off scurvy, though.

I walked into the gym this morning to find that one of my kids had been throwing pennies at other kids. When I asked Braxton why he was literally throwing his money away, he sneered, "I HATE pennies!"

I can only hope he hates ten dollar bills just as much and starts throwing them at me soon.

Later in the day, I was strongly starting to suspect that all of my kids hated quarters. What should have been a simple answer became a never-ending guessing game.

By this point, it should come as absolutely no surprise to you (or me, for that matter) that I have a lot of hopeful guessers among my students. It's always been that way over the years – some kids would rather just guess repeatedly than put any thought into an answer. Even if those guesses are ridiculous, and even if those ridiculous guesses have already been ventured.

I can only assume the thinking behind this strategy is that some words sound so elegant and refined, they are bound to impress somebody in the room, even when used out of context. It would be like you asking how many volts a particular heat pump needs and me shouting, "SEMICONDUCTORS!!"

Today we were working a rather simple addition problem – 75 + 25. I personally find the number 25 easier to work with when I think of it as cents, so I (foolishly) took the opportunity to go off on a teaching tangent.

I said to the kids, "You know, whenever I see the number 25, it makes me think of a small item I can carry in my pocket. This item is something I see every day, and it's something I can actually spend at the store. Does anyone know what 25 reminds me of?"

I should mention here that I have really put a lot of emphasis on vocabulary words this year, and the kids must think one of those words can answer any question.

Kiara raised her hand first, so I called on her. "Sum?" she ventured.

I don't even know why I was surprised by this after teaching for so long.

"No," I answered. "I'm talking about a physical item, something simple and small you can carry in your pocket. Something related to the number 25."

I called on Siddiq next. "Total?" he guessed.

"No," I answered again, mightily resisting the urge to slap my forehead. "A total isn't an object you can carry in your pocket, and it doesn't apply just to the number 25."

"SUM!!!" Eld'Ridge shouted, without even being called on.

At this point, a wiser teacher would have turned around, finished the addition problem on the board, and silently left the classroom in search of the nearest bar. I am clearly not a wiser teacher. Instead, I persisted, but not before threatening to take away recess for a week if anyone guessed "place value."

I reminded the kids that I had mentioned spending the item in question and that I was referring to a piece of money, but the scope of guesses remained wide of the target.

"Twenty-five monies?"

"Twenty-five dollars?"

I told the kids, "Listen, I'm just looking for one simple little object, you can carry it in your hand, and it is linked with the number 25."

That's when Gavin came up with the best guess of the day. He actually stood up, pointed at me in triumph, and confidently declared, "Twenty-five dollars, put on a Visa gift card!"

I couldn't help laughing at that one, but I fear my giggles sounded like the type of hysterical laughter that comes when the voices in your head have told you the only way out of the closed room is to chew off your own arm.

Somebody finally guessed the mystery object – a quarter – after what seemed like a quarter century. I tried to convince the kids that thinking of 25 as a quarter sometimes makes the math easier, especially when adding more than one group of 25. Truth be told, I was hardly convinced of that myself after the ordeal we had just been through.

As a final step, we added and completed the original problem – 75 + 25 = 100 – then I asked the question whose answer had already been shouted repeatedly.

"And now what do we call our answer to this addition problem?"

I stood with my feet shoulder width apart, head bowed, both hands out and wagging, like a comedian begging for laughs after a joke. I was fully expecting the answer of "SUM" to come crashing over me from 20 voices.

Instead, three kids shouted, "QUARTER!"

Now the number 25 just makes me think of how many Advil I need to take this evening.

Talk to you later,

LoneSum Dove

Date: Monday, September 29, 2014
To: Fred Bommerson
From: Jack Woodson
Subject: Naked and Afraid

Hey pal,

No, a quarter horse, a quarter mile, and an NBA fourth quarter are not things you can carry in your pocket. You never miss a chance to pile on, do you?

That's really cool that you and Ron Philby were able to use Reggie's tickets to take some clients out to the Rangers game last night. I saw the highlights on SportsCenter, and it looked like a good one. I'm guessing when it came time for concessions, though, quarters didn't help you much. You needed Gavin's 25 dollars, put on a Visa gift card, just to buy a couple of snacks!

Personally, I would have preferred overpriced peanuts and crackerjacks to what awaited me this morning.

My day started with a kid from one of the bilingual fourth grade classes coming into my room before school even started. He was not there to bring me a tasty breakfast burrito or tickets to a sporting event but rather to report that a boy in the OTHER fourth grade bilingual class had "pictures of naked women in his backpack!"

(At this point, I can practically see Larry drooling, "Go on...")

It had been at least a few hours since I had seen any pictures of naked women, so I felt it was my duty to investigate the story further. When I walked downstairs and into the gym, it was plainly apparent which boy had brought the contraband. His whole face screamed "GUILTY!" while the surrounding kids inched away from him without even trying to be subtle about it.

I took him into a room across the hall and looked inside his backpack. The "pictures of naked women" turned out to be a lingerie calendar, leaving me to wonder if "naked" did not mean the same thing between cultures. Also, this was not a Playboy calendar by any means. The featured women, while not unattractive, could not have been any younger than 50. Ms. March looked like she was pushing 60.

I'm not sure where this kid got the calendar (since I didn't for a moment believe his story that his older brother slipped it into his backpack while he was brushing his teeth), but my guess would be he dug up a time capsule buried by his grandfather in the backyard. The pictures were low rez, the lighting was awful, and the hairstyles were straight from the 70s. 1870s, that is. Mr. Utoobay agreed when I called him into my room to take a look, and Mr. Redd soon joined us and verified my opinions as well. I'm sure Mrs. Bird also agreed by the way she rolled her eyes and said, "You pervs!" when she found us closely examining the evidence. Of course, I had first delivered the student to Mrs. Del Torro, his homeroom teacher, so he could be reprimanded in the proper language.

This kid was not the only one who was busted today. I came down on Lewith and Rodrigo pretty hard for cheating on last week's homework.

I think cheating is a horrible, disgusting, dishonest thing to do – in situations that actually matter. Cheating on Super Mario Brothers? Who cares? Cheating on a diet? Who am I to judge? But cheating on your taxes, on a significant other, or on a test? Prosecute to the fullest extent of the law.

If there's one thing worse than cheating, however, it's cheating stupidly. Lewith and Rodrigo cheated in the stupidest ways possible. Thursday night's homework was an array of 16 clocks, where the kids had to write the time each clock was showing to the nearest minute. We didn't have time to grade the work Friday, so I looked at them over the weekend and was greatly dismayed by what I saw. Lewith had all of the correct answers, but every one of his answers was exactly one clock off from where it should have been. The third clock should have been 4:02, but Lewith's FOURTH clock was marked 4:02. The eighth clock read 6:37, but the NINTH clock was where he had written 6:37.

Rodrigo, on the other hand, had all of the correct times in all of the correct places. He also very clearly had a photocopy of Kirstie's homework, complete with Kirstie's scribbled out name at the top and Rodrigo's name written above it.

I called both boys over to my desk to ask why they had cheated, and they just stood in front of me gasping like fish out of water. They seemed far more upset that they had been caught rather than the fact that they had cheated. They earned the privilege of doing more clock problems during recess. Kirstie was absent today, but I'll be speaking to her about the "loaner" as well.

I don't think RT cheated on his homework, but Siddiq apparently thought he had. RT tends to need a lot more positive reinforcement than most kids, so when I passed his homework back this morning, I made it a point to tell him, "Great job! This is fantastic work!"

As I walked away from his table, I heard Siddiq, sitting across from him, say, "Way to go! Did your mother do it?"

Who knows? Maybe his mom needs positive reinforcement as well.

One last thing, do you remember the first day of school when I told you the people across the street turned on their sprinklers as the kids were being dropped off? This afternoon at dismissal, I saw the lady of the house peeking through a window, taking pictures.

I had no idea why she would be taking pictures – and I tried not to focus on how incredibly CREEPY her actions seemed. Instead, I gamely played along, posing and mugging for the camera. Jill is now worried I'm going to show up online, cheesily giving a double thumbs up, above a caption which reads, "Local teacher approves of crackpot plan to replace marshmallows in Lucky Charms with live scorpions."

I, on the other hand, am guessing she'll somehow use pictures of the school and noisy kids to cheat on her taxes. I'll even go so far as to say I'll bet she cheated on her clock homework when she was a kid. It all starts somewhere.

Talk to you later,

Dewey, Cheetum, and Howe

Date:	Wednesday, October 1, 2014
To:	Fred Bommerson
From:	Jack Woodson
Subject:	Here Comes Money Boo Boo

Hey buddy,

Once again, I have to wonder how you guys have so much free time on your hands. I received multiple pictures of myself with newspaper-worthy captions. I guess if Latya or Winter ever pursue a career in graphic design, they'll be experts in Photoshop.

A few of my favorites:

Man defies centuries-old fashion laws by wearing white after Labor Day.

D.B. Cooper is alive and well and teaching in Dallas ISD – but where is his money?

Soon-to-be father attempts to sell naming rights for future heir to ketchup fortune.

I'll be sure to pass on these great suggestions to Mrs. Voyeur across the street for her secret project. I won't be passing on Larry's tips for cheating on tests to anybody, though. Like anybody's going to smuggle an abacus in their pants.

Today the high point of my day was finding a $20 bill on the floor in the hallway! This was followed shortly thereafter by the low point of my day – turning it in to the office.

But money is what we've been focused on this week, and my kids sure do love money! Anytime they see a multi-digit numeral in class, they mentally place a dollar sign in front of it and salivate over the thought of having that much moolah. They absolutely adore the idea of having a ton of money.

They also have no earthly idea how money works, unfortunately. Sure, most of them can identify coins and differentiate between a dime and a penny, though Raina has tried to tell me a picture of the tail side of a penny – with the words "One Cent" clearly visible – is a nickel. When it comes to how to make change, though, or how much to pay when buying things, the vast majority of these kids are clueless.

These are not new concepts for fourth grade, so I wasn't planning on spending much time on money. But last week's little quiz (and the Great Quarter Debacle of 2014) showed me that I really needed to stop and plug up some knowledge holes. In one question, a boy was buying two apples for 65 cents each and using a five dollar bill to pay for them. To find the change he would receive, some kids added 65 cents + 2 apples. A large group added the prices of the two apples correctly, but then wrote that as their answer instead of following through to find the change.

Another quiz question had a girl buying three items at the grocery store and trying to find her total. Most kids answered this one correctly, but there were still a few – far too many – that have become convinced over the years that the word "spend" in a word problem ALWAYS means to subtract, no matter what. So for them, if the girl buys one item, her total is $3.25, but if she spends money on TWO items, her total is only $1.09. And if she buys all three, I guess the store owes her money?

I always ask these kids if the store where their parents shop follows these crazy monetary rules, because I want to start doing all of my shopping there immediately!

Monday and Tuesday, we had ourselves a couple of pretty intense days of money boot camp. I wasn't screaming like a drill sergeant, but I wanted to at times.

Me: "IF YOU SPEND $15 AT A RESTAURANT AND GIVE THE CASHIER A $20 BILL, DOES IT MAKE SENSE THAT YOU WILL GET $35 BACK IN CHANGE?"
Kids: "SIR, NO SIR!"
Me: "YOU THINK BUYING ONE GUMBALL COSTS YOU 50 CENTS, BUT BUYING TWO GUMBALLS GETS YOU BOTH FOR FREE??"
Kids: "SIR, NO SIR!"

I wrote some menu items on the board today (Coke – two dollars, hotdog – four dollars, frustration migraine – priceless) and assigned mini-projects based on that menu. Each group of kids had a pile of fake money and a food order such as two hotdogs, four cokes, and a cookie. They had to figure out how much change they would receive if they bought that combination and paid with a twenty.

Ja'Kendrick still tried to subtract 40 from 17, and Susana totaled the food and took away the price of one hotdog. But by the third challenge, most of the groups seemed on track.

After a while, I let my higher kids make their own menus with dollars and cents while I worked with the lower kids. When I took a break to check in on them, I found that Rajiv was creating much larger food orders. I asked him who on earth was going to order 348 hamburgers, 967 cokes, and 513 bags of chips. He replied, "The Dallas Cowboys and their families?"

I couldn't argue that one.

Back with the lower kids, I asked Cesar to show me on his whiteboard how much change he would receive from a five dollar bill if he bought two hamburgers that cost $1.80 each. He sat there and stared at me as if I had said, "I want you to show me your best confused face."

On a whim, I decided to try something different. Knowing Cesar's tastes, I asked him to show me how he could find the change he would receive from a five dollar bill if he bought a dozen donuts that cost $2.70.

Without hesitation, he answered, "Two dollars and thirty cents."

And there you have it. Cesar actually DOES have a slight chance of passing the math STAAR (The extra A is for Apple_fritters!) this year. It's a long shot, but who knows? Maybe every question will be about donuts.
Talk to you later,

Doctor Changelove

Date: Wednesday, October 8, 2014
To: Fred Bommerson
From: Jack Woodson
Subject: Snakes on an Inclined Plane

Yo!

You don't need to prove your money prowess with me, pal. I know how knowledgeable you are when it comes to the use and value of the dollar. That Nigerian prince knows just what a fiscal genius you are, too!

I like your idea to start a money boot camp for financially irresponsible adults. I know at least a dozen myself. Let's start those wheels turning. And speaking of wheels, this week, our science topic has been simple machines. You know, those things that make work easier, unless your work involves teaching science to school children.

I started off the first lesson Monday by presenting a problem to solve. I asked the kids to imagine that we had a 200 pound box on the floor that we needed to move to the top shelf of a bookcase. I invited the kids to start thinking about ways we could accomplish this task.

The discussion immediately centered around what was inside the box. 200 puppies? A thousand pizzas? A fire truck? Hannah Montana?

It's a good thing we'll be reviewing reasonable estimates of weight soon.

I tried to quickly refocus the group on the act of actually moving the box. Most of the kids thought lifting the box would be the best solution. One proposed plan had 10 to 12 kids teaming up to lift the box. Omar suggested Big Show of pro wrestling fame could stop by and lift it for us.

RT, future scourge of the ATF, suggested putting small explosive charges underneath the box and propelling it up to the top of the shelf. I took him aside later and pointed out two things. First, explosions tend to destroy objects, not guide them to better placement. More importantly, I mentioned how I was a little concerned that he always seemed so fixated on weapons. We had an interesting conversation.

Me: "RT, sometimes it seems like all you ever talk about are guns, swords, bombs, and other weapons."

RT: "Nuh-uh! Sometimes I talk about monsters, like the Loch Ness Monster, Wolfman, and vampires – which are all real, by the way!"

I'm so glad he set the record straight.

Back to the box, though, some kids did finally voice the idea of using a lever, and I was very impressed. They didn't use the word "lever," but that was definitely what they were proposing. The best of these ideas came from Gavin. He said, "Here's what we're gonna do. We're gonna get a big board and put it on a rock like a seesaw. Then we put the box on one side of the board. Then we drop a BIIIIG rock onto the other side, and the box gonna fly up to the shelf."

I started to congratulate Gavin on his input, but he was already lost in thought, stroking his chin, muttering, "Or maybe we have a really fat kid jump on the other side..."

Yesterday, we delved more into the six simple machines and their uses. We talked about the difference between a simple machine and a compound machine. We talked about how Thomas Edison invented the first machine that could show a movie. We talked about how that first machine was not, in fact, a DVD. We talked about how a DVD is not an example of a wheel and axle, just because it is round. We talked about how Anita's favorite DVD is Madagascar 2.

You see the train of thought here?

Today I gave the kids note cards and asked them to draw an example of a simple machine in use. They needed to have a picture, the name of the simple machine, and a sentence describing their illustration.

Overall, the results were really impressive, mostly involving levers, inclined planes, and wheels and axles. Nobody attempted the wedge, though I was really hoping to see Star Wars fanatic Khabi draw a picture of celebrated X-Wing pilot, Wedge Antilles.

Trevor's submission takes the cake, though, without a doubt. I just showed it to Jill, and she's still laughing. She's laughing for two now, you know. Let's see if I can do Trevor's card justice.

There is a car. There is a stick figure with spiky hair standing in front of the car. There is what appears to be a rope leading from the stick figure's hand to the hood of the car. The caption reads: "Dis boy is pulley da car."

Technically, he met all three criteria I gave him, and his caption did indeed include the name of a simple machine. So I guess I have to give him an A?

Back in class, when I tried to shoehorn the name of a simple machine into conversation, it didn't go over so well. We received a passel of papaya this afternoon, courtesy of my favorite intrusive school program, and while my helpers were passing them out, I said, "Enjoy this week's wedge-tables!"

This triggered no reaction whatsoever from most of the kids. Misaki, though, belly laughed for several minutes and then kept bringing it back up throughout the day.

At least no one asked if I was pulley their leg.
Signing off,

Wheel and Axle Rose

Date: Tuesday, October 14, 2014
To: Fred Bommerson
From: Jack Woodson
Subject: Weight, weight, don't tell me

Hey Fred,

    No, I didn't feel comfortable writing the comment, "Stop screwing around!" on anybody's note card. There are some parents I'm already on a slippery slope with, and I don't want to drive a wedge between them and me, so I have to be wheel careful.

    I certainly do appreciate you offering to consult with noted simple machine experts Pulley Shore and Lever Burton. May I suggest adding Screw Barrymore to that list?

    Jill had her first doctor visit yesterday since the pregnancy confirmation. There will apparently be a lot of these, and so I don't need to go with her every time. I'll definitely go when our little wing nut has grown enough to be seen on a sonogram. At the present time, though, he weighs about as much as a kidney bean.

    It is probably relevant for me to mention here that a kidney bean should not be measured in tons. This is a fact that sadly continues to elude some of my kids.

    We've started to study weight and mass this week, which is really just a review of concepts the kids learned last year. Most of my students do have a pretty good grasp, at least on the customary units of ounce, pound, and ton. A handful of kids, however, regularly confuse the extremes, thinking very heavy things are measured in ounces, while tons are the smallest units of weight.

    Yesterday, when Greyson told me a grasshopper weighed about five tons, I exclaimed, "5-ton grasshoppers? That is not a world I want to live in!"

    I could tell Greyson realized his mistake when he presented me a hand-drawn picture at recess showing a small stick figure labeled "Mr. Woodson" being terrorized by an insect that took up most of the page. I asked him to pencil in a drawing of you so I'd have a friend to sacrifice to the beast.

    Eld'Ridge, on the other hand, clearly does not get the idea. When I asked for something that should be measured in ounces, he said an elephant. I asked for something that weighed a ton, and he said his brother. When I asked what unit would be best to measure a blue whale, he said grams. Grams – when we were only focused on customary units and nobody had spoken the word "grams" all day!

I know all of Eld'Ridge's responses to those questions because he tends to blurt out whatever comes to mind, without ever raising his hand to be called on. There is absolutely no filter between his brain and his mouth. There have even been times when he's blurted out answers during tests!

On the opposite end of the spectrum, we have the competitive hand raisers. They are always the first to thrust their hands into the air after any question. They often do not know the answer, they just want to be called on. To them, being called on is not a request to hear an answer; rather, it is permission to begin the thought process of formulating a response.

Today I asked, "Can anyone think of something that weighs about ten pounds?"

Immediately, several hands shot up, including Anita's, queen of the competitive hand raisers. Also immediately, Eld'Ridge shouted, "A spoon!" but that's beside the point.

I gestured to Anita, and her sounds changed from, "OOOH! OOOH! ME! ME!" to, "Ummmmmm…"

Meanwhile, I have no doubt this was the dialogue that was running through her head:

All right, all right, all right! He called on ME! I'M the chosen one! Phase one complete, now it's time to come up with the best answer ever, one that's going to knock everyone's socks off! They'll be talking about this one for years! Now, what was the question again?

I'm hard pressed not to shout, "Ain't nobody got time for that!" whenever she does this. But it's even more annoying when I ask a math question and the student I call on says, "Wait, I know this one!" then starts to do computation on his or her paper. I'm a big fan of kids showing their work, but not after I've asked, "Who ALREADY knows the answer?"

Back to the current lesson, the kids did make some pretty good flipbooks based on the customary system of weight, and the specific examples for each unit were diverse and thoughtful. I especially enjoyed the cruise liner on Chloe's tons door, the roller coaster on Blanca's, and the Zamboni on Rajiv's. I also liked the ketchup packet on Lewith's ounces door, the wheelbarrow full of bricks on Landon's pounds door, and the beautifully detailed monarch butterfly on Jeauxsifeen's ounces door.

I wasn't as appreciative of the picture of ME on Cesar's tons door, but I guess the fact that he made a flipbook at all is a win. Also that he didn't stick any crayons up his nose while doing it.

One last little story before I sign off.

Yesterday was really hot, and when we came in from recess, I was sweating profusely. D'Qayla had a suggestion.

"Tomorrow, don't wear pants!" she said.

I told her, "I think I would be in a TON of trouble if I came to school with no pants."

Without a trace of shock or embarrassment, she clarified, "No, I mean wear shorts instead!"

Unfortunately, I'll have to pass on D'Qayla's suggestion (even the G-rated version). For one thing, it's against the teacher dress code. For another, I don't need to give Mrs. Voyeur across the street anything else to take pictures of.

Talk to you later,

Ton DMC

Date: Thursday, October 16, 2014
To: Fred Bommerson
From: Jack Woodson
Subject: It's not you, it's your kids

What's up?

I like your suggestion to always speak the word "ounce" in a high mouse-like voice and "ton" in a deep booming voice. If it worked for your teacher, all those centuries ago, maybe it will work for me now. Plus, I always enjoy the chance to show off my Elmo and Darth Vader impersonations.

On the other hand, I definitely will not be warning the kids they'll never be successful drug dealers if they can't even tell the difference between grams and kilograms, as Latya suggested.

Today was an especially long day, as it was our first parent conference night of the year. Fortunately, tomorrow is Fair Day, so I'll have an extra day of messing up my sleep cycle by staying in bed until 1.

Earlier this week, when I announced there would be no school on Friday, Curtiss shouted, "What's Friday?"

I immediately replied, "It's the day of the week that comes after Thursday, but that's not important right now."

While some of the other kids laughed, my homage to Airplane! was wasted on Curtiss as he frowned and slowly wagged his head, the way people do when they see a dog continue to bark at a spot of sunshine on the floor.

Mrs. Bird and I had a good turnout tonight, with most of the parents we wanted to see showing up, and only a few no-shows. Our biggest behavior problems – Braxton and RT – probably never even delivered the invitations to their parents, and we didn't get to meet Andres' mother, either. It all balanced out, though, because Akasha, Beto, and Rajiv all showed up unexpectedly and filled in the gaps.

I was definitely prepared for tonight. Having been a teacher for many years now, I've learned over time what NOT to say during conferences. The worst offenders seem to be, "Excuse me while I polish off this brewski," "Your daughter reminds me of a young Millard Fillmore," and "For a dozen cronuts and a lotto ticket, I can make sure little Johnny gets an A."

Still, I do have a few suggestions for ways we could make the evening more entertaining, and I'll be sprinkling them throughout this email, starting with…

Ways to Make Parent Conference Night More Fun #1
– Margarita Machine

    Margaritas would definitely mellow the mood, especially when you need to discuss a topic such as the one I had with Landon's parents. Last Tuesday during our after-recess restroom break, Tyrellvius rushed out of the bathroom to tell me that Landon had pointed his middle finger at him. My first thought was, "Really? He POINTED it at you?"

    My second thought was that it was an odd thing for Landon, a normally well-behaved boy, to have done. When asked why he flipped Tyrellvius the bird, Landon replied, "My dad said that it's not bad and that it means God."

    Well, that's certainly a new one.

    I asked Landon if he went to church, and when he said he did, I asked how often he saw the congregation giving the minister the Hawaiian Good Luck Sign. He had no answer. I did a Google search for "Our Lady of the Middle Finger," and came up empty. I'm pretty sure there's no story anywhere titled "Are You There, Middle Finger? It's Me, Margaret."

    Landon's dad certainly looked like he would have appreciated a margarita or two when he learned about what had happened. While I don't support the whole "No prayer in public school" thing, I'm fairly confident there will be no more of Landon's middle finger in public school after tonight.

Ways to Make Parent Conference Night More Fun # 2
– Voice Modulators.

    Just think how much more entertaining it would be for parents to hear about bad behavior and poor decision making if the news was being delivered in Morgan Freeman's voice or auto-tuned like a Cher song.

    We conferenced with Alvaro's mother tonight, and I took the opportunity to verify a suspicion I'd had for a while. A few weeks ago, Alvaro came in on a Friday with homework that had answers but absolutely no work shown on it. I asked him why he hadn't shown any work, and he insisted that he was going to do the work the way we had practiced in class but that his mother had adamantly told him not to do it that way. I pressed him for more details, and he eventually said, "She told me not to listen to the teacher."

This being quite possibly the most anti-parental thing I've ever heard a parent being credited with, I asked Alvaro to repeat his statement. Amazingly, he stuck with it.

Finally, I gave him a piece of paper and asked him to write down his claim, explaining that I wanted to be able to show that paper to his mother when we sat down to talk, and that I wanted to be able to show that paper to Mrs. Forest and Ms. Zapata when they asked about his grades, and that I wanted to be able to show that paper to Santa Claus when he started making his Nice and Naughty list.

Most kids would have distanced themselves from such a bold claim long before reaching this point, but my little muppet Alvaro persisted and wrote down his statement, word for word.

Fast forward to the conference with Alvaro's mother tonight, and you'll never guess what happened! She was utterly shocked to hear the story, and she vehemently denied ever telling Alvaro not to listen to his teachers! She then proceeded to give her son a lengthy tongue lashing in Spanish. I couldn't understand half of it, but I kept thinking how great it would have sounded in Alvin the Chipmunk's voice.

Alvaro merely looked shocked that his bald-faced lie had not panned out for him the way he had hoped. He does tend to look shocked all the time, though, so it's hard to tell what he was really thinking.

Ways to Make Parent Conference Night More Fun #3
– Put out a tip jar.

OK, I'm totally kidding about that one. Sometimes when I see a student flashing around a dollar they've brought for a snack, I jokingly ask if they've brought that for me as a tip for being such an awesome teacher. I'll admit, I always appreciate being told I'm doing a good job, even if it's not with a monetary gift. That's why I really enjoy the conferences where we can praise kids for their excellent work habits, stellar social skills, and commendable personal hygiene. The last conference of the night was with Marina's mom, and I received a totally unexpected and completely wonderful compliment. Marina's mom told me that her daughter has always struggled in math. This was a shocker to me, because Marina is one of my top students. Her mom went on to say that she's never seen her so excited about math or truly enjoying it and that it's all because of the way I teach it.

How great is that? Now that's the way to end on a high note!

Jill and I are going to go celebrate another successful conference night with a round of margaritas (virgin for her, of course) and some funny voices. Hopefully I won't wake up feeling the need to point my middle finger at the porcelain god.
Talk to you later,

The Miracle Worker

Date:	Tuesday, October 21, 2014
To:	Fred Bommerson
From:	Jack Woodson
Subject:	Dammit Jim, I'm a teacher, not a DOCTOR!

Hola, mi amigo!

Don't lie to me. You've never seen a margarita machine being used at a business conference or a client meeting. Going out for drinks with the client AFTER a meeting is totally different. And that's a lot easier to do, since they usually don't have their kids with them.

A tip of the hat to Tom Winter for suggesting Paintball guns as another way to make conferences more fun. Heaven knows there have been parents who have wanted to shoot me.

Thankfully, dodging paint pellets is not in my job description. It's amazing, though, how many hats we have to wear when we work in the education business. I'm not talking about fedoras and Kangols; I mean the many roles we have to fill in addition to merely teaching the children.

We take on the role of counselor whenever we talk with the kids about things that are bothering them. We act as coaches when we try to motivate them to do things they don't want to do. We have to be detectives sometimes to track down the truth when stories aren't in agreement. We even play financial advisors when some kid decides to trade his lunch money for some other kid's used Pokemon cards. Last, but not least, we are expected to be doctors and nurses, and in some cases epidemiologists.

We are very fortunate to have a wonderful nurse, Mrs. McCaffrey, on our campus, but those of us with a few years under our belts don't send kids to her unless we've seen blood flowing freely from at least two orifices. Thankfully, most of my kids never ask to see the nurse unless they are truly feeling sick. But there are a few who try every once in a while to use a clinic visit as a way out of a test, or an activity, or a whole lesson. And then there are those who honestly think they have major medical maladies.

Last Thursday, Tommy came inside from recess absolutely certain that he had contracted West Nile Virus or Malaria from a mosquito bite outside. Tommy is the kind of kid who probably spends three hours on WebMD every night, calculating his chances of succumbing to some exotic disease.

I calmly surveyed him then began loudly sniffing the air around him, like a bloodhound.

"Nope, you pass the sniff test," I told him. "You're all clear."

Tommy looked as though he had been given a reprieve from certain death. I should have let it go at that, but I'm a jerk, so I added, "I am 88% sure you are Malaria-free! Congratulations!"

"Wait, what?" Tommy's face grew petrified again. "88 percent? What about the other 12 percent?!?"

See, I can diagnose diseases AND assess math ability at the same time. Tommy, by the way, is the same one who went home and told his parents that a boy had left school early with Ebola back in September. Siddiq had thrown up after lunch that day and did indeed leave early. I didn't do the sniff test then, but I was 100% sure he did not have Ebola. Nevertheless, I received an email from Tommy's dad that night asking, "Is everything ok at the school? We are very concerned here. Tommy said a boy went home sick."

I reassured Tommy's dad that kids went home sick all the time in elementary school and that there was nothing to be concerned about. Maybe my message was a bit brusque, because the reply I got was a terse, "Thank you, Mr. Woodson. Please forgive me for being worried about my family's safety."

I forgave him.

Sometimes, I don't even need to use complicated (made-up) procedures such as the sniff test to make medical assessments in the classroom. Just yesterday, I had this conversation with RT:

RT: "I just heard a loud snap, and I think it was my arm breaking!"
Me: "I see you waving both arms around as you're telling me this, so your arm clearly is not broken."
RT: "But it LOOKS like it's broken, and it really hurts!"
Me: "That's strange, to me it looks totally unbroken. But if you're sure, then you need to ask your mom or dad to take you to the emergency room to see a doctor as soon as you get home."
RT: "Wait, that's weird. Just now, it suddenly stopped hurting!"
Me: "That'll be $20, please."

At times, we have to be amateur optometrists as well. So many kids come to school and complain about not being able to see the board. I usually move them to a closer desk and then send them to Nurse McCaffrey to do a vision test. This often leads to them receiving glasses. But it went a little differently this year with

Khabi, who never complained about not being able to see the board. He would just stand up and walk closer to the board whenever he needed to. I don't know why it took me so long to ask him about glasses, but the other day, after the fourth time he had walked closer to the board, this is the conversation we had:

Me: "Khabi, have you ever gone to the nurse to have your vision checked? To see if maybe you need glasses?"
Khabi: "Yes."
Me: "Oh, good! Did the nurse say you needed glasses?"
Khabi: "Yes."
Me: "I see. Did you ever GET glasses?"
Khabi: "Yes."
Me: "OK. So do you have glasses here at school?"
Khabi: "Yes."
Me: "Can you put them on, please?"
Khabi: "Yes."

This is a kid who is in the Talented and Gifted group! Apparently common sense is not a tested ability during the screening process. Here's hoping his problem solving skills can overcome that nasty bout of Ebola.
Talk to you later,

Dr. McTeachy

Date: Thursday, October 23, 2014
To: Fred Bommerson
From: Jack Woodson
Subject: Don't you know who I am?!?

Hey buddy,

Very brave of you to attempt the sniff test around Larry. We all know you're much more likely to detect Funyuns and coffee breath than any kind of sickness.

Also, I'm psyched that Jacob is coming to visit! I haven't seen your brother since the wedding (mine, not his), and that's far too long. Jill and I would love to meet up with you guys for dinner Saturday. How about McDonalds? Taco Bell? Or someplace classier, like Hooters?

Speaking of classy, Landon showed up yesterday with pink hair. He looked like someone had given him a swirly in a cotton candy machine. When I asked him why he had dyed his hair pink, he said it was because lots of kids told him to do it.

Tomorrow, I'm going to ask lots of kids to tell Landon to learn his multiplication facts.

I've treated myself to a little perk this week, though I don't know how long it will last. A few weeks ago, a fresh coat of paint was applied to all of the curbs in the staff parking lot, and ten or so were labeled with specific designations. The individualized spots include one for "Principal" and a couple marked "Assistant Principal." Mr. Redd and I joked about modifying one of the Assistant Principal spots. I proposed sketching a crude megaphone in front of the title; he suggested painting over the last six letters of the first word.

There are also spots marked "Counselor," "Nurse," and "Office Manager," among others. Sadly, none are labeled, "Genius of Math." However, there is one labeled "Employee of the Month." One would think that one of the teachers would be selected for that honor, but there has been absolutely no mention of it before or since the paint job. And it's not like we haven't had several staff meetings in the meantime.

So I parked there Monday. And Tuesday. And every day this week. I mean, until I'm told otherwise, I kind of have to assume I AM the Employee of the Month, right?

Of course, if there was a spot marked "Anonymous," I might have to start parking there, too. I'm apparently not as well-known around campus as I thought I was.

Yesterday, I was walking down the hall by myself during my planning period when I was passed by a little first grader. I've seen this girl a bajillion times, and I'm sure she's seen me before as well.

As she walked by, she asked, "Who are you? Are you a substitute teacher?"

Only slightly offended, I answered, "I'm President Obama. Don't you recognize me?"

She didn't seem to be impressed, as she kept walking briskly past me. I solemnly proceeded, humming "Hail to the Chief."

As I rounded the corner, I happened upon her again. She was standing in front of a bulletin board with some other kids who were decorating it. One of them asked me, "Does this look good?"

I replied, "It sure does!"

As I walked away, I heard the boy tell his classmates, "YES! We got a compliment!"

One of the other kids replied, "Yeah, because you ASKED for one!"

I was hoping to hear my first grade friend chime in with, "And it was a compliment from the President!" But no such luck.

I really can't be too resentful at someone for not knowing my name when I'm just as guilty of that crime myself. On the long walk back from art today, I had stationed myself near a corner while my class passed by. As I watched, most of the kids walked in a nice straight line close to the right hand wall. Rodrigo, however, was walking smack dab in the middle of the hallway.

When I noticed this, Rodrigo was a good fifty feet past me, so I shouted at him to get back in line. He just ignored me, never responding. I called his name several times, and he never even turned around!

Then Rodrigo, who was near the very end of the line, walked by me, wondering why I was shouting his name down the hallway. I did a double take before realizing it was Beto up at the front of the line, not Rodrigo! They look enough alike to make me look like an idiot, certainly.

Lack of recognition is one thing, but I've had a few more active swipes at my ego lately, too. You'll recall that last week, we were estimating weight and talking about units like ounces, pounds, and tons. We've revisited it a few times since then during warm-ups and spare moments. One point of contention is that my kids tend to think anything over 100 pounds is super heavy or that anything bigger than a sofa weighs a ton. They don't understand the

57

correlation between height and weight, so in an effort to show the kids that heavy does not always mean fat when it comes to people, I told them that I weigh over 200 pounds, but I am also very tall. I then asked if they thought I was fat.

Amidst the resounding chorus of, "NO!!!" I heard someone mutter, "Yeah, a little bit."

This goes hand-in-hand with our end of the day discussion this afternoon. With only a few minutes until dismissal, all of the kids were packed up and ready to go, so there was a lot of random conversation going on. Anita asked if I had ever heard of a type of whale called a dugong. A few of the other kids perked up and said they had seen a dugong in a social studies video in Mrs. Bird's room.

Omar and Marina spoke at the same time. One said, "It's big and chubby," while the other said, "It's about the same size as you."

I guess I'll have to limit myself to thirds at the buffet tonight. Otherwise, I might be taking up two parking spots pretty soon.

Talk to you later,

Thick Jagger

Date: Wednesday, October 29, 2014
To: Fred Bommerson
From: Jack Woodson
Subject: Kids, don't try this at school

Greetings and salutations!

You name the time, and I will definitely be there to help you custom paint some parking spots at HPU. "Employee of the Minute" and "Goatee of the Year" sound like good fits for Tom Winter and Latya, but you might have to arm-wrestle a few people for the right to a spot labeled "Engineer Extraordinaire."

I don't really expect to keep that parking spot for much longer, but every day I go to school, I do expect certain things. I expect that I'll impart a little knowledge, I expect to get to know the kids a little bit better, and I expect I'll probably get a little frustrated, most likely with Braxton and Eld'Ridge. However, I generally don't expect to find my life at risk.

Today, though, as the pictures I texted you prove, I found my life, or at least my skeletal continuity, in great peril! Let me take you back a few days to explain how those pictures came about.

A large part of Monday's staff meeting was devoted to the agenda for Red Ribbon Week, aka "Say No to Drugs Week." Every day has its own theme, giving the kids a chance to wear or do something different. Our counselor, Miss Rooker, walked us through all of the daily themes, such as Sunglasses Day and Crazy Socks Day. I had already suggested Miss Rooker go off book and include a Lederhosen Day or a Star Wars Villains Day, but sadly, neither was included in the agenda. She did tell us, however, not to park in the staff parking lot Wednesday because it would need to be empty for a demonstration.

This morning around 9:30, we were all called out to the parking lot where a couple of ramps and cones had been set up, and two guys about my size (much smaller than a dugong, in other words) were riding around on tiny bicycles. When the whole school was assembled, the guys spoke to the kids for a bit. They introduced themselves as Pete and Vinnie, trick riders who go from school to school spreading the dual message of participating in school and staying off drugs and alcohol. Instead of popping pills, they pop wheelies. Instead of getting high, they get air. Instead of drinking gallons of moonshine, they... Well, you get the idea.

Pete and Vinnie spent the next 15 minutes or so delighting the crowd with jumps, flips, and other tricks. While a few of my kids, most notably Cesar, looked totally unimpressed, most of them were going wild with every new stunt. Trevor screamed himself hoarse, and I'm almost positive Andres peed himself a little.

Then Vinnie announced, "For our final trick, we will need the help of six or seven brave teachers."

Immediately, groups of kids began chanting the names of teachers they wanted to volunteer. These chants seemed to be either for their favorite teacher or for the teacher they most wanted to see beset by some bodily harm.

Both of my sections loudly screamed my name, and kids tried to push me out to the middle. I playfully resisted at first then walked over to the two stunt men. I noticed Mrs. Bird was chanting my name too, making absolutely no move to step forward herself.

Mr. Utoobay was already out in the center, and Mr. Redd soon joined us. Mrs. Keller from special ed and a pair of ladies from second grade rounded out the bunch. Interestingly enough, none of the admin wanted any part of it.

By this point, I think everyone out there knew exactly what this final trick was going to be. My plan of action was to be at the FRONT of the group being jumped over, not at the end. While Pete – by far the bigger of the two performers and definitely the one who looked like he'd had a bad experience in elementary school and was looking for some time-delayed revenge – slowly circled the parking lot on his bike like a hungry shark, Vinnie positioned the teachers and asked us to lie down. As luck would have it, I was indeed right on an end. I didn't know WHICH end, though, since there was no way to tell which way the bike was going to be approaching. Vinnie asked his partner if he was ready, and Pete wheeled around to the side opposite me. I was on the far end! If this guy didn't jump properly, I'd be the one most likely to get landed on!

Vinnie yelled a few things to the kids and scaredy-cat teachers to amp up the crowd, then he must have felt my trepidation, because he laid down next to me, placing himself at the end. I breathed a little easier at that. I was still hoping Crazy Voyeur Lady across the street was rolling film, though, in case Jill needed video evidence in my wrongful death lawsuit.

Suddenly it was happening. I hardly had time to position my hands over the family jewels when the guy was up in the air, flying over us. He was probably in the air for a fraction of a second, but that moment seemed to last an eternity. As I watched the bike rise in slow motion, my brain projected a dashed line showing its path, with the end of the parabola directly on my neck. As the back tire passed inches from my nose, I could clearly make out the word "Chupacabra" stamped on the rubber and a green wad of gum between two of the treads. I have no earthly idea how the bike didn't land on Vinnie, though come to think of it, I truly can't remember seeing him use his right hand after it was all over.

Mrs. Phelps took some great pictures, and she forwarded some of them to Jill before she sent them to me. When I got back to the classroom, I had a text that read, "I am not super happy that you would put yourself out there to almost die. I'm going to need you around to help me raise our child! Also, I'm going to need you to pick up milk on the way home."

Back in the classroom, I thought I'd take the opportunity to talk about mathematical prefixes. I mentioned that "cycle" means wheel, and I asked the kids what "bi" means.

While Eld'Ridge waved his hand and blurted, "Like when you say 'SEEYA!'" the other (more sensible) kids drowned him out with, "TWO!"

Then someone mentioned a tricycle and someone else mentioned a unicycle, and we talked about what those prefixes mean. Beto asked if there was an "octocycle," and if so, would it have eight wheels? Khabi smugly held his pencil out in his hand and announced that he had a "nocycle."

When the kids started asking what other words start with "bi-" I worried just a bit that somebody would say something that might result in parent phone calls. I needn't have worried. Along with a lengthy list of words that didn't really fit the prefix – biography, bitter, big – the kids only came up with one applicable (and very appropriate) word – bilingual.

Nobody mentioned the word I was worried about. I'm speaking, of course, about bifocals.
Talk to you later,

Sean "Huffy" Combs

Date: Friday, October 31, 2014
To: Fred Bommerson
From: Jack Woodson
Subject: Friday the 31st: Jason vs Dyslexia

Hey bud,

I'm going to go ahead and hard pass on your invitation to let you drive a golf ball off of a tee in my mouth. I'm not actively searching for more danger in my life. If I was, I'd do crazy things like skydiving, running from bulls, or letting Larry drive me somewhere. The thing with the bicycle seemed relatively low-risk, so I'm good at least until my child arrives. I did have some crazy dreams over the past couple of nights, though. Most involved getting up, looking into the mirror, seeing bicycle tread marks covering my face, then screaming myself awake.

Hey, here's a question for you. If Friday the 13th is supposed to be an unlucky day, is the reverse – Friday the 31st – the luckiest day of all?

I'd say the fact that there is no school tomorrow, the day after Halloween, absolutely makes this a lucky day! No sugar comas to deal with, no makeup or hair dye that stubbornly just won't come off, no kids packing their own lunches consisting solely of candy corn, gummi bears, and pixie sticks.

I did have a bit of bad luck befall me, though. First thing this morning, Susana gave me a chocolate coin wrapped in foil and wished me a happy early Halloween. I thanked her and put the coin in my pocket for later consumption.

Fast-forward to 3:30 today. I packed up and headed out the door. As I approached my car, I pulled my phone out of my pocket and found it coated in what appeared to be turtle dookie. Lovely sentiment on Susana's part; lousy memory on my part.

Today was also somewhat unlucky for Eld'Ridge, who tried out a new Halloween-themed excuse for not doing last night's homework. He told me, "I tried to do my homework last night, but then a spider crawled across the paper and I got very scared!"

While my sarcastic side wanted to reply, "Much like a vampire bat, that sucks!" I instead answered him, "Well, I guess you'll be safe sitting next to me at recess while you do your work!"

Speaking of undone papers, I have been very tempted to embrace this Halloween season and decorate my room in truly horrifying fashion. Instead of heads on spikes, I feel like I should post student papers with no names, dripping with red ink, at my classroom door as a warning to all who enter.

As I mentioned in my last email, this week was Red Ribbon Week, and it culminated with a short walk around the neighborhood today. Kids made posters and banners, and we carried them and waved as we walked. I guess the idea is to ward off any potential drug dealers or potheads in the neighborhood. When my kids were making their posters and banners, I did have to remind them a few times that there IS a difference between "Drug Free" and "Free Drugs." I also had to keep a close eye on RT and Omar. I noticed they were having a ball drawing what appeared to be a person shooting a needle into his arm and a person smoking a very fat and tapered cigarette. When they saw me looking, they quickly stopped laughing and hurriedly drew a thin circle with a diagonal line through it around each picture, much like the Ghostbusters symbol. Needless to say, those two went posterless on the walk this morning.

Red Ribbon Week has traditionally been all about resisting vices like doing drugs, smoking, and drinking. I don't think anybody has ever said anything about tattooing. I was somewhat mortified yesterday to find a pencil in my exchange cup labeled, "Best Ink Tattoos and Piercing. Ridding the World of Ugly Naked Skin."

Oh boy! One of my kids is a heart-beat away from getting his/her skin blemished with some oriental symbol they think says, "Peace is everlasting" but which really means, "Elephant barf jumps the pretentious camel."

I can't be sure Misaki is the one who brought that weird pencil, but this afternoon, I noticed she had some ink of her own. She had drawn tally marks all over her legs with a marker. Not just lots of random lines, but actual groups of four with a fifth crossing through each group. I only noticed at dismissal, so I left the question unasked. Maybe it goes with a costume for tonight. Or maybe she wanted to be able to tell her friends, "You can count on me."

So what are your plans for tonight, buddy? Jill and I are ready to receive all the trick-or-treaters at our house. I told her I wished she was further along in the pregnancy and much bigger so she could throw on a red T-shirt and I could yell, "Hey Kool-Aid!" every time a kid came to the door. Instead, we're dressing as Penny and Sheldon from The Big Bang Theory. I actually look pretty darn good in the blonde wig and halter top.

Hey, one final note... Don't forget to set your clock back an hour this weekend!

For some reason, Tommy was quite concerned about this today. When I mentioned the time change, he asked, "Is there still going to be school on Monday?"

I answered, "Yes. It's Daylight Saving Time, not the Zombie Apocalypse."

I probably should also have warned him not to go trick-or-treating with Omar.
Peace out,

All Hallow Steve

Date: Tuesday, November 4, 2014
To: Fred Bommerson
From: Jack Woodson
Subject: Mother knows best

What's up?

I'm glad to hear your neighborhood was so heavily trafficked with costumed youths Friday night. We had about 50 or so trick-or-treaters before we ran out of candy and turned off the porch light. Everyone who rang our doorbell after that heard blood-curdling shrieks coming from inside the house but received no goodies.

Speaking of blood-curdling, sure, let's talk about Ron Philby's tattoos. I knew he had a tattooed symbol on his calf, but it's interesting you think it means "Dry green statue bones." I always thought it meant "Hairy wolf potatoes."

Either way, those are not things one hears very often. Which reminds me, here are three things I've never heard my kids utter:

1) This number 2 pencil is clearly of the finest quality!

2) I think I should like to place myself in time out now, thank you very much!

3) My mom says if somebody spits on me, I should spit on them!

Oh wait, I DID hear that last one this morning, from a little girl entering the building. Great advice, Mom!

There are certainly some mothers at this school with interesting thought processes. Take Clara's mom, for instance. If I haven't mentioned Clara to you very often, it's because she has been absent about 427 times so far this year. OK, that's an exaggeration. The actual number is 26. That's more than half the days we've been in school so far! Clara is absent at least twice a week, and some weeks, she misses up to four days.

Dude, she's absent more often than you and I exchange emails!

Very few of these absences are excused, and she almost never brings a doctor's note or any official explanation. She is what we would call a milk carton kid.

"Have you seen me?"

Not very often, no.

    Miss Phelps had Clara in 2nd grade and faced the same problems back then. She was in Mrs. Frosch's homeroom last year and accrued a whopping 82 absences. Since the trend has been going on for years, Clara is woefully below grade level in all subjects. Mrs. Bird and I have called for meetings with Clara's mother many times, but she's only ever showed up to talk to us once. She's almost impossible to reach by phone, so most of our requests have been through notes sent home.

    One day, after our latest note home went unanswered, I suggested to Mrs. Bird that we try a little trickeration and send a note home that said, "Congratulations! You've won the lottery! To claim your prize, come up to your daughter's classroom at 3:30 tomorrow, right after the buses leave!"

    The time we finally did meet with her, we expressed concern over the number of days Clara had missed, and we heard in return a litany of excuses ranging from severe health issues (the mom's, not the child's) to lack of a car. Clara rides the bus to school on days she does show up, so we were confused as to why that would even be mentioned. The mom told us Clara oversleeps a lot, and when she wakes up late, the mom doesn't have a car to take her to school. She also has leg issues so she can't walk Clara to school, either. Nothing was resolved at that meeting. When the mother left – with a neighbor who had driven her – Nurse McCaffrey filled us in. Since this has been going on for years, she has a much better understanding of the full story. Apparently, Clara's mother calls the nurse frequently to report some new ailment, to request medicine for conditions Clara doesn't have, and to complain about how often she receives notes and voice messages from teachers. According to Nurse McCaffrey, Clara's mom asks Clara every morning whether she wants to go to school or not, and when she says no – as kids are wont to do – her mom is happy to have her stay home and keep her company. In fact, there are days when Clara actually wants to go to school, but the mom tells her she will be too lonely and convinces her to stay home. It seems they get a lot of good quality cartoon watching done on those days.

    Coincidentally, today is Tuesday, and I haven't seen Clara since last Thursday.

Moving from a parent who doesn't seem to care much about her child's academic growth to one who cares just a bit too much...

I had an email last week from Anita's mother, very distraught over her daughter's math grade.

"What can we do at home to help bring her grade up, even if just a few points?"

Normally, I would be more than happy to suggest ideas for practice activities at home, overjoyed to see parents caring about improving their kid's scores.

In Anita's case, though, I had to find a tactful way to write back, "Your daughter made a 93! That's really, really good! Keep up the good work! Oh, and maybe pass on your stress and concern to the parents who don't care that their kids made a 50!"

I had a parent conference this afternoon, and this one wasn't about excessive absences or unacceptable grades. Tyrellvius's mom wanted an explanation as to why he had a certain code in his behavior folder.

We use codes like W1, B7, and so on in the monthly behavior charts, and there is a key under the calendar so the parents and kids know what each code means. I wrote a B3 – excessive arguing – in Tyrellvius's folder yesterday.

Tyrellvius is not a terribly behaved kid, but he's not one of the best either. He wouldn't sucker punch you, but he'd have no qualms about stealing your Netflix password. He accrues two or three codes per week, and for the most part they are for not doing work or not following directions. He's not earning codes for fighting or arson or money laundering. Most times, though, the codes on the calendar aren't enough, and Tyrellvius brings his folder back with a note from his mom saying, "What happened?" I wrote short explanations the first few times, but then I asked for a conference so we could meet face-to-face.

Tyrellvius's mother is brusque, to put it nicely. She doesn't mince words. She doesn't hold back. She doesn't practice the fine art of "tactful diplomacy." She started off the conference by letting us know, in no uncertain terms, how displeased she was with me for not including a detailed note in the folder about exactly why Tyrellvius had been given a B3 code.

I can certainly understand a parent wanting to know details, but I also believe kids should be held accountable for owning up to their own actions. I asked, "Did Tyrellvius not tell you what happened?"

"I didn't ask him!" she snapped back, as if I had just suggested she ask a taco for directions to the nearest zeppelin depot.

"Why not?" I asked, very confused by this reaction. "He knows exactly why he got that code and certainly should have told you."

Her response was dumbfounding.

"He's not going to tell me the truth! I wouldn't expect him to! He doesn't want to get a whuppin'!"

I glanced over at Tyrellvius, who sat wide-eyed, nodding his head in agreement. I had to will myself not to shake my own head in disbelief at what I was hearing. Unfortunately, Tyrellvius's mother did not seem like the type who wanted to debate the merits of promoting honesty in one's children, so I explained to her what had happened.

After our conference, I can tell I'll still be expected to write detailed notes every time I give Tyrellvius a code. Though I'm already tempted to add one little question the next time I send her a note.

"Are you sure you wouldn't like to keep Tyrellvius home tomorrow to watch Sponge Bob with you?"

Talk to you later,

The Mom Squad

Date: Friday, November 7, 2014
To: Fred Bommerson
From: Jack Woodson
Subject: State of Confusion

Dude,

    Funny that you mentioned Misaki's tally marks from last week. I know that you use tally marks to count how long you've been stuck at HPU, but I don't agree that was Misaki's motivation. She only had 15-20 on her legs, and we've been in school for much longer than that. Of course, it would be a valid argument if it had been Clara drawing the tally marks, counting missed days of school.

    And no, of course I don't ever expect you to tell Larry the truth about anything. I know you don't want a whuppin'!

    Earlier this week, I was grading some tests at home, and I had a notion to create a new, non-numerical grading system. Instead of points, I could use the names of famous mathematicians to mark how well students had performed. The top tests would be labeled Newton, Descartes, Pythagoras, and Euclid. The geek in me was totally psyched to try this out. Then I actually started looking through the tests, and there were way too many kids I would have had to mark "Larry the Cable Guy."

    Unfortunately, those tests were not the only aspect of this week that proved to be confused, jumbled, or flat out wrong.

    Today I experienced the mother of all "smack my head" moments. At recess, I was talking with some kids, telling them about the basketball game my brother and I went to last weekend. School kids are always immediately fascinated when they discover a teacher has a life or relatives of any kind, so they insisted on seeing a picture of Zack.

    I pulled out my phone and brought up a recent picture of the two of us, taken at my wedding. Alvaro immediately exclaimed, "He looks just like you!" and several others voiced agreement.

    "You think so?" I asked. People have said we have similar features, but it's not like we're twins or anything.

    "He looks EXACTLY like you!" Andres shouted. This caused more kids to rush over to see what the fuss was about.

    Alvaro told the newcomers they were looking at never before seen photos of Mr. Woodson's brother, pointing for emphasis. He put his finger so close to the screen, I could tell he definitely was not pointing at Zack.

    I pinched the screen and blew up the half with just me in it.

"You do know THAT'S me, right?" I asked before swiping to the other half of the picture. "THIS is my brother."

Every single kid shouted, "OOOOOOOOOOHHHHH!!!!" in sudden and inexplicable understanding.

Like I said, smack my head. Then there was the conversation I had with Susana yesterday.

Me:	"We live in Texas, but Texas is not the biggest state in the United States. Do you know which state is the largest?"
Susana:	"The world!"
Me:	"No, I mean the biggest STATE. In the country."
Susana:	"The planet!!"
Me:	"The whole planet is not a state."
Susana:	"The earth!!!"
Me:	"Yeah, you nailed it."

Susana's insistence on her global line of answer choices reminded me of something that happened a few weeks ago. I was down on one knee helping someone at their desk when Carmine came up and asked me if he could use a therapy. I asked for clarification, because I couldn't figure out why a little boy would be asking for therapy. Or even why he would think a teacher could provide it. After he spelled it out for me – T-H-E-R-A-P-Y – I was getting ready to call Nurse McCaffrey or Miss Rooker to see if Carmine needed physical or mental help, but then he told me he wanted to look for other words that mean the same thing, so Mrs. Bird wouldn't accuse him of copying directly from a book.

He was so dogged, persistent, and indefatigable with his request, I finally figured out he wanted a thesaurus, not a therapy. I have to say, my head literally explodes every time I hear a fourth grader use a word incorrectly like that.

Then there are the misspellings. I spotted potential trouble yesterday when the kids were writing their own word problems as a warm up. I was reading over the shoulder of a few kids, liking what I saw for the most part. Then I viewed Greyson's journal. He had written, "Blanca has 32 ___. Rajiv has 17 ___. How many more ___ does Blanca have?"

In recreating this word problem for you, I've replaced Greyson's units with blank lines. I'm really not sure whether he intended Blanca and Rajiv to have pens or pennies, but either way, he grossly misspelled. As a result, his word problem read like a black market report on male genitalia.

I had a case of right spelling, wrong definition today myself. Around 3:30, Ms. Zapata came over the PA system and announced, "Teachers, don't forget to go to the conference room after dismissal to get your shots."

I headed down to the conference room, walked in, and said, "Line 'em up! What's first? Lemon drop? Buttery nipple?"

The young woman in the lab coat smiled obligingly and said, "We're giving FLU shots."

Bummer.

Well, I've decided if there's going to be so much confusion here at the school anyway, I should try to use it to my advantage. For instance, I'm really tired of kids running down the hallway. I shout, "STOP RUNNING!" at them, and it has zero effect. I yell, "SLOW DOWN!" and they keep running. So I think I'll try saying something completely random to see how they react. The next time I see a kid running, I'm going to yell, "GOD SAVE THE QUEEN!" or, "GET TO DA CHOPPA!!"

If initial attempts are successful, I might even take the opportunity to work a little academic knowledge in there and yell something historical like "REMEMBER THE ALAMO!" or "FIFTY-FOUR FORTY OR FIGHT!"

The sheer bewilderment alone should stop them in their tracks. And then they can seek a therapy.

Talk to you later,

Mal A Prop

Date: Tuesday, November 11, 2014
To: Fred Bommerson
From: Jack Woodson
Subject: No, Mr. Bond, I expect you to divide

Hey Fred,

Thanks for sending me those pictures from the latest HPU outing. I can tell you guys had a lot of fun. Also, I can't believe how much Latya looks just like you! Oh wait, that WAS you I was looking at?

"OOOOOOOOOOOOOOOHHHHHHHHHHHHHHHH!!!"

We've arrived at that time in the year where we have to cover the topic that makes so many kids decide they hate math. Sure, nobody's overly fond of measuring perimeter, and fractions frighten some folks. Nothing holds a candle to long division, though. Kids tell me they just don't understand it. Parents tell me they can't do it themselves. Journalists tell me it's to blame for world wars, childhood obesity, and acid rain.

I always enjoyed introducing the concept at the very end of third grade, when I didn't really expect everyone to fully master it. This year I do have to care whether everyone understands, though, because it's officially a math standard!

So far, the class is split (you see what I did there?). We've been practicing the skill for over a week now, with mixed results.

Some of the kids have really taken to the main strategy and the process – what we are told to call "The Algorithm" – and they totally understand what they're doing. On the opposite end of the spectrum, I have some kids who have a hard time copying the problem to begin with, much less knowing how to solve it. We're talking sixth round limbo stick low, academically.

The majority of my kids, though, fall into a third group. They are the ones who seem to understand the process, whether it's the algorithm or another method I've shown them, and who solve most problems correctly in class, but who then don't seem to have a clue when it comes time for an assessment. It completely boggles my mind. These are not kids who copy their neighbor's whiteboard to make it look like they did the right steps. I've got those kids pegged. These kids genuinely appear to have the concept grasped but then just lose that grasp on a test.

I don't think it's just a focus problem, either. I know that my kids face lots of distractions in the classroom – the lingering smell of unscented hand sanitizer, the sound of an ant crawling on the floor three rooms down the hall, remembrances of the funny way Mom said, "Taco Bell? More like Taco Hell!" two years ago – but this seems to go way beyond that.

They're like the pro field goal kicker who puts every ball perfectly through the uprights during practice but then shanks multiple attempts wide left during a game. Maybe if I Google "Cure for the Yips," I'll find some ideas for how to help these kids do better on tests.

I am happy that most of them, even the low ones, at least understand that division makes numbers smaller. Take a bunch of items and split them into equal groups – every group is going to contain less items than the total you started with.

Alas, poor Raina does not seem to understand even this. For her, 456 divided by three is 9,976. 381 ÷ 5 is 002 with a remainder of 140. 6 ÷ 1 is Neptune. Or it may as well be, for as much as she understands the concept. It certainly doesn't help that she's not very strong with her multiplication facts, either, which are such an integral part of the long division process.

I've kept Raina and a few others – Ja'Kendrick, Cesar, Carmine – in from recess a couple of times just to practice multiples with flash cards and sing-alongs. So far, I've seen no real improvement, except maybe in Carmine's pitch and tenor.

I suppose it's a good thing we're starting long division so early, as it gives us plenty of time to practice, practice, practice. Hopefully, I'll be a wizard and give all of these kids the ability to do it in class AND on tests before the big STAAR (the extra A is for Alchemy!).

I've mostly been concerned with the computational form of division in the classroom, but it sure would be nice to see a little more division being applied in the school around lunchtime as well. Have I told you that we have the last lunch period of the day? Or have you just heard my stomach rumbling? We go to lunch at 12:45, and as a result, every once in a while, the cafeteria runs out of food. This has happened four or five times so far this year, including today. While some might see it as a blessing not to be given a "burrito," I find it sad to see the last ten or so kids in line standing there hungrily while the cafeteria ladies scramble to put together a few peanut butter sandwiches and carrot/hummus platters.

This afternoon, Mrs. Bird and I noticed that a few kids who had already been through the line had burritos sitting untouched on their trays, and we asked if they would mind giving them to the kids still waiting in line. Immediately, D'Qayla, Greyson, and several others who had already scarfed down one death bomb started waving and shouting that they wanted another.

This of course earned a bleat from the bullhorn of Ms. Butler, our resident cafeteria vigilante. I really hate that bullhorn, especially when Ms. Butler turns it in my direction. The look she gave me after she told the kids to hush suggested I was nearly responsible for causing a full-blown riot, and that didn't earn her any points in my book either. So I responded in as mature a way as possible. I cupped my hands around my mouth and yelled, "Don't worry, situation under control. Just trying to feed hungry kids."

I quite cleverly began with a short burst of fake static and ended with a little high-pitched feedback. The sound effects guy from the Police Academy movies would not have been impressed with my makeshift loudspeaker, but it did earn me a respectful whisper of, "Don't do that!" from Mrs. Bird.

In the end, a couple of kids did offer to give their burritos to the kids waiting in line. It was a quick fix to a bigger problem, though, and I don't think it's going to go away any time soon. I also have my doubts that there is even anyone working on the problem. I've heard, "Don't worry, that won't happen again," a couple of times now, but I don't see anything being changed that might actually prevent it from happening again. Let's just hope for the best!

Throughout the years, I've had kids who have jumped up and run to the door as soon as the clock struck lunchtime. I've always jokingly said, "No need to rush to be first in line; I heard EVERYONE gets to eat today!"

This year, it seems I won't be able to use that line with any certainty.
See you later,

Starvin' Marvin

Date: Thursday, November 13, 2014
To: Fred Bommerson
From: Jack Woodson
Subject: We interrupt your regularly scheduled lesson

Hey bud,

It's very kind of you to offer to bring meals to my kids whenever the cafeteria is running low. Not that I believe for a second that you'd actually do it, but it's the thought that counts.

Also, in no way do I think school kids missing out on their daily lunch equates to that one time Red Lobster ran out of salmon and poor Larry had to settle for catfish.

Speaking of, did you know that lobsters mate for life? Or that a horseshoe crab is not really a crab? These are just two of the interesting facts that I was told today... as I was trying to teach math.

I really have no idea why Kiara felt the need to bring these things to my attention. It's not like I had given them a word problem about crustaceans. Unfortunately, Kiara is not the only one providing needless interruptions throughout the day. It's a bad habit our administrators routinely demonstrate as well.

Some days, it seems we don't go a solid hour without something coming over the PA.

"Teachers, please send some kids to the office to pick up flyers to go home today."

"It's fruits and vegetables time again!"

"Whoever left the rotting pumpkins in my marked parking spot – I do not appreciate it."

Yesterday, we were asked via the loudspeaker to "write all of your students' names on a piece of paper and send it to the office by 2:00." Somehow, the technology used to print off class rosters vanished or was made unavailable for office use later in the day.

This request was made at 1:53, by the way.

It's not always requests or information on the PA, though. Many times, we experience what Mr. Redd refers to as "DJing," where one of the administrators comes on through the speakers and just rambles on and on, talking far longer than necessary. It really is like the DJ at a wedding who only needs to introduce the bride and groom and then step aside but who instead tries to make a joke about the new couple's name that somehow involves his trip to Vietnam and his side business renting hot air balloons. Or the radio DJ who is just so excited to explain to everybody just how excited she is to be playing this certain song. If only we could just change the channel here at school.

We had a classic example of this today, when Mrs. Forest not only broke into our lesson, but then proceeded to talk incessantly for several minutes. Today's topic was alleged misuse of the copy machine. Despite this being something more appropriate to an email or a staff meeting, AND despite her claim, "I have a feeling I know who did this," she spent the next four minutes and nineteen seconds berating the entire school population over someone running labels through the copier and jamming it. After this initial tirade, someone must have whispered in her ear, because her whole tone changed, and she exclaimed, "Oh, it was you, Ms. Butler? Well, we all make mistakes!"

We then heard riotous giggling for about ten seconds, at which point she finally remembered to turn off the microphone.

Gavin beat me to the punch by slowly whispering, "What just happened?"

Sadly, I had no answer.

Mrs. Forest was not the only one who seemed lost today. My new kid, Mateo, forgot where he was again. Mateo enrolled last Monday, and while he does possess some math aptitude, he usually walks around in a fog. Whenever it's time to switch classes, he is always the last one out of the room, no matter what order I call the kids to line up. I guess it just takes that long for his muscles to fire and start moving.

Today, Mrs. Bird and I were in sync, our classes exiting our rooms at almost exactly the same time. While my homeroom entered Mrs. Bird's room, I stood in the doorway greeting my second class for the day. As they came into the room, I offered each student a fist bump and a "Good morning!"

I used to do high fives, but I switched to fist bumps in the hopes it would lower my chances of catching mumps, measles, or pinkeye.

Mateo, standing at the end of the line that had just left my room, saw me standing there with my fist out, and walked over to give me a fist bump. He then started walking into my room again. I had to gently remind him that he had already had his math and science for the day and that he needed to go into Mrs. Bird's room now. He's been here less than ten days, and this is the third time he's done this.

Maybe I'll see if Mrs. Forest can remind Mateo, via loudspeaker, which room to go to each day. That would at least give her a reason to interrupt class. Maybe she'll also tell us all what a horseshoe crab actually is.
Talk to you later,

Captain Oblivious

Date: Wednesday, November 19, 2014
To: Fred Bommerson
From: Jack Woodson
Subject: Everything floats down here

Good evening, pal!

I took yesterday off so I could accompany Jill to her doctor's appointment. It was time for the first ultrasound, and I didn't want to miss out on that! Ultrasound, not to be confused with Needless Sound, as you so eloquently termed the recent PA abuse here at the school.

The picture itself certainly didn't give us many details, and at this early stage, there are no indications of the baby's gender (it's going to be a boy). Jill thought it looked like a little cookie crumb. I thought it looked like a screenshot of the classic Atari game Yar's Revenge.

The technician doing the ultrasound was highly trained, though I'm not sure whether she was trained in the art of ultrasound reading or the art of BSing. She was pointing to various blurry spots on the screen that all looked the same to me, saying, "Look, there's the head!" or, "Here we can see an elbow!" or, "Poor little baby has an ingrown toenail!"

I couldn't see any of that, but I took her at her word that our little quark was doing well, and we certainly heard a healthy, hummingbird-esque heartbeat.

Things are getting exciting now! Exciting, but not terrifying. Despite my subject line, we haven't had any Pennywise the Clown sightings at the school for several years. And as the kids found out today, there are plenty of things that don't actually float.

First though, breaking news. This morning, a bird pooped on my classroom window. Naturally, this means no work whatsoever could be accomplished until every single student had informed me about the incident. In Eld'Ridge's case, three times.

While not pleasant to look at, the bird crap was weirdly timely, as my planned science lesson was titled, "Will it sink or will it float?"

My inner child came down with a big case of the giggles when I first read that in the planning guide, but I spent the day dreading immature reactions from my kids. Thankfully and shockingly, my students seem to be more mature than my inner child.

Buoyancy is just one topic in the standard from this year's science curriculum that focuses on properties of materials. Last week, we looked into magnetism, where I brought a small collection of items and asked the kids to predict which were magnetic and which were not. Ja'Kendrick was the only one who thought a Pokémon card would attract a magnet, while Raina indignantly insisted balloons are magnetic because they rise towards the sky. I've had kids who thought the sun was a planet, but Raina might be the first to think the sun is a magnet.

Most of the kids intuitively recognized that non-metallic objects would not be magnetic. Very few recognized that not all metallic objects are magnetic. Of the items I placed on the table, only the nail and the paper clip were magnetic. The kids' mouths dropped in amazement when I ran the magnet over the penny and the nickel and they remained unmoved.

Not as many were shocked when the magnet didn't move the empty Coca-Cola can, though Gavin kept licking his lips and making weird moaning sounds of desire until I finally hid the can from view. I even put my wedding ring in the collection – it's made of titanium – and its non-magnetism drew more gasps of disbelief. It also earned me a strong rebuke from Olivia, who asked, "What would Mrs. Woodson say if she knew you were using your wedding ring in a science experiment?"

She'd probably ask why I hadn't found a way to transmute it into gold yet. But even then, it would still be nonmagnetic.

Today's experiment involved buoyancy. Once again, I put out a small collection of various and sundry items, this time next to a tub full of water. When I did it with Olivia's class, I made a show of grinning widely, slowly pulling the ring off my finger, and adding it to the pile. This earned me a disgruntled "Harrumph."

Before any of the items actually went into the tub, several kids had interesting facts to share.

Braxton informed us that a person can float in a swimming pool, but a dead body will sink to the bottom.

Jeauxsifeen told us ice will float in water, but she's also seen ice sink in the stuff that looks like water but is not water that her mom likes to drink.

RT let us know an iPhone most definitely sinks, and then you get into a whole lot of trouble.

There didn't seem to be as many "shocking" discoveries during the buoyancy lesson as there was during the magnetism lesson. There weren't any gasps of surprise, anyway, when something floated or sank. Not genuine gasps, anyway. Khabi did take it upon himself to make exaggerated, overly loud, completely insincere sounds of shock every time something was placed in the water, whether it sank or floated. He only stopped once a particularly violent intake of air caused him to have a coughing fit that lasted for several minutes.

The final step in the lesson – which I copied directly from the district planning guide, I should mention – called for me to ask the kids the cringe worthy question, "Can we change an object from a floater to a sinker?"

I shudder to think just how high whoever created this lesson was when he wrote it.

But hey, despite all that, we somehow had a full day of hands-on exploration without anybody making a toilet reference.

Until now, anyway.

Talk to you later,

Wrong John Silver

Date: Friday, November 21, 2014
To: Fred Bommerson
From: Jack Woodson
Subject: The Girl with the Turkey Tattoo

How's it going?

    Somehow I just knew that last email would be a popular one with the guys at HPU. While Larry gave me an unwanted list of disgusting items and asked me to categorize them, Tom Winter wanted to know why I was classifying my students as sinkers or floaters now.

    Some people are just so dense.

    By the way, I really appreciate the set of word problems you guys made up to help my kids. I could totally use those questions once tutoring starts! All I'd need to do is reduce the numbers by a factor of ten thousand, change "heat pumps" to "cookies" or "marbles," and take out all of the swear words.

    Speaking of word problems, a few days ago, I had the kids using their workbooks, and I saw this challenging question:

A man and his 2 sons want to cross the river. The man weighs 150 pounds and each of his sons weighs 75 pounds. Their boat can hold no more than 150 pounds. How can the man and both sons get to the other side of the river, using only the boat, without sinking it?

    I noticed most of my kids either skipped this question entirely or wrote something that merely proved they had not read the question at all.

"152."

"The 2 sons."

"Long division."

    Curtiss, however, had given it some thought and written down a sensible answer.

    "The dad will have to lose weight."

    I can guarantee the dad is not going to lose any weight with Thanksgiving right around the corner. There will be much eating and drinking, and anybody who wants to cross a river in an inadequately prepared boat is on their own.

Smart teachers, like Jill and I, who fulfilled the required professional development hours over the summer, have the whole week of Thanksgiving off, and I couldn't be happier. And apparently, I'm not alone in that joy. I'm always amazed how even the kids who have trouble putting one and one together can tell me exactly how many days are left until Thanksgiving break. Trevor has given me a countdown every morning since the beginning of November.

Today he was practically bursting with excitement.

"What do you like so much about Thanksgiving break?" I asked him this morning. "Is it the turkey and dressing?"

"No, it's not having to go to SCHOOL!" he sighed dreamily.

I must have looked offended, because he quickly sobered up and added, "And it's the turkey, too."

The other day, I made a holiday-inspired pun, and it was received with mixed reviews. The kids had spent a couple of days completing a self-paced scavenger hunt for math answers around the room, and my afternoon class was preparing to switch back to homeroom. I was standing near Kirstie and Arianna's table, and I asked them, "Was the scavenger hunt fun?"

Kirstie replied, "Yeah, but kind of stressing!"

I remarked, "Stressing? Isn't that a Thanksgiving meal? Turkey and stressing?"

Arianna, who is totally the most angsty 16-year-old in a 9-year-old's body there ever was, rolled her eyes and muttered, "Why do you always have to say bad jokes?"

Hey, why does the sun rise in the east? Why does a scorpion sting? Why is the Statue of Liberty somehow the mascot for every single income tax return company in the country? Why ask why?

Moving on from bad jokes to bad science, our focus for the week in science has been strength and direction of forces. Something only moves when the forces acting on it are unbalanced, so a stronger push or pull makes a big difference. Ja'Kendrick rarely moves, so clearly, the forces acting on him are balanced.

One of the related vocabulary words associated with this lesson is "strength," and for some reason that word has posed a massive challenge. At least the kids are pronouncing the word correctly. I still have not so fond memories of Ron Philby bizarrely leaving the "g" out of the word "strength" and mispronouncing it as "strenth." Though that did lead to Larry's finest moment – hanging the "Stay Stron, Brother!" poster on Philby's door.

Pronunciation aside, the knowledge has not come easy. Earlier in the week, when I asked my homeroom what "strength" meant, I was met with a sea of blank faces. I'm used to this; I see these same blank faces when I ask what "subtraction" means.

I prodded the group by asking, "Doesn't this word sound a little bit like 'length?'"

"Oh yeah!" they replied in unison.

"And do we remember what 'length' means?" I asked, fully expecting the zombie stares again.

A few surprised me by hesitatingly asking, "How long something is?"

"Yes! So if 'length' means how long, and 'length' and 'long' both start with the same letter... Then 'STRENGTH' – which starts with S-T-R – must mean...?"

The kids grinned wildly and proudly shouted, "How long!"

I'm going to need some extra length Tylenol to make it through this year.

I'll see you after the tryptophan coma wears off,

Long Arm of the Straw

Date: Wednesday, December 3, 2014
To: Fred Bommerson
From: Jack Woodson
Subject: The Silence of the Spams

Hey Fred,

    Tom Winter told me Larry kept cracking up during your status meeting last week, and Steve and Reggie weren't too pleased with him. Apparently Larry blames me for his meltdown, because he kept thinking about the decree from Curtiss that the dad would have to lose weight to cross the river. What I don't understand is why Larry doesn't hold YOU accountable for telling him that story 30 seconds before the status meeting began.

    I'm sad to report that I lost a really good kid over the holiday break. Beto was an extremely polite and respectful young man and a model student. He told Mrs. Bird and me about a month ago that he was going to be moving to Coppell so his parents could open an empanada store. They even brought us a few of the tasty treats a few weeks ago, and I predict they are going to do VERY well with that store. Still, I hate losing such a wonderful kid.

    Maybe I need to open an empanada shop. Or something that will make me rich. You know I'm always looking for an idea to rake in the bucks or a gadget that will land me a spot on Shark Tank. Unfortunately, my prior track record has been less than stellar. My super soaker for salad dressing – the Ultra-Rancher (TM) – just never took off, and the Toddler's First Welding Kit was rife with safety issues.

    So instead of an invention, I've been thinking about creating some math-related websites where I could use the click-bait tricks and lures I see every day in my junk mail (I'm not including the spam from Latya here). I envision a picture of a child in safety goggles, mouth gaping, above the caption – "The teacher put a division problem up on the board. What his kids did next will blow your mind!"

    Of course, when they click on the link, the follow up will be, "They solved the division problem. Well, some of them did. Most got it wrong. A few subtracted instead of dividing, because that was easier. Cesar took 20 minutes just to copy the problem. Mind blown?"

    My mind was a little blown (or shot, at least) by something Carmine told me earlier this week. That kid is a total space case, and he seems lost most of the time. I think I actually had steam coming out of my ears when I overheard him say, "What does multiply mean?" earlier in the year. To give him his due, though, he does know a lot of science facts.

Monday, Carmine heard Khabi talking about black holes and how nothing can escape from them, not even light. Carmine spoke up and said, "Well, a famous scientist told ME that black holes used to be stars, but then they shrank into massively dense singularities."

Talk about mouth gaping! I'll admit, I've associated the words "massively dense" with Carmine a time or two, but I never imagined I'd hear him use those words correctly in a sentence.

Once I picked myself up off the floor, I asked him, "Who was the famous scientist that told you that?"

"I don't remember his name," he answered.

"That's OK," I assured him, knowing that half the time, Carmine can't remember MY name.

I continued, "Did he come to your old school to talk to your class?"

"No, he never came to my school."

"Oh, did you meet him at a museum or a science lab somewhere?"

"No, I never met him."

My mind was becoming less blown and more jumbled the longer our conversation went on.

"If you never met him, how did he tell you about black holes?" I asked.

"He told me on YouTube!" Carmine proudly announced.

Yes, and a famous actor once told ME that two Excedrin would work wonders on the headache I was experiencing just then.

Staying on the subject of Internet-related headaches, our district has its very own spam email making the rounds. It's probably malicious and virus-riddled, so we have that going for us as well.

Over the weekend, we all – meaning everyone at the school I've talked to – received an email with the subject line, "I need soup cans and pantyhose for fabulous Friday." This was followed up by 19 messages with that same subject before noon Monday.

I know what you're thinking – "Well, duh! How could you possibly have a fabulous Friday WITHOUT soup cans and pantyhose?"

I didn't recognize any of the senders, though, so I never opened any of the emails. Sadly, many of my district colleagues were not so savvy.

This clearly was a worm that, once opened or clicked, replicated and sent itself as an email to everyone in that person's address book. Since all of us are in the DISD address book, we received another email anytime someone's computer was infected. I stopped counting after receiving the fifty-third one.

This morning, we received an email from someone in the IT department with the subject line, "Do not open the 'Soup Cans and Pantyhose' email!" In it, the IT guy explained the worm just the way I did, adding that the infected computers would be treated as quickly as possible.

Then the replies began. People started replying (to All – that's every single person who works for the district), complaining that they had opened the email and unleashed the worm, and now their computers needed to be fixed. So I was getting worm-infested emails AND complaints about those emails from people I had never even met. This afternoon, a new email went out from IT, titled, "Stop replying to the 'Do Not Open the Soup Cans and Pantyhose' email!"

I've counted 12 replies since then. I've heard people say kids are just tiny humans, but truly, an event like this goes to show that adults are just large children. Same mentalities, same inability to follow directions.

You should be proud of my restraint, though. Because I've been tempted to reply to All, saying, "Now that I have everybody's attention, does this tie make me look fat?" – with an attached picture of a 200 pound tabby cat wearing a bowtie.

I won't do that, though. Jill just reminded me that she'll be on maternity leave soon, and one of us does need to have a job.
Talk to you later,

L'eggs Campbell

Date: Friday, December 5, 2014
To: Fred Bommerson
From: Jack Woodson
Subject: Homework, it's what's for dinner!

Hey buddy,

I had completely forgotten about Larry and the Wahoo virus. I'm sure he'll go to his deathbed claiming he was just opening a link sent by one of his clients, but we know better. Having the word "Wahoo" randomly inserted into outgoing emails is certainly not the worst thing we could have experienced. And if memory serves, we caught it quickly, before any of our customers had to wonder why we were asking about their Wahoo voltage requirements.

I've felt like a Wahoo myself lately. Once again – for the twelfth time, I suppose – I find myself waging a losing battle when it comes to the homework front. What's new this year is that I'm really only struggling with one of my classes. Mrs. Bird's class has actually been known to give me a standing ovation when I pass out homework, but my own class? Not so much.

Over the years, I've heard a myriad of excuses. Some were sincere, some were ridiculous, and some were inspired.

"Oh, I thought this homework was merely a symbolic gift, not a mandatory assignment!"
"I was at church all night, and the Bible says doing homework in church is a sin!"
"I wanted to do the homework, really! But last night, my two-month-old baby brother climbed out of his crib, crawled over to my backpack, unzipped it, carefully took out my homework without disturbing anything else, removed his own diaper, and peed on my paper!"

Man, if I had a nickel every time I heard THAT one…

Every year, at least one student trots out a brand new excuse to run up the flagpole and see who will salute (as my grandfather used to say). This week, it was Lewith, and while his excuse involved a class assignment and not a homework, it was quite a doozy.

This particular assignment had been made the Tuesday before Thanksgiving break and was due that Thursday. Lewith did not turn it in Thursday or Friday. I told him if he didn't turn it in first thing Monday morning – after a full week off – he would receive a zero.

This Monday, I first had to spend a couple of minutes reminding him what the assignment even was, then he told me he didn't have any time to work on it because his dad made him help remodel their bathroom the whole break.

Must be one heck of a new bathroom!

Having heard the multitude of excuses doesn't make me any more lenient or patient with the offenders each year, though. This morning, I blew a fuse when I discovered that only five of my homeroom kids had done their homework correctly. Three hadn't done it at all!

I don't know a single teacher who passes out homework along with the pep talk, "OK kids, we just spent the majority of class practicing strategies and showing how we solve our problems. Now forget all that, and just fill in some bubbles!"

Yet you would think that was exactly what they had been told by the looks of their finished work. To make matters even more infuriating, I had done two of these problems with the kids at the end of class yesterday so there could be no way for them to forget the correct steps. I was very vigilant in checking each person's paper to make sure they were doing the steps with me. I had to get on Eld'Ridge's case several times.

The first homework I looked at this morning was Kiara's. Not a fantastic start to my morning. Kiara had done the two problems we did together in class and nothing more. She hadn't even filled in bubbles for the others. She looked surprised when I pointed this out to her.

"Oh, were we supposed to do the others?"

I have no words.

I know I just need to adopt the "Any homework turned in is gravy" attitude, but I'm stubborn. I just can't do it. Especially when some of these kids have put NO effort into it whatsoever.

There were two other kids who had done only the two problems we worked in class. Three claimed to have done the homework – and to have shown all of their work, of course – but had merely forgotten to bring it. Crazily enough, they all had their homework folders, just not the actual assignment. I asked how often they bring a lunch box with no food in it, but I think the sarcasm was lost on them.

Cesar was one of the three who didn't bring his paper. I think he realized quickly that his claim of having done the work was highly dubious given his track record, so he changed his story to say that his pencil had broken and he therefore could not finish the problems. According to his excuse, he only had the one pencil at home, and his one and only pencil sharpener was in the shop as well.

I once read that Abraham Lincoln, as a kid, never let the lack of a pencil prevent him from completing his work. Whenever he ran out of pencils or paper, he was known to use coal or chalk on the back of a shovel. Honestly, I always wondered what his teacher thought about that.

"Oh, fantastic. Yet another shovel from our young mister Lincoln."

After lunch, I took the five kids down to Mrs. Zapata's office so they wouldn't just hear it from me. Mrs. Z asked them when I had given the homework, and none of the kids could even tell her that! I asked the kids what days I always give math homework, and they looked at me cluelessly, before beginning to guess. Wednesday? Thursday? Saturday?

Yes, Andres said that I give homework on Saturdays. I almost asked Mrs. Z right then and there if she really needed me to formally turn in my predictions of who would not be passing the STAAR (the extra A is for Acetaminophen!).

Next, Mrs. Z asked the kids one at a time what their excuse was. Kiara, Cesar, and Tyrellvius fell back on the old standby, "I forgot." Olivia chose to blame her mom. "I gave it to my mom to check, and she never gave it back!"

Andres matter-of-factly stated, "Because I was too lazy."

Mrs. Z said to him, "Well thank you for your honesty," but when Andres started to beam with pride as though he had just pulled two drowning kittens out of the river, she added, "but that doesn't excuse you from not doing your homework!"

I suppose if there's any silver lining to the story, it's that I saved on candy. I give a piece of candy to everyone in my homeroom who didn't receive any marks in their conduct folder at the end of the week. Not bringing homework earns a mark, so today I only gave out two Jolly Ranchers in my homeroom.

Now if you'll excuse me, I need to go prepare some of my infamous Saturday homework for tomorrow.
Talk to you later,

The Great White Gripe

Date: Tuesday, December 9, 2014
To: Fred Bommerson
From: Jack Woodson
Subject: Welcome to the 12th annual Stresscapades!

Hi Fred!
    When you realize some of your 4th graders can't count by sixes, is it more acceptable to weep openly or to bang your head repeatedly against a desk? Asking for a friend.

    I appreciate your treatise on the evils of homework, but I'm going to be honest here – I'm not going to stop giving homework just because you had a bad experience with a book report back in the 6th grade. Quite frankly, if I had been your teacher back then, I would have given you grief for choosing the TV Guide as your "book" as well. Also, I guess I truly can't claim to have heard every excuse, since Tom Winter's suggestion of "Homework was too soggy to write on after being dropped in the toilet" was a new one for me.

    Let's drop the homework debate, shall we? There are much more pressing issues here on campus. We have been informed that we are lacking sense. One sense in particular.

    I think it's safe to assume most people have more than the basic five senses. We may not have Spidey-Sense or see dead people with a Sixth Sense, but I try to maintain my sense of humor while promoting a sense of decency. Any time I see Carmine up on the monkey bars, I feel a sense of foreboding. Now we have a new sense to consider. For the past two weeks, we've been hearing a lot about a sense of urgency in the classroom. Mostly how our principal doesn't think we have one. And how her bosses don't think we have one either.

    Apparently, our lack of urgency has kept us from getting the ratings we strive for so very earnestly. Our school has not merited "Exemplary" or even "Recognized" for some time, instead languishing in the dreadfully named "Acceptable" rating. This is certainly not a ranking we assign ourselves; rather, schools are rated every year based on test scores. On the other hand, we do have more control over our individual ratings. Whenever I fill out my Teacher Self-Evaluations for the year, I always like to set a goal to reach "Effing Outrageous" status, but all that really does is prove that nobody reads my self-evaluations. I guess I should have been writing goals about urgency instead.

I've been wondering exactly how a sense of urgency is measured. I haven't seen any kind of barometer on the wall in the office (Urgency Level Purple today!), nor do I get updates on my smart phone. Is someone who is running up and down the rows of desks – with or without scissors – sweating profusely, eyes bulging, yelling basic factoids at the kids demonstrating an appropriate sense of urgency, while someone enjoying an even-paced lesson while smiling at their kids is dropping the ball? These are things I'd love to know as I'm being told again and again in staff meetings that I do not possess this coveted sense of urgency.

The best guess I can come up with from what we're being told is that a teacher's true sense of urgency can only be gauged by how well his students do on tests. That somehow if a teacher has a sense of urgency, he can transfer that urgency over to the students who will then feel compelled to perform faster, higher, stronger.

I know for a fact that I have a strong sense of urgency about wanting and needing my kids to do better. Not just on tests, but in life in general. I will admit, however, I've been somewhat deficient in transferring that sense of urgency over to the children. It's a very hard thing to transfer, because it's not like an auto title or power of attorney that one can just sign over to somebody else.

I've tried direct skin-to-skin transfer – but high-fives and fist bumps seem to only make the kids happy instead of stressing them out more. I've tried Vulcan mind melds – but thoughts of Hot Cheetos and My Little Pony have forced my mind back like a brick wall. I've tried lecturing – but judging by the quickness of eyes glazing over, it's obvious my sense of urgency just didn't take. So I continue to be one of those teachers labeled with the NSU (No Sense of Urgency) stamp.

Our super fun and increasingly frequent staff meetings have presented us with new programs and directives that are guaranteed to universally ramp up the urgency level at our school. I was sitting next to Mrs. Fitzgerald at the latest meeting and jokingly asked her if there wasn't just a pill we could take to boost our urgency. I must have said it a bit louder than I intended, because I noticed Ms. Butler glaring at me, no doubt wishing she had brought her bullhorn to the faculty meeting.

One of the new directives is "Learning Walks," where teachers visit other teachers' classrooms to observe their strategies and methods. Mrs. Zapata has been in charge of this program, and this week, we are doing math walks. For the past couple of days, Mrs. Z and most of the other math teachers – one at a time – have visited my room. They've stayed for five to ten minutes, observing my word wall, anchor charts, student work displays, general set up, etc.

For my part, when guests enter the room, I've done my best to continue doing what I was doing, whether it was leading a lesson, working with an individual student, or pouring myself a cocktail. There's always something nerve-wracking about being observed, though, even when it's a friend like Mr. Redd or Miss Phelps.

The kids didn't seem bothered in the least. I had forewarned them that we would be having guests and that they needed to ignore the visitors and continue working. I may as well have passed out markers and glitter and asked them to make big welcome signs. I think some kids feel they gain some sort of street cred if they can be first to greet a teacher by name. As soon as Mrs. Z and Miss Phelps entered my room, it was a race to see who could shout, "Hi, Miss Phelps!" first and loudest.

Yesterday afternoon, I was working with Ja'Kendrick at my small group table, trying unsuccessfully to get him to work with numbers AND to stay awake at the same time. When Mrs. Z walked in with Mrs. Fitzgerald, though, you'd have thought he was hosting a housewarming party.

I certainly hope they sensed my urgency!

Today, I got a chance to visit other classrooms. A substitute watched my kids while I was out for about half an hour. I saw some great teaching and some effective lessons, as I knew I would. I also made a bit of a commotion in one room.

Mr. Santos is a second grade math teacher on Miss Phelps' team. I had never been in his room before, but today's journey passed through his wing so we stopped in. In the back corner of his room, up on a bookshelf, Mr. Santos had a Captain America shield. After spending a few minutes doing the obligatory math search, I went over to take a closer look at the shield and to see what it was made of. I VERY gently touched it to see how it felt, and the whole thing fell off the shelf with a loud crash. This of course caused all the kids to spin around and stare while I turned red, mumbled, "Sorry," and tried to put it back.

Props to Mrs. Z for not immediately declaring, "And THIS is why we can't do math walks more often!"

I did ask her, "Did you see how urgently I put that shield back in place?"

I came back to my room to find a note from Clara that said, "Mr. Woodson, you're the best! And I am the best!"

Nothing like a nice little affirmation with a side of cockiness. And for Clara to be present today!

At least the kids still think I'm great, even if the front office is not so sure. I think my Stuart Smalley mantra for tomorrow will be, "I'm good enough, I'm smart enough, and doggone it, the administration tolerates me!"
Later,

Vitamin Urgent C

Date: Thursday, December 11, 2014
To: Fred Bommerson
From: Jack Woodson
Subject: Yippee-Ki-Yay, Math Instructor!

Hey Fred,

I see I caught you on a good week to discuss urgency. I honestly do not miss the ridiculous deadlines some clients would set nor the stressful rush to get their product out the door. Once you've met the demand, see if you can bottle up some of that urgency and send it over to me. Come to think of it, I may just find a large bottle, write "Sense of Urgency" on it, and then attach a big tag that says, "DRINK ME." If I keep this on the shelf near my classroom doorway, maybe Mrs. Forest will think her pep talks are having an effect.

I was asked a couple of unusual questions today. The first came from my favorite 4th grade muppet, Alvaro. At recess, he asked, "Mr. Woodson, back when you were a kid, did they have math?"

Why, yes they did, thanks for asking! We also had reading and music, but we had to do without science, as that hadn't been discovered yet.

The second odd question came just before 3:00 from Andres, a well-known curator of bizarre remarks. I have no idea what kind of side conversation he was having with his neighbors, but when I walked past, he suddenly turned to me and asked, "How many catch-phrases do YOU have?"

I looked him straight in the eye and asked, "What you talkin' bout, Willis?"

At that, he looked confused and answered, "My name isn't Willis! And I'm talking about if you have any catch-phrases!"

"Fifteen," I answered as I walked away.

If anything, I suppose I say, "Show your work!" enough for it to be considered a catch-phrase.

Or perhaps my catch-phrase could be the response I've given at least three kids over the past few weeks – "It is 8:05 and lunch is over four hours away, so don't ask me if we're going outside for recess!"

I should be happy that I'm not in a position to use the Arnold Schwarzenegger catch-phrase, "It's not a tumor!" Today absolutely reaffirmed my belief that I would be a terrible and miserable kindergarten teacher.

Don't get me wrong, I enjoy SEEING the kindergartners; for the most part, they are adorable. The very tallest of them comes up to my ankles, and they tend to be either afraid of me because I'm a fearsome giant or in awe of me because I'm a mighty giant. As for the little girl who cheerfully shouted, "Hi, Mr. Big Head!" at me in the hallway the other day? I'm not sure yet which camp to put her in.

I know for a fact that I would not want to be alone in a room with 25 of them attempting to get them to pay attention to me. But I saw a small sampling today of what the bathroom breaks would be like.

I had dropped my class off at the cafeteria and was headed back to the teachers' lounge for lunch. As I rounded the corner, I made the mistake of glancing down the adjacent hallway and, more precisely, at the restroom area at the beginning of that hallway where a class of kindergartners was gathered. And lo, there I beheld a tiny kindergartner walking out of the boys room with his pants down around his ankles and his tightie whities visible for the whole world to see.

This kid wasn't showing the appropriate level of embarrassment that one would expect from someone with his drawers hanging out. He wasn't looking around the hall wild-eyed shouting, "LOOK AT ME!" but he also seemed ready to drink some water and shuffle back into line as he was.

I didn't see a teacher (she was probably handling a similar situation in the girls room), so I figured I should step in and limit the exposure to a few giggling kids that had already spotted the Fruit of the Looms. I gently escorted the lad back into the bathroom, telling him, "Come on, man, nobody needs to see that."

Potential catch-phrase?

Unfortunately, taking care of the situation was not as easy as asking the kid to pull his pants up. For one thing, his pants were down below his knees, but they were still buttoned up and belted. He started tugging them up, but they wouldn't go over his hips. I'm at a loss as to how he pulled them DOWN over his hips like that in the first place. He also proved to be lacking the manual dexterity to undo his belt so that he could pull the pants back up himself. I finally accepted the fact that this was not going to be a spectator sport. I undid the kid's belt, and then he was able to unsnap his pants and get the zipper down so he could pull his pants back up to acceptable pants levels. But then he couldn't get the zipper back up, so I had to help him with that. And then with buttoning up his pants again. And then with securing his belt again.

I feel like I should've offered the kid a moist towelette and a selection of colognes to complete my services as a valet. I suggested he look into elastic-band pants and then I resumed my lunch break. Mrs. Bird told me the experience was good practice for when I was a dad. I asked if her son had still needed help going to the bathroom when he was five, and she blurted, "Oh, hell no!"

As soon as I returned home, I told Jill potty training and bathroom etiquette are high on the priority list once our little Quark arrives.

Our catch-phrase will be, "Once you've turned three, and you have to go pee, you'll do it without me!"
Talk to you later,

Kindergarten Copout

Date: Tuesday, December 16, 2014
To: Fred Bommerson
From: Jack Woodson
Subject: Giving your True Love the bird

Hey buddy,

Just so you know, "Quark" is not our officially settled on name. Nor is "Wing Nut," "Tic Tac," "Peanut," or any of the other names I may lovingly bestow upon our little guy. I'm not ruling anything out as a middle name, though.

It was certainly interesting to read through the plethora of catch-phrases I received from you guys – most of which I have never ever heard any of you utter. Tom Winter wins the Most Random Award with "Raise your popcorn before I shave the goat!"

I most definitely will not be passing on your suggestion of "It's Juice-Box Thirty somewhere!" to Andres, or anyone else for that matter.

No. Just no.

Actually, if frequency is any indication, I may need to adapt "That doesn't make any sense" as a catch-phrase soon. My Challenge Question this week asked how many total days the kids would be out of school over the holiday break if they were off for two full weeks plus two more days. Clara said 10,363 days. For anyone else, this answer would be ludicrous. For Clara, it's merely absurd. I think if I won the Powerball lottery, then I'd be out of school for that many days, but my chances are slim, seeing as how I never buy a ticket.

Speaking of money, I'm happy to hear that you got a raise. I'm sorry to hear it wasn't the amount you had wanted. If it's any consolation, your meager raise was more than the combined total of my fourth grade team's individual bumps in salary this year.

I shouldn't complain, seeing as how I can now buy one more Subway sandwich each month, but it still irritates me. I've been thinking about this a lot lately, and I believe it's high time we move teacher pay scale over to a model similar to professional athletes. Many NFL players have a set base rate, but then they earn a little extra every time they reach a rushing milestone, make an extra tackle, or refrain from drunken public brawls.

I'd like to apply that sort of structure to MY paycheck. I suggest a base salary of $30,000, which can be increased by documenting events from the following list. We would of course get paid for every occurrence of the event, not just the first time.

Staff meeting –	$200
Fire drill –	$150
Classroom observation –	$100 per observer
Student talking back –	$20
Student cussing at you –	$75
Student giving you the bird –	$50
Student giving you the ring finger and then saying, "What? It's not the middle finger!" –	$49.50
Student disrespecting your lesson –	$20
Student disrespecting your hair or clothes –	$15
Student disrespecting yo momma –	$100
Administering a standardized test –	$250 per student per test
Student slapping you –	$2000
Student punching you –	$4000
Student kicking you –	$3000
In the nads –	$15,000
Student whining, "They're skipping!" –	$15

    I think teachers would totally support this salary schedule. Heck, I could retire after a year based on the "They're skipping" rider alone!

    Alas, I remain consigned to teaching money, not making it, and my kids were having money issues of their own this week. With Christmas break fast approaching, I put the kids in small groups, gave them lists of the items bought in the song "The 12 Days of Christmas," and asked them to estimate the total cost of these items. Never mind that Carmine immediately asked if Halloween was one of the 12 days of Christmas. Enough of the kids were familiar with the song, so it was an enjoyable project. Thankfully, no one guessed that a partridge in a pear tree would cost a bajillion dollars.

    I wandered around the room giving tips and assistance and greatly enjoying the conversations I was hearing.

    In one group, I caught a bit of this conversation:

Landon: "Hmmm... Two turtledoves? Let's say five dollars."

Marina: "But they're SPECIAL birds!"

Landon: "Oh. OK. Six dollars then."

Later, I heard Tracy Jane tell a partner, "The 10th day is going to be expensive. Lords cost a lot!"

Once they had estimated everything, I showed the kids a pricing sheet I found online that listed current market value for each item. Without exception, the kids overvalued the five gold rings by a mile. I think the lowest estimate I saw all day was $500,000, and guesses went as high as $8 million!

Actual retail price? $750 for the set.

Once the shock and disbelief of that wore off, the rationalization began.

"Maybe they're fool's gold."
"Or just gold plated."
"Must be rings for a baby!"

More shockingly to me, the most expensive item on the list was the seven swans a-swimming. Those dirty birds will cost you over thirteen thousand dollars!

At the end of it all, I saw Curtiss intently studying the list and muttering, "My friends would have to be happy with eight maids a-milking and a partridge in a pear tree, because I'm not spending more than a hundred bucks!"

Stay frugal, Curtiss. Stay frugal.
Talk to you later,

13 Nerds a-LARPing

Date: Friday, December 19, 2014
To: Fred Bommerson
From: Jack Woodson
Subject: The Little Dumber Boy

Sum, they told me, pa-rum-pum-pum-pum.
I have no clue on this, pa-rum-pum-pum-pum.

    This is just an excerpt from the new math-themed Christmas album I'm working on. Hark the Acute Angles Sing is in the can, and I'm still trying to make "Decimals" rhyme with Jingle Bells.
    I'm sorry to burst your bubble, but the nine ladies dancing were pretty darn expensive. Maybe you can add just one to your Christmas wish list, but you'll probably have to settle for the more reasonably priced three French hens.
    I also appreciated Tiffany's suggestion for my proposed teacher pay schedule. I think receiving a new student within two weeks of any standardized test should definitely be worth $1000 a pop.
    Today was the last day of school for the year 2014! Whatever anybody wants to call this break – Christmas, Yuletide, Holiday Extravaganza, Winter Sales Event – let it now begin!
    By the way, eating a chocolate rum ball at school doesn't count as drinking on the job, does it? I hope not, because I had about 50 of those bad boys today.
    I know that a lot of my kids aren't exposed to much culture and are thus unaware of many things you and I take for granted, but I was stunned this morning at their ignorance on Christmas-themed literary characters. I wrote a word problem for today's warm-up, and in the problem I included the names of three of Santa's reindeer – Blitzen, Comet, and Dasher. When it came time to discuss the solution, I asked, "You guys DO know these names, right?"
    The kids had no earthly idea. I might have had better luck including Larry, Moe, and Curly in the problem.
    To my utter shock and amazement, Akasha and Rajiv were the only two kids in either of my classes that had even heard of Rudolph. They were all aware of Santa (thank goodness), and they knew he had reindeer; they just didn't know the names.
    I suppose not knowing who Blitzen, Comet, and Dasher were might be why Trevor thought they had seven legs in all.
    As I mentioned, they're all aware of Santa, but they don't necessarily know what he does. Earlier this year, when I overheard

Alvaro talking about Christopher Columbus, I asked him, "Do you know an explorer who went to the North Pole?"

He excitedly replied, "Santa Claus!"

When I said, "No, a real explorer," Andres chimed in with, "Indiana Jones!"

I didn't get many gifts from the kids, but Kiara did give me a candy bar early in the morning. It had a weird name – something like Bubu Jubu or Loobee Boobee – but it sure tasted good. It contained marshmallow, jelly, and chocolate on a crispy wafer. On our way to PE, I thanked Kiara again and told her how tasty it had been. Marina, who was walking right behind Kiara, overheard and said, "Hey, I gave her that candy bar this morning!"

Kiara, the regifter, just sheepishly grinned.

Doesn't matter. I still want to get my hands on some more of those delicious Loobee Boobees.

During our shortened science period, I asked the kids to write one thing they had learned about Force (our science focus for the past few weeks) on a note card. Mateo's entry stood out from the rest. It read, "I lern Force is so good to hos."

Images of Little Red Riding Ho flashed back into my mind, this time with gravity and friction aiding and abetting her. I asked Mateo to read his sentence to me out loud, and he said, "I learned Force is so good to us."

Mental Note #1:	Talk to Mrs. Bird and Mrs. Karras about implementing more spelling tests.
Mental Note #2:	Maybe stop capitalizing Force, because you're making it come across as some sort of benevolent presence.

I was looking for a sentence that at least included words like "gravity" or "push" or "pull," so I'm afraid Mateo is going to find my red pen is not so good to hos.

Speaking of Christmas-themed literary characters, our principal decided to channel her inner Scrooge and gave us all a big Humbug today. She had very clearly mandated the official holiday party hours as 1:00 to 2:50. All of the teachers had planned activities, snacks, and the likes in their rooms during this time. Our party was going to start a little later, since our lunch runs until 1:15, but nobody seemed to mind. When I went to pick the kids up in the cafeteria, I was really hoping to hear Ms. Butler singing Frosty the Snowman through her bullhorn. No such luck.

We had barely arrived back upstairs to our classrooms when the fire alarm sounded. Principal Scrooge ran a fire drill at 1:30, smack dab in the middle of the designated party time. What a Grinch!

When we finished the drill and could actually begin the party, Mrs. Bird showed a movie in her room, and I had games in my room. We let the kids migrate between rooms based on their interests.

Rodrigo asked me at one point if he could have an empty bottle to play Truth or Dare. I asked him (for my own curiosity) how one played such a game, and he basically explained the rules for Spin the Bottle (minus the kissing). I doubt any parents would be keen on either of those games being played at school, so I recommended some alternatives to him.

Later, Greyson came up and complained, "We don't have any sense!"

I bit my tongue and tried not to shout, "I know! It's driving me crazy!"

Instead I asked Greyson to explain the problem. He and a few others were playing a game that involved money, and they only had bills, no coins. They didn't have any CENTS.

Our two week break starts now, so let the good times begin! Merry Christmas Break, and I'll see you tomorrow night at Nancy's party. Jill is anxious to show you our newest ultrasound pictures! Be ready to tell her the embryo looks just like me!
See ya,

Boozer, the 9th (and seldomly called into service) reindeer

Date: Wednesday, January 7, 2015
To: Fred Bommerson
From: Jack Woodson
Subject: The resolution will be televised

Heya Freddy,

You've had plenty of time to recover from our New Year's Eve bash last week, so I'd better not get an Out of Office reply when I send this email.

The Christmas break was wonderful, but Jill and I once again fell back into our bad habit of staying up late and sleeping in late. The alarm yesterday morning hit us like a ton of bricks. You know you're super tired when you find yourself repeatedly trying to jab your house key into your classroom doorknob.

The kids didn't seem any worse for the wear after the extended vacation, but you can never tell just how much they may have forgotten during the downtime.

A few questions I'm never surprised to hear:

"Which one is the denominator again?"
"What's a hypothesis?"
"Which end of the crayon do I use?"

I always like to ease the kids back into the groove with some activities that will not overly tax their brains. I started off yesterday's lesson with a project titled "Harvesting Corn for Maximum Output."

Just kidding. I let them write in their journals about what they did over the break. I was intrigued to find out that Arianna traveled with her family down to central Mexico to visit a cattle farm. I was amused to discover Rajiv spent the break creating a new board game. I was slightly disturbed to learn that Siddiq used his time putting on puppet shows for his bulldogs who then tore the puppets' heads off and buried them in the back yard.

After the kids shared their writings, I tasked them with writing New Year's Resolutions. I explained what they were and gave a few examples, like exercising more or not watching as much TV.

Here are a few of MY resolutions by the way, which I am wholeheartedly committed to keeping, at least until I'm finished writing this email.

1) Cut back on my daily breakfast of Mountain Dew, chocolate mini donuts, and unfiltered cigarettes.
2) Stay awake during faculty meetings. OK, stay awake during at least 75% of faculty meetings.
3) Stop confusing my kids in class so much with outdated phrases they don't understand, like "Beam me up, Scotty," "Come on, no Whammy!" and "Your homework was due today."

Care to share any of your New Year's resolutions? I know Larry has resolved to run eight miles every morning – he always makes that resolution, and he always gives it up around noon on January 1. Jill resolved to silently curse at me less as I'm still sleeping and she's on her way to work. So what are YOU committing to?

As the kids wrote and shared their resolutions with their partners, I walked around and observed. Some resolutions were very focused – "To clean my room on Wednesdays and Fridays" – while some were incredibly generic – "Learn so much things."

Veena had a good one with, "I have to stop eating stuff that makes me fat," while Kirstie was even more specific – "I'm not going to eat tacos."

RT wrote "I need to play my games," which is technically a resolution, I guess, but not exactly a life changing decision. On the other hand, Landon wrote, "Be good at basketball, baseball, tennis, and foosball," which is a nice goal, but not really a resolution. (Also, foosball?)

Kiara declared, "I would like my mom and dad to help me study more."

Leave it to Kiara to make resolutions for other people.

Phil Collins wrote he would "Do the homework of my brother."

I suggested that he HELP his brother with his homework, but that he not DO it for him.

Another very specific one was Lewith's – "I'm going to watch TV from 3:00 to 3:50."

I saw that and asked him, "Is that when Wapner is on? Definitely gotta watch Wapner. Definitely."

And there goes Resolution #3!

Marina, who is a model student, resolved not to run and scream in the classroom. This is like Andres resolving to eat more pizza. By the way, Andres resolved to eat more pizza.

Lastly, I noticed a list of goals in Trevor's journal, beginning with "Get a dog," and closing with, "Get a girlfriend." All he needed was, "Get a pickup," and he'd have the makings of a killer New Year's themed Country-Western hit.

Honestly, I was hoping for more resolutions along the lines of "I will pay more attention in class," or "I will show my work," or "I will stop violently arguing with my classmate every single time we discuss who would win in a fight between the Hulk and Godzilla."

I can only hope the kids who did write thoughts like these will stick to them and the other kids will follow suit.

Oh, and that everybody will get better at foosball.

Later,

The Commitment-phobe

Date: Friday, January 9, 2015
To: Fred Bommerson
From: Jack Woodson
Subject: Hey, heater, leave them kids alone!

Hey bud,

  Vowing to play more practical jokes on Latya isn't really a good resolution. It's a GREAT resolution! One I sincerely hope you do not break.

  Oh, and by the way, you're an idiot if you really think Godzilla could beat the Hulk, especially the one from World War Hulk, where his strength was super-enhanced by his time off the planet and his growing anger, and also, oh my gosh, we are nerds!

  Have I told you how much I love it when a student gives a correct answer to a math question I've asked and correctly explains his thought process? The only thing better than that is when said student burps loudly midway through the answer then keeps on explaining.

  Gavin did just that today, and if his had been the only noxious belching of the day, I would have been a happy man. However, the new HVAC unit under my window decided today would be a good day to explode, and around 2:30, it began billowing out smoke.

  Don't worry, I'm all right, and most of the kids got out alive. OK, all of the kids. It was a scary moment, though, and it made me long for the older unit that, while being decrepit and crappy, tended not to threaten fatalities.

  We were told that the old units would be removed and replaced with new ones over Christmas break and, technically, what we were told was correct. The physical removal and replacement did occur while we were gone. Clearly, though, the new units were never run or tested until this week. Also, there is now a gap between the A/C unit and the wall big enough to fit a small child into, and I can't wait to see what falls down there by June. Or whom.

  I came in on Monday morning, the day without kids, to find a brand spanking new unit – pretty nice looking on the exterior – blowing cold air. Even with a new machine, my room would still be a meat locker, it would appear, and I was just fine with that. When I came back to my room after lunch, though, hot air was blowing, and my room was a fiery furnace. The heater was burning up all of the dust particles, rat turds, and asbestos inside the unit, adding a particularly lovely odor to the environment.

It quickly became obvious that this process was going on in all of the 4th grade rooms, because the upstairs hallway became a hazy nightmare – or the ideal setting for an 80s rock video. I told Mr. Utoobay if Quiet Riot or Bon Jovi suddenly materialized out of the smoke, I was putting them to work planning a lesson on estimation. Thankfully, by the next morning, the haze had dissipated, and the kids were not affected.

Tuesday, when the kids returned, my room was way too hot. The kids were begging for a return to the glory days of freezer-like temperatures. Wednesday, their wish came true – the room was way too cold. Of course the kids complained about this, too.

Too hot one day, too cold the next – I was totally expecting to see Goldilocks walk into my room today and declare the temperature just right. Instead, it was freezing cold again. I advised the kids from now on they might want to dress in shorts and T-shirts but keep thermal underwear and parkas in their backpacks.

These new units don't have on/off switches on the outside where we can control them. And we certainly don't have access to the room thermostat to regulate the temperature. Monday, when I came in to find my room fifteen degrees hotter than the surface of the sun, I found a screwdriver, opened up the unit, and flipped the internal on/off switch. I was promptly told never to do that again.

Jump to this afternoon and our wild, panicky exodus from the room. Class had been going well. We were talking about force and motion, even mixing in a little math with decimals. Suddenly and without warning, the outside wall seemed to explode with a horrendous sound. It was like an elephant was right outside the classroom, hitting an extended G-flat to warn its troop of danger from intruding poachers.

At the same time, a huge cloud of white smoke billowed forth from the HVAC unit like the smoke monster from Lost come to attack, and it hadn't even appeared to me in the form of dead loved ones first.

I rushed to evacuate the kids from the room as quickly as possible. Most of them looked like they were scared out of their wits, though Greyson and Ariana appeared not to care, and D'Qayla was laughing. The image that remains etched into my brain is Blanca wincing in terror, looking like aliens had just abducted her best friend.

I took the kids down to the end of the hallway to regroup, and Kirstie started shouting, "Tracy Jane! Tracy Jane is still in the room!"

I pointed out that Tracy Jane was standing right behind her.

For the remainder of the day, we stayed out in the hallway. I sent Rajiv down to the office to report what had happened, but apparently it wasn't deemed important enough for anybody to come investigate. When dismissal approached, I let my homeroom kids run back into the room, four at a time, to retrieve their backpacks. I told them to hold their breath and to be in and out in under 30 seconds. Even Cesar, who takes seven minutes to find a pencil in his backpack every morning, didn't linger any more than necessary.

Strangely, the explosion in my room seemed to set off a chain reaction of full bladders upstairs. The other 4th grade teachers told me later that nearly every one of their kids asked to use the restroom around 2:45. I successfully kept all of the looky-loos out of my room at dismissal, and my class went downstairs last.

After the kids left and I returned upstairs, I was kind of scared to enter my classroom. I pray to God the smoke that came out of the A/C unit was just steam and not some kind of toxic gas. Unless I wind up getting superpowers out of it, and then I'm OK with toxic gas. I'll take an origin story involving toxic gas over markers up the nose any day. I don't think harmless steam is supposed to have an odor, but there was definitely a bad smell in my room. It wasn't the usual mix of body odor and dry erase marker, and it wasn't the chili I ate yesterday.

The 3rd grade teachers had heard the kaboom as well, and they came up after school to see what had happened. Hank Redd walked into the room to take a closer look at the unit. I told him he should hold his breath, just in case, but he ignored my advice. He made it halfway across the room then collapsed to the floor in a heap. 99% of me was laughing at his shtick along with the other teachers; 1% of me feared I'd be writing a strange and tragic obituary tomorrow.

Before I left for the day, I stopped by the office to make sure they knew what had happened. I was hoping for some kind of reassurance from the principal that the situation was under control and was not going to be repeated. Instead, Mrs. Forest told me not to worry, because the same thing had happened in one of the kindergarten rooms this week.

That's not at all the reassurance I was looking for. If the engine falls out of my car as I'm going 75 mph on the highway, I want the mechanic to tell me it will be fixed and that it will never happen again. I don't want to be told not to worry because three other people had their engines fall out.

Right now, I don't even know if my room will be habitable Monday or not. We may have to study dynamics of the swing set and diameter of the tetherball path all day long.

If Mrs. Forest asks why I think spending a full day on the playground is acceptable, I'll tell her not to worry because I heard a Kindergarten class spent the whole day out there, too.
Talk to you later,

The Steam Team

Date: Tuesday, January 13, 2015
To: Fred Bommerson
From: Jack Woodson
Subject: All signs point to maybe

Hi pal,

    Thanks for taking the time to locate and send me that "Do you or a loved one suffer from mesothelioma?" commercial. Was that for me as a potential sufferer, or for Jill as my loved one? I think we're going to be okay, though. No one showed up yesterday morning with any unusual growths or missing appendages. And thank goodness Tommy wasn't in my room when the event happened, because he probably would have shown up in a full radiation biohazard suit instead of just a surgical mask over his mouth.

    You read that correctly. Tommy wore a surgical mask all morning long and then most of the afternoon in Mrs. Bird's class as well – just to be safe.

    Everything seemed to be working the right way today, and the room was quite comfortable. Yesterday was not the most pleasant, though.

    As you might have expected, absolutely no work was done on my faulty HVAC unit over the weekend, but first thing Monday morning, two guys were up on ladders directly outside my window doing some kind of "repairs" that sounded more like they were trying to summon Cthulu from the bowels of the earth. Next time, I hope they have the common decency to hold up posters with math facts while they work so the kids might actually learn something while completely ignoring me.

    This morning, Anita approached me and asked if it would be all right if she didn't talk too much today because her throat was sore. My poker face got an intense workout as I slowly replied, "I think that would be okay."

    I figured it would be very unlikely for her to stick with her vow of silence, and it proved to be darn near impossible. She was her usually chatty self by 9:30. Interestingly enough, we started a unit on probability yesterday, so Anita's silence was not the only impossible event of the day. I started the lesson by asking the kids what the word "probability" sounded like, and instead of "probably" – the springboard I was hoping for – they all said "problem."

    A problem indeed.

    Yesterday, we focused mainly on the ideas of possible, impossible, and certain. The difference between possible and certain is especially difficult, because to a 4th grader, why wouldn't something that is true right now be true always? To them, going to bed at 9:00 is certain, math being hard is certain, and me being a teacher is certain.

"But what if I decided tomorrow that I wanted to be a famous actor?" I asked.

Arianna immediately sneered, "You're not a famous actor! You're a teacher!"

"Thank you, Arianna, you just provided a great example, because that was CERTAINLY rude!"

They have a much better grasp on impossible, because it's easier to think of things that could never happen. Like a dragon becoming the principal. Or Cesar ever saying no to a donut.

More confusion arises with things and events that are possible, but not likely. They all told me it was impossible when I asked if the Queen of England might visit our school tomorrow. Andres insisted it was impossible that the cafeteria would serve pizza for lunch that day – because of course they only serve pizza on Fridays.

Then things got personal. I asked if it was possible or impossible that it would snow that evening. Because of our discussion, a lot of kids were coming to understand the possible but not likely angle. Not Raina, though. When I asked my question about the weather, she immediately blurted, "You're WRONG! It's not going to snow tomorrow!"

I tried again to explain to her that it probably was not going to snow, true enough, but that as long as there was even a tiny chance, it was not an impossible event. Raina wouldn't have any of it. "No, you're wrong! Way wrong!"

Sure enough, when Raina saw me in the gym this morning – after it had not snowed – she jumped up with glee and shouted, "You were WRONG, Mr. Woodson! It didn't snow today! HA!"

I'm quite CERTAIN she doesn't understand the concept just yet.

Today we reviewed the "likely" group – less likely, more likely, and equally likely. I gave each group of partners a paper sack with six red cubes, three blue cubes, and one green cube in it. I asked them what color they were most likely to pull out if they reached in without looking. Ja'Kendrick amazed us all by saying, "It's gotta be red, cuz there's a lot more reds than blues or greens."

The other kids were stunned that Ja'Kendrick had even said anything, much less given a correct answer, complete with rationale.

None more so than Olivia, though, who exclaimed, "Mr. Woodson, he's actually right!"

When the thunderous applause died down, the project began. The kids took turns pulling a cube out of the bag without looking, making a mark on their tally chart, then putting the cube back in the bag. Each group did this 20 times. At the end, most groups had a much higher amount of tallies in the red column, as one would expect.

When we did the experiment a second time, the cheerleading was in full effect. I heard Siddiq say, "This time, I'm going for green!" and whenever the green cube was pulled, there was loud cheering. I walked by one group only to hear, "Red and blue are tied!"

It always turns into a contest, with the kids rooting for one color to "win." I almost told Raina, "I'm rooting for snow. Come on snow!"

Tomorrow, we'll look at spinners. Remember Chutes and Ladders and Hi-Ho Cherrio? Instead of dice, games like that have spinners, with an arrow you flick. Grade school probability questions with spinners have the same number in more than one space or colored portions that are different sizes. The number that appears the most or the color with the largest piece is most likely to be landed on, while burnt sienna is almost always impossible to land on.

When I mentioned we'd be using spinners, Eld'Ridge nearly erupted out of his seat, thinking I was going to lift the schoolwide ban on the annoying little paper doohickeys the kids are always passing around in the gym. He's going to be very disappointed tomorrow.

Later,

Les Lyklee

Date: Thursday, January 15, 2015
To: Fred Bommerson
From: Jack Woodson
Subject: Random Acts of Mindless

Howdy!

    I think you know we only have one or two field trips each year, and they are to local places and budgeted carefully. So while you're right that it would be a valuable learning experience in the real-world applications of probability, we will most definitely not be taking a class field trip to Las Vegas.

    On a side note, you and I could do our own probability investigations at Winstar sometime soon. I'll ask Jill.

    To paraphrase Forrest Gump, Mama always said school is like a box of chocolates – there's always going to be more nuts than you expect.

    We've certainly come to expect nuttiness from Carmine, though ironically, he can't be around nuts, as he's allergic to them. In fact, according to the health survey his mom filled out at the beginning of the year, he's also allergic to blueberries, strawberries, milk, chocolate, honey, and probably every food item that starts with A through T. I think his mom just checked every box there was on that form. He's not supposed to eat anything that wasn't handed to him directly from his parents, so anytime someone brings birthday cupcakes or cookies, he can't partake.

    Today, he almost didn't eat lunch (which he had brought from home) because he forgot to bring a fork. When Mrs. Bird and I suggested he go to the front of the cafeteria and use a set of plastic utensils, he told us, "No, I'm not supposed to touch anything in the cafeteria."

    He then argued with me for several minutes until I finally convinced him I would much rather call his mom and let her know I had allowed her son to use a plastic utensil than call her to let her know her son had not eaten all day.

    I get the feeling Carmine's parents are ultra-germophobes. I suppose it's a good thing they can't witness how gleefully he fondles and chews on the markers and crayons in the community supply on his desk.

    My newest nut is a boy named Dodd who was placed in my class yesterday. He brought a bad attitude with him, and he acted mopey the whole day. He even told me at one point he didn't like my room. Apparently my feng shui doesn't quite live up to that of his previous classroom. Ever since he dissed my work environment, I've had a hard time not referring to it mentally as "my Dodd-forsaken classroom."

I wish I would get a new kid named "Mitch." Actually, I wish I'd get two or three. Then I could walk in every morning and shout, "Whaddup, Mitches!"

After-school tutoring began this week, so since Monday, I have been asked, "Is today tutoring?" about 512 times. Normally, I would expect my kids to remember that Tuesdays and Thursdays are tutoring days, but since I have some kids that cannot even remember how old they are, I'm not holding out much hope. Seriously, I have a kid who doesn't know how old she is. We went to the library to browse at the Book Fair yesterday, and Raina brought a book to me. She wanted to write down the price so she could remember how much to bring the next day (or maybe tattoo it on herself, like the guy in Memento). I saw that the book was priced at $8.99, so I had an idea.

I asked Raina, "How old are you?" thinking she would say nine, like most 4th graders, and I could tell her to bring that many dollars. Instead she replied, "I do not know. My mother never told me."

Mrs. Drogz, the librarian, looked at me in horror. I just sighed and said, "I wonder what else her mother is keeping from her?"

During tutoring today, I worked with Raina and other victims of Youth Alzheimer's. On one end, there are Ja'Kendrick and Cesar who flat out don't care to remember anything. On the other end, there are kids like Susana and D'Qayla, who truly want to do well and who participate mightily – but who just can't retain the skills for very long. Then there's Eld'Ridge, who seems to want to learn but seems to have no short term memory at all.

Here's an actual conversation from Tuesday's tutoring:

Me:	"How do we check the answer to our division question?"
Eld'Ridge:	"Uhhhhhh…"
Olivia:	"Multiply?"
Me:	"That's right, we multiply! And on the next division problem, how will we check our answer?"
Eld'Ridge:	"Uhhhhhhhhh…"
D'Qayla:	"Multiply!"

Me: "Correct! And what about the one after that? How will we check our division answer?"
Eld'Ridge: "Uhhhhhhhhhhhhh…"

We spent the majority of today's tutoring time on addition with regrouping. By the time tutoring ended, most of the kids had solved at least seven addition problems and shown the regrouping on their whiteboards. Except Ja'Kendrick, who barely finished one. The very first problem was 37 + 16. After what seemed like several ice ages, Ja'Kendrick had the two numbers stacked up properly on his white board and began drawing tally marks to add the 7 and the 6. His first answer was 11, but I convinced him to recount until he arrived at 13. He then wrote 13 underneath the 6 and a 4 (3 + 1) under the 1. This gave him an answer of 413. As in 37 + 16 = 413.

I silently made a mental note to bring my quizzes home to grade tomorrow night, so I could scream from the comfort of my own home, "How on earth do you not know how to add in the 4th grade??!?"

I pointed to the 13 and told Ja'Kendrick that there were too many for the Ones place and that he would need to regroup. I then asked him how many Ones we needed to regroup into a Ten.

With his typical bear-awakening-from-winter-hibernation speed and enthusiasm, he answered, "Five?"

I replied, "Think about the name of the place value. It's the TENS place. FIVE Ones don't make a TEN. How many Ones do we need to make a Ten?"

Ja'Kendrick shrugged his shoulders and guessed, "Three?"

He spent the rest of tutoring time using the place value blocks – which had been on his desk the whole time – attempting to see how many Ones blocks it actually took to make a Ten.

So tutoring is off to a fantastic start – maybe next week I'll throw a flaming helicopter into the mix. I came home with a pounding headache, and I am super thankful tomorrow is Friday. Which, despite the confusion, is NOT a tutoring day.
Later,

Forget Me Not

Date: Tuesday, January 20, 2015
To: Fred Bommerson
From: Jack Woodson
Subject: How the test was won

Hey man,

Yeah, Dodd is kind of arrogant, but he also seems very intelligent. I could totally see him going down the evil genius path. So you're probably right, it won't be long before I see him out on the playground shouting at the other kids, "KNEEL BEFORE DODD!"

I kind of hope he does, just so I can call my timeout corner The Phantom Zone while he's imprisoned there.

And I did indeed bring my tests home to grade this weekend. Thankfully, I was only driven to yell at two or three tests in the pile. Jill, on the other hand, was on the opposite side of the room, cussing like a sailor as she graded her tests. I kept hearing, "No, no, no! Christopher Columbus did NOT invent the telephone!"

Sometimes it seems like all we do is give tests. It's a defining feature of the educator. Just like scorpions sting, doctors heal, and Larry giggles whenever he hears the phrase "Number two pencil" – it's just what we do. Big comprehensive tests at the end of a unit, simple oral questions, sniff tests – you name it, we're constantly assessing.

It's certainly great (and easy to grade) when all of the kids answer every question correctly. But come on, that rarely happens. Sometimes the wrong answers are frustrating, often they are informative. And then every once in a while, the answers – right or wrong – are highly entertaining.

I gave a short note card quiz yesterday where one of the questions asked for an explanation of a remainder in division. RT wrote, "A remainder is what you get when you forget to do something and your parents have to tell you again, like cleaning up your room."

RT obviously needed a remainder on what we discussed earlier in class. Phil Collins, on the other hand, had clearly been listening. He wrote, "A remainder of two means there are two left over after you divide. Like maybe two pencils that can't be given out, or two marbles. Sometimes you can split up those two things into pieces, like cookies or brownies. But not if you're dividing people for soccer teams. No one wants just an arm and a head on their team!"

The kids have to take a wild and wooly writing STAAR this year (the extra A is for Alliteration!), so I try to assess their sentence-writing abilities as well. Whenever I give the kids a word problem, they have to write a complete sentence as the answer. They can't just write "18" or "295 minutes." They have to write something like, "Mary has 18 apples left," or, "Ja'Kendrick will take 295 minutes to solve that basic addition problem."

Early on each year, some kids think ANY sentence will suffice, so I'll see answers like, "I added the 2 and the 7 first to get 9, then I added the 6 and the 5 to get 11, so my answer is 119 marbles."

Or sometimes I'd see "I added and got 488 pencils, and I checked my work, so I know it's right."

This far into the year, most of the kids have the correct procedure, using words from the question to answer it. As I was grading today's test, though, I came across a few answers that looked like they had been written by Master Yoda.

Olivia wrote, "32 pieces of cake will she bring to the party."

On another problem, Jeauxsifeen's response was, "Still left 120 miles does Terry have to drive."

Complete sentences? Check.

Keywords from the question? Check.

Proper syntax? Still getting there, we are.

One girl who does plenty of writing on math tests is D'Qayla. She is the sorriest test taker I've ever encountered. I don't mean that as an insult; rather, the girl is always apologizing! Anytime she doesn't know the answer to a question, she writes some sort of mea culpa statement. On the test from last week, there was only one instance of, "Sorry, don't know that." But there was a test from a few months ago that had at least three, with each getting progressively sorrier.

First, it was, "I don't know this one. Sorry!"

Then, "Aw man, I'm really sorry!"

Finally, "I am sooo sorry, I should know this one!"

I was tempted to write, "I'm so sorry, too!" next to her grade.

I'm always writing complete sentences on tests myself while grading. Whether it's praise for correctly using a strategy or a note to tell a student which strategy they SHOULD have used, my red pen routinely gets a workout. And occasionally I write notes for my own amusement, like when I wrote, "You're missing the point" on the decimals tests where an answer said 327 instead of 3.27.

Unfortunately, convincing some kids to write full sentences is still like pulling teeth. Cesar is a prime example. His answer on today's free response question was frustrating, though totally unsurprising.

Since I've taught the kids several different ways to multiply, I put a question on today's test that said, "Explain the steps for your favorite multiplication strategy."

There were a smattering of kids who appreciated the standard algorithm the most (I refer to them as the Algo-Rhythm Nation), and a handful who chose the distributive property. The vast majority of both classes liked the lattice method the best, though Trevor and Raina wrote it as the "Lettuce Method."

Then there's Cesar. Cesar's response was, "I don't really have a favorite."

That's it. Nothing else. I told him he'd have to choose one and explain the steps, but that just caused him to put his head down and refuse to write anything else.

So it's not just teachers who are constantly testing. Cesar continues to test my patience every day. It's probably pointless, but I really should send his mother another "remainder" that we'd like to conference with her sometime.

Talk to you later,

The Quizzer of Oz

Date: Thursday, January 22, 2015
To: Fred Bommerson
From: Jack Woodson
Subject: The Running of the Bullies

Hey dude,
 Everybody already knows your favorite multiplication strategy is "Use a calculator." I will also be sure to pass on to Jill all of the wildly inaccurate statements about who exactly invented the telephone. My favorite answer was Lady Gaga, but Davy Crockett and Chuck Norris were good guesses, too. Gold star to Tiffany for coming up with Alexander the Great Graham Bell. I'm impressed!
 We found out this week that next Wednesday, there will be a mandatory bully training workshop after school. Oh, goody! I can't wait to learn how to be a bully!
 Actually, it's coming at a really good time, as I recently learned about a case of bullying that's been going on right under my nose.
 Mrs. Bird and I met with Julio's parents after school yesterday. Julio is new to our group, and his English is very limited. His parents told us he had complained to them about other boys in my class bullying him in Spanish. They have been calling him names like "gordo," "feo," and "cabeza cuadrada."
 Slowed down and over-enunciated, I can recognize those words and what they mean, despite my less than stellar grasp on the Spanish language. Spoken rapidly, though, I guess the insults have just blended into what I thought was these boys – Lewith and Alvaro – translating my directions to help Julio do his work. They must be translating to some extent, because most of the time, Julio does appear to be keeping up with us, but apparently my instructions have been accompanied by childish insults.
 I pulled Lewith and Alvaro aside this morning, and I could immediately tell they were guilty of bullying. Neither one denied it. They both apologized to Julio, but I rearranged my seating chart so that Julio was closer to Blanca, who can speak to him in Spanish and who I know would never call him a blockhead in any language.
 I was shocked because both of these boys are generally very friendly and sweet. They both seemed truly remorseful and went out of their way to include Julio in their recess activities this afternoon.
 Nevertheless, this incident necessitated a complete change in the seating chart. Over the years, I've realized rearranging a seat-

ing chart is like solving that logic puzzle which involves getting a fox, a chicken, and a bag of corn across the river. You just can't put certain kids with certain other kids.

Speaking of bullies, today I had what can best be described as an "outburst" with another one of them towards the end of the day. Braxton is a kid in Mrs. Bird's homeroom who has worked his way under my skin all year long. He calls other kids names when he thinks I'm not listening (and sometimes when he knows I'm listening), he hits or kicks kids as they walk by, and I've even seen him rip a tablemate's homework then laugh about it. On occasion, he's even tried to bully ME – once snapping a pencil in half while he glared at me. I just told him he'd have to do two assignments, since he now had two pencils.

This afternoon, he was in a foul mood, and when I asked him to stop sulking and start working, he said he needed to go to the bathroom. Since it was obvious he just wanted to leave the room to avoid working (and maybe to rip up a hallway bulletin board or two while he was at it), I told him no. He snarled at me then stood up anyway. As he walked to the door, I told him to sit down, but he acted as if he hadn't heard.

I spoke louder.

"Braxton, sit down."

He still pretended that he didn't hear and kept walking. Just as he was about to cross the classroom's threshold, I used a volume level I normally reserve for sporting events and search-and-rescue efforts. All I said was his name, but it was far louder than Ms. Butler WISHES her megaphone could go.

That certainly caught his attention. He stopped in his tracks and slowly turned around, lip trembling, while I gave him the glare of a thousand suns. He sat back down, and I didn't hear a peep out of him for the rest of the day. I actually didn't hear a peep out of ANY of my kids for the rest of the day. I think they were worried I might turn my banshee wail on them next.

Come to find out, my vocal outburst acted like an EMP down the whole hallway. Mr. Utoobay told me his kids thought it was the voice of God shouting at poor Braxton. Mrs. Bird and Mrs. Karras said their kids were quiet and well behaved for the rest of the day, stealing scared, furtive glances at the door.

As a secret weapon, it was effective, but I certainly wouldn't want to rely on that every day. Besides scaring the crap out of the other kids (possibly literally in Trevor's case), it certainly did my larynx no favors. My tutoring kids had to suffer through a very raspy Mr. Woodson after school, and my throat-clearing to math-teaching ratio was disturbingly high.

After tutoring, I was really anticipating the golden sound of silence. I might have let it show a bit too much. While waiting to be picked up, Olivia asked me, "Mr. Woodson, what's your favorite animal?"

I replied, "A fourth grader, sitting quietly."

She said, "Hey!" then laughed, so I think it's ok.

I may need to brush up on my mime skills or make a few Wiley E. Coyote signs to use in class until my voice recovers. I've been sipping herbal tea all evening and hoping not to be too gravelly-voiced tomorrow.

I don't want Alvaro or Lewith to start calling me Senor Voz Tranquilla.
Talk to you later,

The Hoarse Whisperer

Date: Friday, January 30, 2015
To: Fred Bommerson
From: Jack Woodson
Subject: The Fall of the Bouncy House of Usher

Hey bud,

    My voice has fully recovered now, thanks for asking. And yes, I thought I'd give my online voice a rest for a week as well. Sorry if you've missed me. It's not just been me that's been technology-dark, however, because the copier AND the internet have been down at the school all week long, and that's practically apocalyptic.

    Things have been crazy at home, too, and by "things," I mostly mean "my wife." It's been a rough couple of weeks for her, so I've been picking up a lot of the slack around the house in the evening. I've taken on all kitchen duties, because she's easily nauseated by the smell of raw meat (and vegetables, and can openers, and dish detergent, apparently), and I've done all of her grading this week because she's told me repeatedly it's the least I could do in exchange for putting her in this condition.

    I thought about asking her to attend this week's bully seminar with me, but then I decided I enjoy having two arms.

    Aside from the aforementioned bullying seminar Wednesday, where a few teachers took just a wee bit too much glee in role playing, the week at school was relatively uneventful. Until today, that is, and then it got interesting.

    For one thing, you know it's going to be a good day when it starts with someone asking her friend, "Am I possessed?"

    I'm really not sure which aspect amused me more – the off-the-cuff, "this is a totally normal question" way Kiara asked it, or the utterly nonchalant way Susana shrugged her shoulders and answered, "Maybe."

    On top of that, today I had one kid out for truly bizarre reasons, one kid tattling on another for something he didn't even witness, and one horribly written Benchmark test. Yes, this has been Benchmark week (remember, everybody loves a good BM!), and they saved math for last. Curtiss was the one who first called me over this morning to complain about two of the questions on the test.

    "Look!" he cried. "They didn't even ask this question right, and there's no correct answer on this other one!"

In addition to being a future grumpy old man yelling at kids to get off his yard, Curtiss tends to be a whiz at math, and sure enough, he was correct on both counts. First, the grammatical mistake was glaringly obvious in the question, "How many pages do Bertram still needs to read?"

Throughout the duration of the test, several other kids brought this error to my attention as well. It didn't interfere with the math involved, though, so I told the kids, "You're right, it's not worded properly. But you knows what they means."

The other issue was a little harder and quite a bit more infuriating. The problem read, "Patricia invited 20 friends and five relatives to her birthday party, where there will be pony rides and a bouncy house. Only 13 of her friends could come to the party. Which is the best way to find the total number of people who came to Patricia's party?"

The answer choices were:

A) 20 + 5 - 13
B) 20 - 5 - 13
C) 20 + 5 + 13
D) 20 - 5 + 13

I'm sure the writers thought they were being clever and creative, adding details about a pony and a bouncy house. Unfortunately, that sort of extra detail tends to throw some of my kids off and cause them to fixate on something that has no real relevance to the math whatsoever. In fact, I heard Trevor at lunch today wistfully remark how much he loves bouncy houses.

As far as the math error goes, I'm pretty sure the writer meant to say 13 of her friends could NOT come to the party, which would then make A the correct answer – IF we assume Patricia attends her own party and one of her 5 invited relatives does not. Presumably Aunt Doris, who hates everybody and totally ruined Christmas of '11, so her absence would not cause any sorrow at all.

Later in the day, I overheard Curtiss and Greyson griping about the test, asking, "Who the heck writes these things?"

Good question, young men. Good question.

Mr. Redd and Mrs. Jones told me they found a few mistakes in the 3rd and 5th grade math benchmarks as well. Good thing we're not paying anyone to make these tests. Oh wait...

Speaking of "Who writes these things?" I received a very bizarre excuse note this morning. Veena has been absent since

Wednesday, but her mother just brought a note up to school today. Mrs. O'Reilly shared its contents with me.

It was from a doctor's office in almost illegible handwriting, and it said this:

Please be advised Veena has been under my care. Veena has suffered an allergic reaction to a non-nut, non-dairy food product resulting in hive-like rash with colored discharge emitting from the nasal and ocular passages. She can return to school after three days with no discharge and no fever.

Yikes! "Non-nut, non-dairy food product?" We can only guess at what food product THAT might be! Mustard? Pickles? Sesame seed bun? Whatever it is, I'm sure Carmine's mom would like to declare him allergic to that as well.

It sounds like Veena will recover from this soon, but I'm certainly not going to mention these symptoms to Tommy or his dad!

As for the tattling incident, it involved Eld'Ridge, who has always valued speed over accuracy. He was sitting with me at my small group table, going over some practice problems, when we heard a crash on the other side of the room. Eld'Ridge's head whipped around towards the sound then whipped right back instantaneously. He blurted, "Siddiq dropped Marina's pencil box!"

Despite being the same distance away from the event as me, despite being just as involved (or uninvolved) in the event as me, he still wanted to be the first one to tell me what had happened. Or what he THOUGHT had happened, anyway.

He told me this news with a hungry look in his eyes that said he hoped to be rewarded handsomely for being the fastest to parlay this piece of important information. If there is ever an Olympics for tattletales, Eld'Ridge will be its Usain Bolt.

As it turns out, Marina had accidentally knocked over her own pencil box and Siddiq had absolutely nothing to do with the crash. Not that trivial details like that matter to Eld'Ridge.

After a day like today, there's really nothing to do but find a nice bouncy house to chill out in. And unlike Patricia, I won't be inviting any friends or relatives. Especially not Aunt Doris.

Talk to you later,

TGIF Scott Fitzgerald

Date: Monday, February 2, 2015
To: Fred Bommerson
From: Jack Woodson
Subject: Quoth the raven, I'm a bore

Hey Fred,

If I ever truly set up a bouncy house in my backyard, I will be sure to invite you over, I promise. Plan on attending Quark's second birthday party. You might want to make sure you're free later today to celebrate Groundhog Day, as well.

By the way, even though it's non-nut and non-dairy, I doubt you can have an allergic reaction to solder. Sounds more like lead poisoning to me. Tell Larry to stop eating on the factory floor.

Today's lesson is on the topic of vocabulary. As you may have guessed, grade school children are not always master linguists, and many times, they mispronuncify words or say things that just don't make sense. With the kids, the mistranslations are often adorable, like when Susana changed "intersecting lines" to "interesting lines." Or like when I overheard Mateo referring to a wall with no windows as "unseethroughable."

In reality, it's not just the kids who get lost in translation – Mrs. Forest insists on using the word "segue" – often – and instead of pronouncing it "seg-way," she pronounces it "seg-you." As a side note, Mr. Redd and I have frequently proposed having a secret drinking game where every time she says segue incorrectly, we take a shot.

I have a whole lot of kids for whom English is a second language, and so the number of malaprops goes up even further. Rodrigo, for instance, had quite a doozy last week.

Wednesday, I was calling on kids to go up to the board and show how they had done their homework problems from the night before. As usual, I had to remind everyone that math is not a spectator sport – when they work a problem, they have to vocalize the steps as well. When I called Chloe up to the board, I could see her mouth moving, but I couldn't hear her. Chloe does tend to be a very quiet girl, so I told her she needed to be "Loud Chloe," and to make it shorter, I'd call her "L'Chloe."

All of the kids laughed when I said this, so I continued with the apostrophized names. I said, "Make sure we can all hear you, like we could totally hear L'Dodd and L'Anita earlier. And talk loud enough for Omar to hear you, because he looks like he's about to fall asleep. I'll call him Sl'Omar."

The kids all laughed again (even Sl'Omar), and they started adding an "L" to the front of their own names. We soon had L'Gavin, L'Susana, and even L'Cesar proclaiming their names proudly. Then Rodrigo brazenly announced, "Well you can call me B'Rodrigo, because I am so boring!"

I'm pretty sure I'm not the only one in the room who at that moment mentally heard the needle being dragged across the record as Rodrigo made his announcement. He obviously meant "bored" instead of "boring," and I had a hard time not becoming Cr'Jack, cracking up big time right in front of him. The other kids also recognized that he hadn't quite said what he meant, and they looked at him like he had grasshopper legs sticking out of his ears.

Rodrigo – or "Boring Rodrigo," as he prefers – was not the only one saying things he probably did not mean. My ears witnessed a severe idiom transgression last Friday during the Benchmark test. In my afternoon class, the kids had been working for about twenty minutes when Alvaro raised his hand. I had been watching him for a while, because he kept grimacing and squinting his eyes, occasionally letting out a little grunt. I approached his desk and asked him if he was OK. He responded, "Mr. Woodson, I don't know how to do number two!"

I promise I was not being sarcastic at all when I replied, "Uh… You are talking about the test, right?"

Thankfully, he nodded and pointed to the second problem.

That same test showed me I need to be clearer with my verbal instructions. I hadn't seen Andres write anything at all on his test for quite some time, and after I watched him gazing at his pencil for about five minutes, I went over to talk to him. I leaned over and said, "Andres, I need you to focus, please!"

Andres looked up at me, nodded his head in understanding, then went back to staring at his pencil even more intensely. I had to make a second visit to follow up with, "Focus on your TEST, not on your pencil!"

Like I said, the students aren't the only ones with unintended phrases coming out of their mouths. Adults can be guilty sometimes as well, and not just me. Today when we were coming back inside from recess, a few of the 4th grade boys continued dribbling their basketballs as they entered the building. This visibly agitated Mrs. Karras, and she yelled, "Boys! Hold your balls!"

I turned to look at her, and I could see she wanted to take the words back immediately. Her face was bright red, and the look in her eyes said, "Just let me die now." The boys followed her directions to the letter, though, halting their dribbling immediately. Mrs. Bird and I exchanged a look and somehow kept from giggling.

Of course, in the interest of equal coverage, I have to tell an embarrassing story on myself as well. It's amazing how some things that are intended so innocently can come out so very very wrong.

As part of my lesson plan today, I set a block of time aside to let the kids play math games as a skills review. During this time, I rotated from group to group, sitting nearby and observing. When I sat down next to Akasha and Chloe's group, they asked if I wanted to join them in playing the game.

I said, "No thanks, I just like to watch."

I then immediately felt dirty. I guess I know what my new name will be.

Talk to you later,

Awk'Jack

Date: Friday, February 6, 2015
To: Fred Bommerson
From: Jack Woodson
Subject: The City Health Inspector is not going to be pleased

What's up, man?

     Listen, I understand where you are coming from, but the thing is, Larry constantly says things that come out wrong. He just can't help it. Whereas Tom Winter thinks things through very carefully and THEN says something inappropriate. You see the difference?

     I tell you what, Fred, it's a good thing we're going over fractions in class right now. Half of my kids have it down cold, but I'm having trouble reaching the other 4/5.

     I had the kids working on a project this week aimed at reviewing several math concepts. The theme was designing and running a pizzeria, so needless to say, Andres – aka Pizzaking123, aka The Mayor of Pizza Town, aka The Big Pepperoni (I just made that one up) – was in heaven. We had fractions and mixed numbers worked into the recipes, decimals in menu prices, and area and perimeter with the layout of the restaurant.

     You should see some of the schematics and floor plans the kids came up with. There was a lot of creative thinking going on, although the idea of scale proved elusive by and large. I passed out graph paper, expecting the grid to help the kids calculate perimeter, but I had to point out to several groups that their kitchen couldn't be only 4 feet long, or that a 2' x 2' room would hardly hold a toilet, much less accommodate patrons as a bathroom. Greyson's group had a long rectangular floor plan where the restaurant was just one giant room filled with tables, except for the miniscule square smack dab in the center of the room, marked, "PRIVATE." When I asked what was inside that room, Greyson whispered, "That's where the magic happens!"

     The math has been sketchy throughout the project, to put it nicely, but some of the periphery activity has been good for a chuckle. Every group had to prepare a newspaper ad, enticing people to eat at their pizzeria. I listened in on several conversations involving this part of the project and came away with some real gems.

"Come and eat our pizza and ride a donkey!"
(For some reason, Arianna is obsessed with donkeys.)

"Eat here, and you'll die of happiness!"

"We have super cheap pizza and tons of TVs!"

Another requirement for the finished project was to include a set of job postings, with the intent to hire waiters, chefs, etc. Here are a few comments I heard and/or read:

"Hey you, do you want a job where you won't get paid very much?"

"Now hiring security guards – comes with a free suit."

"For managers, you have to have a PhD."

"Must not have Ebola or back, neck, or skin disorders."

"Must have good credit."

That last one made me wonder if it was a help wanted ad or a home loan application.

Throughout the week, I met with representatives from each group to give instructions, hear feedback, and answer questions. Most of the time, though, I just observed and listened. There were some very insightful (and hilarious) conversations going on. For instance, Marina's group spent some time debating store hours.

Marina:	"Let's say we're open from 12 to 1."
Siddiq:	"Only one hour?"
Marina:	"No! 12 PM until 1 AM!"
Siddiq:	"Nobody wants to eat pizza at one in the morning!"

Siddiq, my friend, just wait until you go to college and you'll see how very wrong that statement was. I'll bet you'll be eating pizza at one in the morning the very first week!

I listened in on Landon's group discussing salaries for their employees. Opinions varied wildly regarding compensation.

Landon:	"For waiters, let's give them $20 an hour."
Curtiss:	"HECK NO!! Are you crazy?"

Old Man Curtiss, vehemently against raising the minimum wage.

Chloe's team thought about incentives and ways to get customers. They had an interesting discussion about just how much some restaurant chains really care about their customers.

Chloe: "Let's have a 'Kids Eat Free' deal!"
Gavin: "Dominos and Pizza Hut don't do that."
Andres: "That's because they hate kids!"

They weren't the only ones to consider the merits of a kids eat free deal. My favorite conversation came from Lewith's group.

Lewith: "We need to say only kids under eight can eat free, because nine- and ten-year-olds like us eat a lot of pizza!"
Braxton: "Not as much as teenagers! Teenagers eat a TON of pizza!"
Lewith: "OOOOOH, we should charge MORE for teenagers!"

Unfortunately, the teacher, yours truly, was not nearly as funny. I started off the project by telling a fraction-related joke. I said, "A man walks into a restaurant and orders a pizza. The waiter asks if the man would like the pizza cut into four pieces or eight pieces. The man replies, 'Better make it four. I could never eat eight pieces!'"

Tumbleweeds drifted across the room as my joke bombed. When I explained that the guy was going to eat the WHOLE pizza, no matter whether it was cut into four pieces or eight, a few kids started to politely laugh.

Not Dodd. Dodd raised his hand to ask, "How old is that joke?"

I said, "I'm not sure, but it's pretty old."

He nodded and said, "Oh, no wonder it's not funny."

Hey, you can't please them all. At least not without a donkey ride and a free suit.
Later,

Yuck E Cheese

Date: Wednesday, February 11, 2015
To: Fred Bommerson
From: Jack Woodson
Subject: Bad add-itude

Hey buddy,

OK, I will admit that was an old and cheesy (no pun intended) joke. But I figure what's old for us might be brand new for them. Thus my decision to slowly introduce old jokes, Polaroid cameras, and Members Only jackets into the classroom.

To answer your other question, I can only assume that yes, the donkey would have to have a PhD and no back or neck disorders to get the manager position.

My most exciting event today was that Olivia gave me a very special award. It was on a full sheet of paper with a lovely border of glued on construction paper stars, and it said:

> This certifies that
> Jack Woodson
> Is the Best Math
> Teacher of all times!

It's not my job to research or prove the accuracy of this statement. It's just my job to frame it and hang it in a high-visibility location. Like the teachers lounge. Or my Employee of the Month parking space.

Olivia has been a superstar herself this week when it comes to adding fractions, and she's not the only one who's shown a lot of promise with that concept. We've been working on comparing and adding fractions with different denominators, and at first, the kids all wanted to just add the numerators and the denominators in turn. $3/4 + 2/3 = 5/7$ and $4/5 + 1/8 = 5/13$. But now that we've practiced the skill, a lot of the kids have become quite proficient at finding a common multiple for the denominator, creating equivalent fractions, and then adding properly.

One of our practice problems today was $1/2 + 1/5$. After we found the least common multiple together, I quipped, "Better concentrate, kids. Things are about to get in-tenths."

One class laughed appreciatively and gave me a round of applause. When I used the same pun with the other class, they actually winced in pain. I suspect Dodd and Arianna have formed a secret club to badmouth my bad jokes.

I was doing some wincing myself during tutoring yesterday while dealing once again with Ja'Kendrick and his (lack of) addition skills. Ja'Kendrick has no hope with fractions, let's just get that out of the way. He's 9/10 clueless when it comes to regular addition as well.

I worked with him one-on-one for a little while when he was stuck on 15 + 4. I helped him to remember to stack the numbers vertically so he could just add the five and the four in the Ones place, but even that still stumped him. He sat there and stared at the paper, not writing anything, not making any move to write anything, appearing not to even contemplate the solution. I always wonder where his thoughts wander to when he is so clearly zoned out, and in my mind, I have a mental image of Pong.

I asked Ja'Kendrick what 5 + 4 was, and he still just stared, saying nothing. Most kids I've worked with, even the ones who have really struggled, would start counting on their fingers or drawing tally marks on their paper at this point, but he was showing no signs of having any addition experience at all.

I asked him to hold up five fingers on one hand. He did so slowly. Then I asked him to hold up four fingers on the other hand. Finally, I asked him how many fingers he was holding up.

"Five on this hand," he replied. "And four on this one."

"OK," I said, feeling the spike driving even deeper into my brain. "And how many is that altogether?"

"Five and four."

When I glared at him with my patented, "Are you freaking kidding me?" look, he quickly revised his answer.

"Four and five?"

Fred, it took me three and two minutes to finally coax a total out of the kid.

So it's no surprise Ja'Kendrick is not the sharpest pair of scissors in the drawer. But the kids certainly know who is.

Last week, in our opening review of fractions, I asked the kids to count all of the students in the room. While kids like Phil Collins and Veena calmly swiveled their heads and counted internally, Andres and Eld'Ridge acted as if they had been granted the title of Royal Court Counter – jumping out of their seats, running around the room, counting loudly as they tapped each person.

On a related note, when I did this exercise with my other class, I don't think Ja'Kendrick advanced past counting the kids at his table.

Next, I asked the kids to tell me what fraction of kids in the room were boys. Again, this instigated a flurry of exaggerated counting before the answers started. I had to remind the first few that I wanted the fraction of boys, not just the number of boys, but most of the kids told me the correct fraction.

"Now," I continued. "What fraction of kids in the room are girls?"

Once again, there was the standing, jumping, wild finger pointing, and loud, confident counting. After they had a chance to answer my question, I told the kids I had figured out the fraction of girls without actually needing to count the girls in the room.

Ms. Whitney, our TA/bus driver, was in the room at the time, and she spoke up to say, "Me too!"

I asked the kids to turn to their partners and discuss how Ms. Whitney and I could know the fraction without needing to count.

Rodrigo and Eld'Ridge immediately shouted, "BECAUSE YOU'RE SMART!"

Well, sure, I'm not going to deny that, but that's not exactly the answer I was looking for. I suspect it may be what lead to my new complimentary certificate, though.
Talk to you later,

The Last Fraction Hero

Date: Friday, February 13, 2015
To: Fred Bommerson
From: Jack Woodson
Subject: It gives me great measure

Hey dude,

Happy Day Before Valentine's Day! Or, as I like to call it, The Friday of Terrible Stomach Aches!

The amount of sweet, sugary goodness I received today would give diabetes to a brontosaurus! And since tomorrow is the international day of love, I will overlook and ignore all of your commentary, corrections, and redactions in regards to the award Olivia gave me.

Did you guys have the usual V-Day celebrations at HPU? I assume Nancy baked cupcakes, Larry handed out creepy cards, and Latya mumbled about our ridiculous American holiday parties?

We had one such ridiculous American holiday party at school today. It was nothing out of the ordinary, really, aside from the kids being nice to each other. Our party was in the afternoon, so I still squeezed some math in, and I started with this reflection prompt – What would you say to someone who told you they were going to measure the length of a football field in inches?

One of my biggest soapbox issues over the years has been the importance of units, especially in measurement. Maybe it's the small shred of the former engineer lingering deep within my soul, but this has always been a crucial aspect I've stressed to the kids. After all, in the real world, there is a huge difference between 4 inches and 4 feet. Even more so between 4 feet and 4 miles!

In the reflection journal responses to my question this morning, I saw a whole lot of statements along the lines of, "YOU'RE CRAZY!"

Hopefully they meant the person was insane to choose such a small unit of measurement, and not just that the person was crazy to want to measure a football field.

There were a very satisfying number of answers along the lines of, "Well, I guess you could measure in inches, but that's not the best unit. Feet or yards would be better."

I'm so happy nobody said pounds would be better.

Then there was my absolute favorite answer of all, from Curtiss. In typical crotchety 70-year-old fashion, he wrote, "Better bring a whole bunch of rulers and some sunscreen, because you're going to be out there a long time, idiot."

This group is doing pretty well with measurement, though we've had our struggles. Every year, it's a major battle to make the kids understand how important units are. The mentality so often seems to be that as long as the number is correct, the unit doesn't matter, or worse, isn't even necessary!

This boggles my mind. If someone asked, "How long is this pencil?" I can't imagine anyone would answer, "Seven."

Not verbally, anyway. On written work, it happens all the time.

A few examples from this year:

On a quiz, I asked, "What's the area of this square?"
Susana answered, "16."
No.
On a test, I asked, "How tall is this plant?"
Trevor answered, "10."
No!!

The kids are shocked (and often angry or annoyed) when I tell them their answers of 25, 47, or 6,219 are flat out wrong and that the number means nothing without the unit. This year, with area and volume, we have an extra degree of complication with labels like "square" and "cubic" to change the flavor of the unit. I'm a stickler, though. They have to give me the number AND the correct unit to earn full credit.

I'll admit, I do take a kind of devious pleasure in walking around the room and telling kids who have the right number but no unit, "Sorry, that's not it." Meanwhile, I'm going overboard to give a thumbs up to a kid at the same table who has the complete answer.

It's kind of fun to see the first kid glance at the second kid's board, see the same number, and go from confused to indignant to understanding. Often, they're indignantly understanding. Or understandingly indignant, take your pick.

On word problems, I'm a stickler for complete answers, whether we're doing measurement or not. When tests come around, I won't accept incomplete answers. While I'm passing the tests out, I remind the kids that points will be deducted if answers don't include units. I put the words, "Remember the units!" ON the test when I write it. Yet a lot of kids still fail to follow directions. Of course, I go through exactly the same thing with some of them just getting them to write their names on tests.

On one recent test, I posted this free response question:

"Sammy and Tina are measuring a square piece of carpet which is 8 inches on each side. Sammy says the area is 32. Tina says the answer is 64. Who is correct and why?"

As you may have guessed, since the question included no units, the correct answer is that they are both wrong. I was very pleased to see how many kids were not fooled by this trick question and how many even explained that Sammy had fallen victim to the classic blunder of of calculating perimeter instead of area (second only to getting involved in a land war in Asia). About 70% of my students wrote something about how Tina would have been right if she had added "square inches" to her answer.

Then there was D'Qayla, who answered, "Tina is wrong, because 64 is much bigger. So Sammy is right. So do you see what I'm saying?"

I wrote back, "Yes, I do see what you're saying. Unfortunately, it's not what I'm looking for."

I'm going to keep fighting the good fight when it comes to units, but I'm happy with this group's progress. I just don't ever want these kids to grow up and design their own dream home, only to find a very lovely dog house when it's actually built.
Talk to you later,

The Unitard

Date: Tuesday, February 17, 2015
To: Fred Bommerson
From: Jack Woodson
Subject: Sibling rivalry

Howdy!

Dude, I know you're on the same page with me when it comes to specifying units. You don't want to put 1.21 as a power spec assuming your customer will know you mean watts. They might read it as 1.21 gigawatts and think they've got enough juice to travel back in time!

And the next time Larry "boasts" about measuring a football field in millimeters, tell him I'd like to film him doing it. A video example of such an incredibly foolish act could have a huge impact on the kids so they won't want to be THAT guy.

It's nice to see that with a little under two months left in the school year, some of my kids have almost learned our standard morning procedures. Better late than never, right?

Seriously, here's what I say every day – "Good morning! Come in, sit down, and get started on the warm-up problem."

Here's what the kids seem to hear every day – "Good morning! Come in, mingle with your friends on the far side of the room, and discuss at length your favorite movie, cartoon, or pro wrestler. Oh, and if you could make a whole lot of loud farting sounds while you're at it, I'd really appreciate that!"

Last week, a couple of new kids enrolled in the 4th grade. Graciella and Enrique are brother and sister – fraternal twins – and thankfully they were not placed in the same class. I say that not because they are awful kids, but because it always seems to be better when siblings are not in the same homeroom. Mr. Utoobay and Mrs. Karras also have a pair of twins – theirs are identical – and their mother specifically asked for them to be put in separate classes. They look so much alike that I could never tell them apart, until one day their mother told me one always wears red shoes while the other always wears green. Now I make it a point to look down at their feet before I speak to either one of them.

Fortunately, I don't have to remember footwear preferences with my new kids. Enrique is in my homeroom, and Graciella is in Mrs. Bird's. The first day they were here, I spoke with Enrique as school was getting started. I asked where he came from, what he liked about school, whether or not he liked ketchup – the usual barrage of questions.

Enrique told me, "I am very nervous about being bullied here at this school."

When I asked him why he felt that way, he answered, "There are some very suspicious looking people in this class."

I advised him that step number one to avoid bullying is not to call people within earshot "suspicious looking."

Aside from a little healthy paranoia, Enrique and Graciella are bright, friendly, and mature. However, they are constantly checking up on each other.

Every day, when Mrs. Bird and I switch classes, I can count on Graciella to ask me, "How did he do today?" while glancing sidelong at her brother. Likewise, if Mrs. Bird has given a test, I'll hear Enrique asking, "What did Graciella make?" as he enters her classroom.

Today when Graciella asked, "Was Enrique good today?" I replied, "Schedule a conference soon, and we can discuss it."

The twins were involved in an incident during recess this afternoon. Kirstie and Tracy Jane came rushing over to me yelling that Graciella had fallen while running on the field, that she was bleeding, and that she was practically on Death's door step. By the time I reached her in the far corner of the field, Enrique had long since been there, and he was holding his sister's hand. He looked like he was in as much pain as she was, and I wondered if they had some kind of Corsican Brothers connection. I knelt down to talk to Graciella, and she cried, "I think I can see my bone!"

That is quite possibly the worst statement you could ever hear at school, right up there with, "I think I'm contagious, sorry for licking you," "My bowels be runnin'," and, "Don't be ridiculous, of course you are not Employee of the Month!"

I glanced briefly at Graciella's knee, which was indeed bleeding freely. It looked like a really nasty and possibly deep scratch, but I didn't see any bone. Graciella was in no condition to walk, though, so I picked her up and started to carry her inside. Thankfully, she weighs about 50 pounds dripping wet. If it had been Greyson or Cesar out there, they would have had to wait for a stretcher.

Even with Graciella weighing next to nothing, I was still huffing and puffing by the time I arrived at the clinic. Nevertheless, my kids were all very impressed that I had carried her inside. Please tell Ron Philby I'm now rumored to have "super strenth."

Nurse McCaffrey checked Graciella out and patched her up. She confirmed there was no bone visible – just a particularly white piece of grass that had stuck to the scratch. Graciella's parents picked her up and took her home, and Mrs. Bird said Enrique looked grief-stricken for the rest of the day.

It's nice that they care about each other.

While we're on the topic of brothers and sisters, I forgot to tell you about the disturbing conversation I had about a month ago at the end of class one day. It started off pleasantly enough, involving one of my favorite subjects. The kids love Star Wars, I love Star Wars, so we often discuss Star Wars at the end of the day while packing up and getting ready for dismissal. Khabi started it off by talking about the proposed new trilogy, but things went off the rails quickly.

Khabi:	"Did you know they are making Star Wars episodes seven, eight, and nine?"
Chorus of kids:	"YEAH!!!"
Tommy:	"What will they be about?"
Khabi:	"I think they'll be about Luke Skywalker's kids."
Me:	"Well, if they follow the books, they'll be about Han and Leia's kids."
Kiara:	"Han Solo and Princess Leia?"
Omar:	"Oh yeah, they got married!"
Carmine:	"I thought Luke Skywalker married Princess Leia."
Me:	"No, Luke and Leia are brother and sister. They can't marry each other or have kids."
Carmine:	"Why not? Brothers and sisters can have kids sometimes!"
Me:	"Uhhh... no. Don't take life lessons from Game of Thrones."

Thankfully, he let it drop at that, and I didn't delve any further to try to find out which scientist (through the magic of YouTube) had told Carmine inbreeding was OK. I was fully prepared to shout, "I think I can see my bone!" or, barring that, "I see some very suspicious looking people in here!"

Talk to you later,

Your Twin from Another Kin

Date: Thursday, February 19, 2015
To: Fred Bommerson
From: Jack Woodson
Subject: Acute-iful Mind

Whazzzzzzup?

Given Jill's total absence of knowledge (and interest) when it comes to Star Wars, I can see your confusion. But no, she never thought Luke and Leia were married. She did think Indiana Jones and the Big Bear were married, however.

Graciella returned to school yesterday with a bright yellow bandage around her knee, a theatrically exaggerated limp that seemed to come and go, and an undiminished need to check up on her brother. She had hardly limped out of the gym in the morning when she asked, "How was Enrique after I went home?"

Ignoring that, I asked how her knee was and she replied, "It hurt sooooo much yesterday! They said I might have to have surgery, but I said I would be ok."

I silently mouthed the word "Courage" then let her go with Mrs. Bird to ride the elevator upstairs.

She looked to be in perfectly fine shape to me, and speaking of shapes, we are focusing on geometry this week. While most of the kids (though sadly not all) know their basic 2-dimensional shapes, the world of polygons is proving to be tricky. I am often tempted to draw a big multi-sided outline around my room and call it a vexagon.

The kids are used to seeing octagons that are shaped like stop signs and hexagons that look like cells in a honeycomb. This year, I need to make sure they understand that there are many other configurations these shapes can take. A block L can be a hexagon, and an octagon can also resemble an hourglass. They have to know that a square is a polygon but can also be called a rectangle, a rhombus, or a parallelogram.

We went over the basic definition of a polygon last year in third grade. Closed shape, straight line segments only, two-dimensional. No cubes or pyramids, no circles or open boxes, no symbols for The Artist Formerly Known as Prince. For the most part, they seemed to follow along. Not always, unfortunately.

I gave a quiz today and had this conversation with Anita:

Anita: "For number three, can my polygon have nine sides, or only eight?"

Me: "The directions say, 'Draw a polygon with more than eight sides.'"
Anita: "So it has to be eight?"
Me: "It says, 'Draw a polygon with MORE than eight sides.'"
Anita: "I know. Uh… so… eight?"

She was not the only one that just didn't get it.

While grading the same quiz, I got to the last question, which asked the kids to label the angles in a figure which had one 90 degree angle. I was very pleased to see everyone had labeled "right angle" in the proper spot. Then I saw a few kids had labeled the opposite side with "left angle."

This unit is chock full of vocabulary terms. Some of them are long words, as well. Words like "perpendicular" and "parallelogram" are difficult even for my non-ESL kids to say. We practice saying them every day, though, with a few minutes of choral response in the morning. I've let certain students take over leading the vocabulary practice, although that took a little trial and error.

I chose Dodd to lead first, hoping the responsibility would make him feel more integrated into the class. Turns out, he didn't want to feel integrated; he wanted to point out just how incorrectly Mateo was pronouncing the words. If I'd had a gong in the room, I would have clanged it within two minutes of Dodd's debut.

Akasha proved to be a much better choice for leader and a far less caustic choice as well. Just saying the words is only half the battle, though. Gone are the days when it was enough to merely know that a triangle has three sides or a square has four equal sides. Now shapes need to be identified by their attributes – sets of parallel sides, types of angles. Not that there's anything wrong with that, it just makes it harder to teach when the kids have to learn so many new terms.

The kids have to identify three types of angles – acute, obtuse, and right. There is a triangle of each type as well. Yesterday, I asked the kids to draw an obtuse triangle during the warm-up. Three kids just drew obtuse angles, while two drew triangles that filled the page. Their reasoning was "obtuse = big, so let's draw the triangle as big as possible!"

I want obtuse triangles, kiddos. Not obese triangles.

On a related note, Rodrigo told me yesterday he hopes to play baseball for the California Angles when he grows up. He can be somewhat obtuse at times.

During tutoring, we also had some issues with three-dimensional shapes. I asked Raina why she had labeled one shape a cube.

"Because it looks like a cube!" she replied.

I asked her to explain her answer, using attribute words.

"Um, it's obtuse…" she started. "And it has right angles, and edges. So it looks just like a cube."

In case there was any doubt, it was NOT a cube. It was a pyramid.

I reminded her that pyramids are readily recognized by their one base, while prisms, such as a cube, have two bases. I followed this up by quipping, "You know I'm all about that base, 'bout that base."

I know you're disappointed with that, and I am, too. Disappointed I didn't save that line for the main lesson!

In addition to having to know the definitions of right angles, acute angles, and absurd angles (as they've been mispronounced more than once by Alvaro), the kids also have to know how to measure an angle to the nearest degree. Pardon the pun, but this presents a degree of difficulty I've rarely seen before.

For one thing, many of my kids are having trouble just pronouncing the name of the measuring tool. I've heard "Tractor," "Protector," "Proctor" and strangest of all, "Perstanker."

For another, since there are two sets of numbers that run along the top arc of the tool (so you can measure angles from either direction), I'm constantly seeing kids choosing the wrong measurement. I think it's fairly obvious to see whether an angle is more or less than 90 degrees and apply the logic test to an answer, but when have my kids ever used common sense?

No, that angle that looks like Larry attempting a sit-up is not 3°, it's 177°!

I think we'll be continuing this topic next week. At the very least, that will hopefully give RT plenty of time to get the word "crapazoid" out of his system.

And at least I know how I'm starting class tomorrow.

"OK, boys and girls, take out your perstankers now, it's time to measure some absurd angles!"

Talk to you later,

Parall-el, Son of Jor-el

Date: Tuesday, February 24, 2015
To: Fred Bommerson
From: Jack Woodson
Subject: Encyclopedia Brown and the Worst Mystery Ever

Hey Fred,

Ugh. With all of the other wrong names, how did I not foresee Larry making some kind of a "prophylactor" joke?

I took yesterday off for a nice long birthday weekend and so I could go with Jill to her checkup yesterday. This time, we could really make out features much more clearly than the last time. The lad is really making progress! We could see his hand up near his face, and it looked like he was rubbing his nose. We could also see a certain feature that proves without a doubt that he is indeed a he.

Jill was slightly disappointed, as she was so positive that she'd be the one to break the "Woodson curse." But she was also a little relieved as this at least cuts our name dilemma in half. So long, Cruella, Flo-Jo, and Baroness; hello, Hieronymus, Megatron, and Gandalf!

This morning, I faced a dilemma of a different sort.

Taking a day off always seems so nice until I return to the classroom the next day and invariably find my room in shambles, supplies missing, and visible evidence of ritualistic animal sacrifice. Just once, I would like to come back to school and find a glowing note about all my students, completed work with all steps and strategies shown, and/or a winning Mega Jackpot lottery ticket sitting on my desk. This morning, however, what I found was a time-wasting exercise and a mystery with plenty of suspects and opportunity galore, but little to no motive.

You know how every once in a while someone unknown steals your lunch out of the break room fridge? Or do you remember a couple of years ago, when somebody took my bottle of ketchup from the teachers lounge and I never figured out who it was? Well, those mysteries look like fully developed Agatha Christie novels compared to the one I had to deal with today.

Friday, I assigned science homework, so the sub collected that for me yesterday and placed it in a stack on my desk. As I looked through the stack this morning, I took note of who had not turned in their assignment. I called six kids up to my desk to ask why they had not done the work over the weekend. Siddiq blanched and immediately told me that he HAD turned one in. I let him look through the stack of assignments (it's true, I DO sometimes miss things), and he pulled out the one with Anita's name on it. Siddiq insisted that it was his work. Sure enough, when I looked really REALLY closely, I could see Siddiq's name had been erased from the top of the paper.

Having already chastised the non-submitters, I sent them back to their seats and kept Siddiq with me. I called Anita over, wondering if it was worse that she had cheated or that she had done it so lazily. I was quite surprised when Anita glanced at her name on the paper and nonchalantly announced, "I didn't do that. That's not even how I write my name."

Thus began the long, arduous detective work. After a short talk, I sent Anita back to her desk, figuring she was innocent of cheating (though not of neglecting her homework). I asked Siddiq to tell me exactly how he had turned in his homework yesterday, and he told me that Kiara had come around to pick it up. When questioned, Kiara denied having picked up any papers, instead pointing at RT and Khabi.

Now in case you weren't sure, Kiara looks absolutely nothing like either RT or Khabi. Differences include, but are not limited to, height, weight, hair color, skin color, and gender. If this really were a mystery novel, Siddiq would be termed an "unreliable narrator." It really muddies the waters when your eye witness doesn't have all of his facts straight.

By the way, NONE of the kids involved in this story are supposed to be picking up papers. The names of this week's "Administrative Assistants" (we're not supposed to call them "helpers" anymore) are written nice and large on the board in front. RT and Khabi confirmed that they had convinced the designated assistants to let them pick up the homework and that Kiara had not been involved at all. With a little further questioning, Khabi admitted he and RT had erased Siddiq's name and written in Anita's.

The reason behind it all? Turns out back in 1976, Siddiq's grandmother's butler turned state's evidence against RT's uncle, who also happens to be Khabi's second cousin. This was their grand plan to exact revenge and restore their family's dignity.

I kid, of course. There's nothing so grandiose. I told you there was no motive whatsoever. Nothing. Just random foolishness.

Completely unrelated to the novel titled "The Case of the Missing Home... No, You Know What, Just Move Along and Find Something Else to Read Because This Story is Totally Stupid," there was one other nasty surprise awaiting me upon my return. My

Rubik's Cube – which I've owned since I was a kid and have kept in my classroom for kids to enjoy during inside recess – was sitting in a jar on my desk. It had been completely taken apart.

This one did not remain a mystery for long. All of the kids told me it was Greyson who had taken the Rubik's Cube apart, and he admitted to it quickly enough. He certainly didn't seem very remorseful about it, though. His "Oh yeah, that was me," was spoken in the exact same tone as if I had asked who played soccer at recess that day.

I may or may not have given Greyson a speech about how that Rubik's Cube was handed down to me from my Great-Great-Grandfather, who found it in Brazil during the Hundred Years War, and how that puzzle and a picture of him bungee jumping with the original Ronald McDonald were the only mementos I had of my revered ancestor.

OK, I didn't do that, but I did tell him I was going to think long and hard about whether or not he'd have to buy me a new one. Which of course he won't. No mystery there.
Talk to you later,

Hercule Pirouette

Date: Friday, February 27, 2015
To: Fred Bommerson
From: Jack Woodson
Subject: No pain, no Gauguin!

Hey man,

Normally, I would agree with you that having Greyson reassemble the Rubik's Cube would serve as a good punishment/life lesson/vocational training. The problem is he didn't just take it apart. He broke several of the pieces. Little shards of plastic from the central core were among the colored cubes on my desk. It cannot be reassembled. I'm pretty sure Greyson was using it to perform gravity tests.

He can't put it back together into usable puzzle form, but perhaps I can have him put it into some sort of abstract work of art. That would fit in well with what we did as a grade level today.

This morning, we went on a field trip into downtown Dallas to hear the Meyerson Symphony play and then to visit the Dallas Museum of Art. All of the kids had the privilege of attending, since Mrs. Forest would not let us leave any of the kids back at the school for any reason. The "No Child Left Behind" policy was especially good news for RT and Braxton, who otherwise would have missed out for sure. It was also good news for RT's mother, who we asked along to be a chaperone. Our hope was that surely RT wouldn't be his usual troublemaking self with his mother right there watching. More on that theory later.

We weren't at the school for long in the morning, not even long enough to catch the 9:00 announcements. The symphony appointment was for 9:15, so we jumped on the school buses around 8:15. Good thing Mrs. Bird decided to do another headcount once we were on the bus, because Carmine had chosen to run back inside to use the restroom again without telling anyone.

We arrived at the symphony at 9:00 on the dot and were in our seats about six minutes later. Shortly after sitting down, I saw texts from Mr. Redd and Mrs. Fitzgerald saying that according to the announcements, some paperwork needed to be done and turned in by 1:00, no exceptions.

It's not like this field trip has been on the school calendar for months or anything.

The symphony was awesome. They played several pieces of instantly recognizable classical music, and I think the kids really enjoyed it. Except for Rodrigo, who kept falling asleep in the row behind me. After I woke him up for the third time, I just stopped trying.

The conductor of the symphony spoke to the audience in between each musical piece, giving the history of the song and introducing essential instruments. I was very glad she did not take any questions because I'm sure all the kids wanted to ask how much money she made, what her favorite pizza topping was, and why the oboe player didn't have any hair.

RT sat next to his mother a few rows ahead of me, and he really did seem to be behaving better than usual. I only saw him hit the kid next to him twice.

After the performance, we all walked a few blocks over to the park directly across the street from the museum. Here we had to split up, since the museum couldn't accommodate everyone all at one time. Three sections of 4th grade went to the museum, while my homeroom and two others had lunch in the park. We had about an hour to kill before it was our turn in the museum, and that time was pretty uneventful. The kids wolfed down their sack lunches then ran around the park. We had to ask them to throw away the trash, stop hanging on tree branches, and not to play in the sidewalk fountain a few times, but that was it.

When it was our turn to take the museum tour, we lined up in the lobby and waited for our docents to come and greet us. Our docent was decent, let's get that pun out of the way right now. Not as decent, RT's mom was on her phone texting pretty much from the time we started lunch until after the museum tour was over. At one point, I even heard RT hiss, "Come on, Mom, get off the phone! You're a chaperone!"

Not a great sign, if HE was telling HER how to behave.

For the most part, the kids were very well behaved in the museum. I never had to tell anyone not to touch anything, and I only had to remind Dodd twice that he wasn't the docent. Each class was on a different tour, so we only caught sight of another group every once in a while, as we were moving to another gallery. At one point, I did see a parent chaperone escort Rajiv out of one gallery in search of a restroom, because he wasn't feeling well. I don't know if he ate something that disagreed with him or if post-impressionism makes him sick to his stomach, but he didn't look good.

We saw a few paintings with nude figures, and the boys I knew would have an issue with that of course had an issue with that. Thankfully we just saw them during transitions. I wonder what the kid in the bilingual class who had the lingerie calendar earlier in the year thought of them.

Mrs. Bird later told me a question had come up during their gallery walk that the docent was unable to answer. Something about one of the figures in an old Egyptian glyph drawing. Mrs. Bird said Raina had turned to her and exclaimed, "Let's ask the smartest teacher we know – Mr. Woodson!"

I'm sure she wasn't overly offended. I eased her feelings by telling her about how I had overheard the tail end of a conversation between some of our kids at lunch. All I heard was, "Even Mr. Woodson knows that!"

And you know, that's saying something, because Mr. Woodson doesn't know his Cassatt from a hole in the ground!

We got back to the school around 2:15, with just enough time for a restroom break and some end of the day recess. With all six 4th grade teachers outside, we were able to take turns going up to our rooms and putting together the paperwork Mrs. Forest wanted. I was tempted to splatter red ink all over my papers before turning them in, ala Jackson Pollack, but I decided not to since she was for some reason very upset that none of us had turned it in by the 1:00 deadline.

I can already feel the extra "Sense of Urgency" meetings being scheduled for next week. I wonder how much the bald oboe player in the symphony makes and if he's looking for a replacement.

Talk to you later,

Vincent van Gogh Home

Date: Monday, March 2, 2015
To: Fred Bommerson
From: Jack Woodson
Subject: Full quart press

What's up, man?

Yes, I did see the news story about a crane falling over in the museum parking lot and causing a lot of damage. That happened several hours after we left the museum, and I am 99% confident that it wasn't a result of anything any of my kids did. I can't vouch for RT's mom, though.

We had some discussion this morning about the field trip with several questions that had gone unasked Friday. Andres added his own query – "How come we're always learning new stuff every day in school?"

I answered, "I dunno. School is just funny that way!"

Speaking of funny, apparently I've been pausing for dramatic effect way too often when I speak, because the kids are starting to interject things into the middle of my sentences. Today this happened twice, and both times made me giggle.

We've been doing a unit on measurement, and we're up to the point of talking about capacity. When it comes to the customary system of capacity, there's a wonderful graphic organizer called "Gallon Man" to help kids remember the relative sizes and ratio of each unit. The big body is the gallon, the two arms and two legs (four total) are quarts, and cups make up the eight fingers and eight toes. Gallon Man is not human, obviously, and I'll grant you the pints are kind of awkwardly shoehorned in there, but as memory devices go, it's pretty efficient.

Every year, I show the kids what Gallon Man looks like and how to put the parts together to construct him, and then I have the kids either draw him themselves or cobble him together out of colored construction paper. Each student has complete control over the head, since it is not representative of a unit. I typically draw a slim, rectangular, robotic head with antennae, but the kids are wildly diverse and imaginative. I've seen Charlie Brown heads, alien heads, chicken heads, and snowman heads, among others.

One year, I had a kid in my homeroom who was a particularly gifted artist. He drew an eerily accurate picture of MY head atop Gallon Man. I still have that one hanging on my wall of fame. I was hoping my superb artist Jeauxsifeen would use her insane talents and the inspiration from last week's museum visit to draw a

Mona Lisa head or a Frida Kahlo head, but strangely, she opted for a generic smiley face.

This morning at the break for music class, I spoke to the kids, fully intending to say, "When we get back from Music, I'm going to introduce you to Gallon Man!"

Despite knowing many, if not all, of the kids had seen Gallon Man in 3rd grade, I used all the requisite flair and showmanship such an announcement requires by necessity. However, I only got as far as, "I'm going to introduce you to…" when I was interrupted by Eld'Ridge, who blurted out, "Mr. Snowflakes?"

Not being at all familiar with Mr. Snowflakes or his resume, I was a bit befuddled for a moment. After that, my grand announcement about Gallon Man lost a bit of its luster. Of course, with that class, the lack of any reaction is normal and probably would have occurred with or without the interruption. On the other end of the spectrum, my afternoon class had a different reaction. I had already introduced my good friend Gallon Man before we took a break for lunch. As we lined up, I said, "When we come back from lunch, we are going to continue talking about…"

I trailed off because at that moment I noticed Kirstie, who was sitting closest to me, having what appeared to be an epileptic seizure, albeit the goofiest, most attention-seeking seizure ever. As I arched my eyebrows and gave her "The Look," Rajiv tried to finish my sentence.

"Math?" he ventured.

I couldn't help but smile. "Well, yes, we ARE going to continue talking about math," I began, "but more specifically…"

Again I was interrupted, this time by a smattering of applause. The kids were clapping because we were going to continue talking about math. In math class! Hey, I aim to please.

Speaking of providing great entertainment, I certainly brought the noise for Misaki today. At the beginning of each class, when kids finish the warm-up problems early, I always encourage them to make up their own problems to solve. Most kids take this request with a grain of salt, but Misaki is really good about practicing long division or drawing huge polygons to practice area and perimeter.

Today, after finishing what was on the board, Misaki called me over and asked, "Can you give me a problem?"

"OK," I replied. "The financial situation in Greece."

She looked completely bewildered then said, "I don't even know the answer to that one!"

I told her, "No one does! That's why it's a problem!"

Misaki broke into uncontrollable guffaws. She laughed harder than I've ever seen a kid laugh. We're talking tears streaming down her cheeks. I must have really touched her funny bone.

I appreciate Misaki's capacity for laughter. Now if I can somehow convey the concept of LIQUID capacity to some of the other kids, I'll be golden.

Talk to you later,

Goofus and Gallon

Date: Friday, March 6, 2015
To: Fred Bommerson
From: Jack Woodson
Subject: 4th graders without borders

Hey buddy,

You know what? That's really a pretty good idea about making Gallon Man out of actual containers. However, I can't very well hang up eight pints of blood or Jack Daniels!

And no, I never followed up with Eld'Ridge on who or what Mr. Snowflakes is, so I can't help you out there. Wikipedia, maybe? Knowing Eld'ridge as I do, I'm guessing Mr. Snowflakes is his version of the Tooth Fairy and the Easter Bunny, rolled into one.

I gave the kids a fun assignment this week called "I Want to Go There" which involved choosing a vacation destination and then making a travel brochure about their choice. The brochure needed to include travel costs, population and area of the destination, a table showing sightseeing locations, and so on.

Monday, I assigned partner groups and they decided where they wanted their vacation spots to be. Most of them were really good choices like New York City, Miami, Paris, and Australia. Some of the choices were even made based on touristy attractions the kids knew about like the Statue of Liberty and the Eiffel Tower. One group, however, after choosing Jamaica as their destination, had a slight issue spelling "beaches."

Ever the helper, Carmine shouted out, "I know! It's B-I-T-C" before I cut him off with, "Nope! That's not it!"

A few groups weren't quite sure what their attractions would be. Phil Collins and Susana's group chose Mexico as their location. When I asked what people might go there to see, they replied, "Mexican people?"

Um, we can see plenty of them right here!

Graciella convinced Alvaro to choose Japan, seemingly for the sole purpose of promoting the ease with which one can (allegedly) acquire bootleg movies. "You could get any movie you want for three dollars!" she insisted, as I carefully scanned the room for hidden cameras.

There were certainly a few unorthodox choices. Lewith and Tracy Jane asked for permission to look at some maps on one of the classroom computers then wound up selecting Ruston, Louisiana. They were quite pleased with themselves for choosing a location that would only take a few hours to drive to, thus saving a lot of money on travel. They're going to have to do a lot more research to find anything worth doing in Ruston, I think.

Wednesday, I asked the kids to estimate the cost of airplane tickets (or gasoline, in the case of Ruston) to their destination. It was really interesting to see how much they think travel costs. Olivia's group said a ticket to New York City would be two bucks, while Akasha's group had a ticket to China rather underpriced at $50. Maybe that's the price for a slow boat to China.

The assignment lead to some very interesting conversations about travel experiences. I shared my story about taking a trip to Japan when I worked for Heat Pumps Unlimited. The kids all thought it was hilarious that I had to duck to go through doorways. They gagged and made faces when I told them about eating raw squid. Their mouths gaped in wonder when I told them how I was the only American ever to become an official ninja.

Kirstie shared with the class that she once traveled to France and had stopped in Corsica for a weekend. Because I'm a history nerd and a glutton for punishment, I asked if anyone knew what famous person from history had been born in Corsica. Trevor raised his hand and blurted, "Betty White!"

Later in the day, Misaki told everyone she had flown to Hong Kong over the holiday break. She said the flight took 24 hours. Landon stared at her in disbelief and asked, "How could someone stay alive for 24 hours?"

It's really not that difficult, Landon, unless your name is Jack Bauer.

I have a hard time believing that any flight would last 24 hours, but Misaki's comment did make me decide to add a component to the assignment. Each final product had to include the total travel time from Dallas, TX to the destination. This ties in nicely with elapsed time, a concept many kids have trouble with.

I had a conversation with Omar the other day that makes me think he understands the concept just perfectly.

Omar: "What does elapsed time mean again?"
Me: "It's how much time has passed between two events. Or like when you're in a class you hate and you figure out how much time is left until the class is over."
Omar [looks at the clock]: "Oooh, there's 32 minutes left before we switch to Mrs. Bird's class!"
Me: "Congratulations, you're an expert on both elapsed time AND hurting my feelings."

Truth be told, we were all watching the clock for most of the day, counting down the minutes until Spring Break began. As soon as the last kid was picked up, I sprinted out to my car, gave a big showy wave to Crazy Voyeur Lady across the street, and high-tailed it out of the parking lot.

I always love it when the school break coincides with the start of the college basketball tournament. Spring Break and March Madness colliding to make... Spring Madness? March Breakness? Breaking Mad?

Whatever it is, I'll be celebrating it down south. Sunday, we're headed down to Hill Country (or Jill Country, as I like to call it) to visit the in-laws. It will take about five hours to drive there and cost around $35 for gas and lunch. Local attractions include the new Sonic and the town's recently added second stoplight. I'll be sure to show you the full brochure once we're back.

Talk to you later,

Jack the Tripper

Date: Thursday, March 19, 2015
To: Fred Bommerson
From: Jack Woodson
Subject: Random House on the Prairie

Dear Sir or Madam,

    It wasn't easy coming back to school after Spring Break, and I've been kind of a zombie for the past few days. We had a nice relaxing time at Jill's parents' house, but the visit started off a little weird. We walked into the bedroom we'd be using to find a rifle lying on the bed. If this was my father-in-law's way of warning me to keep my hands off his daughter, he is WAAAYYY too late for that!

    It sounds like, if anything, your work picked up even more than usual last week! I suppose it's a shame none of your customers observe Spring Break.

    There have been a lot of tired faces in the classroom this week. The faces that showed up, anyway. Both of my classes were a student smaller today, as two kids moved over Spring Break. Trevor always struggled in class and didn't always seem to mind that he was behind, but he was a super sweet kid nevertheless. He was one of the most cheerful kids I've ever met, and what he lacked in computational ability, he more than made up for in super hero knowledge. He once told me he and his dad enjoyed watching old reruns of Wonder Woman with Lynda Carter. When I said I used to like that show, too, he confided, "I'd like to go on a date with her!"

    How can you not love a kid like that?

    As for the student I lost from my own homeroom, where do I even begin? Marina was quite literally one of the best students I've ever had. She was friendly, hard-working, witty, and all around fantastic. The class just won't be the same without her. I certainly can't begrudge her parents wanting to move to a better neighborhood, though.

    Clara didn't withdraw, but we didn't even see her until today. At least there's SOME normalcy in my life.

    I didn't see any point in pushing the kids too hard this week, and as such, it's been a slow couple of days around here. I don't have anything specific to share with you, but I thought I'd share some of the funny/weird/off the wall things my kids have said over the past few weeks.

    Back before Spring Break, when we were investigating capacity, I brought out my set of liquid measurement containers. The container that measures a cup fits inside of the pint container, which fits inside the quarts container, and so on. They're kind of like Russian nesting dolls, only more educational and far less creepy. When I pulled them out, only the gallon container was visible, so there was no real reaction from the kids. I unscrewed the lid and pulled the quart container out, and suddenly there were gasps and cheers of amazement. For the most part, the "oohs" and "aahs" continued as I kept pulling out smaller and smaller containers, with one exception. Gavin, who looked almost scandalized, kept muttering, "You gotta be kidding me."

I would have been very worried if he started slapping his head and shouting, "This is not happening!"

Gavin was all smiles at the end of class today, though. I always pass out conduct folders Thursday so the kids can have them signed and bring them back Friday. As the kids pack up their belongings, I walk around the room calling out names and handing out folders. Today when I called Gavin's name, he replied, "Right here, my good man!"

When I chuckled, he continued, "I learned that from TV! It was a spy movie!"

I mentioned this anecdote to Mr. Redd after school, and he said I should have asked Gavin if he had learned it from "Quotient of Solace," the undiscovered Bond film.

The strangest non-sequitor came the last time we had inside recess. It was raining, so we couldn't go outside, and a group of my boys was playing one of my math bingo games. Not so much playing, really, as sitting around the board, chatting about random topics. As I wandered closer to see what they were talking about, Andres saw me and asked, "Have you ever almost been in a coma? I have!"

I find that sometimes it's best just to look off into the distance, pretend to see Genghis Khan, and wander over to the doorway.

Andres is full of strange questions and comments, but at least he stays away from the most common statement that drives me bonkers – "I gotta use it!"

I am so tired of kids asking me/telling me about their bathroom needs with that phrase! This afternoon, it was Alvaro who exclaimed, "I gotta use it!" and I came super close to snapping back, "Use what? Your pencil? A crescent wrench? Proper syntax?"

OK, rant over. I'll stop complaining and move on to complaints from the kids.

I'm used to hearing groans and grumbles from kids who don't want to do work in my class. I usually respond, "I know, right? I want you to do math in math class! I'm such a monster!"

Earlier this week, though, Chloe provided the best in-class whine ever. It was funny, and she said it so good-naturedly, everyone couldn't help but laugh.

We were practicing various strategies for solving multiplication problems, and I had just written "482 X 37" on the board. While a few of the boys gave the obligatory wheeze of shock, Chloe called out, "Aw, come on! I'm just a little girl!"

Like I said, everyone laughed at that, even Chloe, and even me. I looked at her and said, "Oh, sorry. Too hard?"

Then I changed the 7 in 37 to a 6 and said, "There ya go!"

Chloe gave me a playful little pout and was then one of the first ones done. Correctly.

On the topic of multiplication, I've been starting each of my after-school tutoring sessions with a sing-along of some of the multiplication songs from 3rd grade since so many of these kids have forgotten their basic facts. Cesar and Ja'Kendrick are always lost and seem to be mouthing "watermelon" instead of the numbers, but Rodrigo really gets into it. Tuesday, after a particularly rousing chorus of the sevens song, Rodrigo winced and said, "I think I pulled a hammy!"

I guess my new motto should be, "Time to Learn, Feel the Burn!"

Speaking of singing, I've learned recently that I'm not the only one in the class who likes to change the lyrics for a laugh. Khabi has been doing that with the school song.

Yes, we have a school song this year. This is one of Ms. Butler's pet projects – she wrote or found the words – though she's left it to Mrs. Halloran the music teacher to teach the kids how to sing it. Since January, Ms. Butler sings it at the end of morning announcements every Friday, and the kids (and teachers) are expected to sing along.

One verse includes the line, "Where the kids are smart, and they do their part." A couple of weeks ago, I swear I heard Khabi sing it as, "Where the kids are smart, and they like to fart."

Since then, I've been conflicted over whether to reprimand him for being crass or to commend him on his fantastic wit. Truth be told, I've been singing Khabi's modified version in my head ever since I heard it.

And lastly on the random story list...

On the way out to dismissal Monday, Mateo asked me, "Mr. Woodson, do you have a fantasy world inside your brain?"

"Of course," I replied. (Really, could there be any other answer?)

"Good," Mateo continued. "I thought maybe some people did not have a fantasy world inside their brain."

If pressed for details, I doubt our inner fantasy worlds would have much in common. His is no doubt full of flashing lights, sparkling colors, and cartoon dragons, while mine mostly involves Spider-man and Boba Fett fighting Skeletor while Shakira dances.
Talk to you later, my good man!

The Tan Gents

Date: Wednesday, March 25, 2015
To: Fred Bommerson
From: Jack Woodson
Subject: Phrase it in the form of a question

Hey Fred,

Sorry buddy, I'm not going to teach you the school song. It's so long, I honestly haven't learned it all myself. Just know that Khabi made at least one definite improvement to the lyrics. Also, your mental fantasy world sounds a lot like Minecraft.

I may have mentioned that my kids are super immature this year. Some of the boys especially, who will go off on a giggling fit at the most inappropriate times. This morning, we were working through a few word problems and came to one containing the word "balls." The context was certainly innocuous enough, with someone playing games in gym class, but this one problem completely derailed the class, as RT and Eld'Ridge just would not stop laughing. Several of the other kids gave the obligatory chuckle but then started to exchange concerned glances when RT and Eld'Ridge kept going.

I can't believe how crude their little minds are, thinking the slightest reference to anything even possibly related to a slang term for a body part is the most hilarious thing ever. It's quite pathetic, really. But I think I only threw fuel on the fire when I said I hoped the next problem wasn't about a squirrel hiding his nuts.

I used to always start the day with a word problem. This year, I've tried to incorporate different types of questions as warm-ups. Sometimes they're visual problems, sometimes they're straight up computation, and sometimes they're open-ended questions that require writing.

Once or twice a week, I like to make the warm-up a reverse question. I write the answer on the board, and I ask the kids to tell me the question. It's kind of like that game show, Jeopardy! Man, it would be really cool to be a contestant on that show some day. I wonder if they do anything special for teachers?

Anyway, as an example, I might write, "The answer is 42. What is the question?"

If anyone ever knew the true question to THAT one, we'd all be blissfully set for life!

I encourage the kids to write as many appropriate questions as they can think of during the warm-up time, so they are not limited to one. The first few times the kids saw warm-ups like this, they thought they had to be strictly arithmetic. If the answer was 15, the questions would be, "What is 14 + 1?" or, "What is 20 - 5?"

Or, infuriatingly (from both Braxton AND Ja'Kendrick), "What is 15?"

I had to train them to be more creative and write things like, "What is my basketball jersey number?" "How old is my sister?" or, "How many IQ points does watching an episode of Keeping up with the Kardashians take away?"

Now that we're much further along in the school year, most of the kids understand the gist of it and enjoy these warm-ups immensely. I always make sure to take time to share out lots of questions, because the kids can be hilariously creative.

A while back the warm-up was, "The answer is 27. What is the question?"

Anita from my morning class wrote, "How many cats have I had in the past six months?"

Ironically, Tracy Jane, in my afternoon class, wrote that same day, "How many cats do you have to have before you are considered a crazy cat lady?"

Other times, this type of warm-up demonstrates whether a child really does or does not understand a certain concept. Before calling on individual kids, I have the kids share their responses with a partner. I like to walk around listening to partners share. Yesterday, my warm-up was, "The answer is 0.25. What is the question?"

I overheard Raina say, "How many puppies do I wish I had?"

Her partner, Arianna, looked at her in horror and asked, "You wish you had PART of a puppy?"

Obviously, Arianna understands decimals. Raina, on the other hand, either does not understand decimals or she is a sick, twisted individual. I choose to believe the former.

It doesn't matter if the answer is 2 or 222, one of Andres' questions (and often his only question) will be, "How many slices of pizza did I eat last night?"

Along the same lines, Gavin has taken to making, "How many ninjas did I defeat last night?" his go-to question whenever we do a warm-up like this. When the answer was 8½, Gavin was clever enough to add a footnote – "*one ninja was missing an arm and a leg."

Among the memorably funny answers, one time, when the answer was 16, Rajiv wrote, "How many eggs would I like to throw at Justin Bieber?"

Another time, the answer was 21. D'Qayla wrote, "How many rooms will I have in my mansion when I am rich?"

When she shared this with Misaki, her partner, Misaki asked, "Oooh, can I live in one of those rooms?"

D'Qayla graciously answered, "Yes. You can stay in the servants' quarters."

Yet another instance, when the answer was 821, one of Khabi's questions was, "How many pieces of broccoli will be in Friday's Fruits and Veggies bag?"

Sadly, he wasn't far off.

I'll leave you with an answer and question relevant to me personally. The answer is 31. The question is, "How many weeks pregnant is Jill?"

Talk to you later!

Question Marky Mark

Date: Friday, March 27, 2015
To: Fred Bommerson
From: Jack Woodson
Subject: What goes up, must…well, who knows?

Hey buddy,

I like that you threw my answer of 31 out to your coworkers and invited them to come up with questions. I liked Nancy's response of "How many flavors does Baskin-Robbins offer?" I enjoyed Tom Winter's response of "How many days has Latya gone without eating an entire party-size bag of Skittles?" I did not particularly care for Larry's response of "What is ten years older than the girls I like to date?"

BLAAAARRRRGH!

Dude, it's a Friday night, and I've been grading. And by grading, I mean writing a variation of the same message on lots of note cards. The general gist was, "Remember, we saw in our experiment that gravity pulls things down at the same rate."

This went on 18 out of 19 note cards in my afternoon class.

We've been talking about gravity all week long. I started early in the week by showing the kids three water bottles of the same size but with different masses. One was empty, one had wet tissue paper in it, and the third had sand in it. I asked the kids to write a prediction for what order the bottles would hit the ground if they were dropped at the same time from the same height. Most of them said the heaviest would hit the ground first. This seems intuitive at that age. Some of them said the lightest would hit the ground first and qualified that by saying that since it didn't weigh as much, it could move faster. That's reasonable, too, especially after witnessing Eld'Ridge (tiny and quick) and Greyson (large and plodding) on the playground. Hey, there are no wrong hypotheses after all.

Then the kids did their own experiment involving three items of different mass. They worked in groups and dropped the items repeatedly, recording the results.

A few kids seemed out to prove that heavier objects fall faster. These kids tried to hold the lighter objects a little longer before releasing or threw the heavier objects down instead of just letting them fall. Olivia approached me with a die in one hand and a math book in the other.

"Watch this, Mr. Woodson!" she challenged.

I watched as she released both items at noticeably separate times then shouted in triumph about how the book hit the ground before the die.

"Yes," I acknowledged. "But you didn't drop the die until you heard the book hit the ground."

I'm pretty sure she missed the point, since her reply was, "What's a DIE??"

There were a few sticklers who, during our discussion afterwards, still insisted that the heaviest item was hitting the ground first. But for the most part, the kids understood the items fell at the same speed, and we had a nice little discussion about gravity.

I asked if anyone had ever heard of Galileo. Alvaro immediately shouted, "Princess Leia?"

I told them about his famous experiment and said that if we went up to the roof of the school and dropped a bowling ball and a grape over the side at the same time, they would hit the ground at the same time. Of course, all the kids immediately wanted to go up and drop stuff off of the roof. Honestly, so did I.

But everyone had to settle for demonstrating the concept in the classroom again, this time by dropping a tiny eraser and Rajiv's backpack.

Today, for the note card quiz, I brought out three items with different masses. There was a big Baby Care book that a fellow teacher had loaned me (for some reason, the kids found this hilarious, with Raina even shouting, "HA! BABY!"), there was a partially filled water bottle, and there was a little binder clip. I asked the kids to write the order the items would hit the ground, if dropped at the same time from my desk, and to explain their reasoning.

Curtiss was the only one – out of 19 students in that class – who wrote that all three items would hit at the same time because that's how gravity works. The other 18 reverted back to their original hypotheses, with most of them saying the baby care book would land first because it is heavier. Raina went a step further, saying even a baby weighed more than an empty bottle or a binder clip.

I wrote a very clear note to her (and her parents) on the card that said, "I DID NOT DROP A BABY DURING THIS EXPERIMENT."

I don't know why the kids are having such a hard time with this concept. I feel like they've been conducting gravity experiments all year long. Judging by the amount of food and trash that winds up on the cafeteria floor, they should be experts. Especially Tyrellvius, who can't ever seem to keep items on his desk. Every day, he inadvertently knocks books, pencils, and papers off his desk. I guess no one was paying attention to how they fell together.

    I suppose it's true what they say – You can lead a horse to water, but you can't drop it off the top of a building.
Talk to you later,

Sir Isaac "I Don't Give a Fig" Newton

Date: Wednesday, April 1, 2015
To: Fred Bommerson
From: Jack Woodson
Subject: The Seven Habits of Highly Infectious People

Hey Fred,
    Wow. The past couple of days have not been fun, unless you consider suffering from a major stomach bug fun. I certainly don't. Everything was fine Sunday night. Jill and I went out to eat, our meal was great, and I even had some ice cream for dessert before bedtime. Then around five the next morning, that Tour of Italy came back up for its own Tour of Porcelain. With several encore performances.
    Around 7am, I willed myself to be upwardly mobile just long enough to call Mrs. Forest and let her know I'd be out and would need a sub. I also quickly emailed Mrs. Bird some sub plans before collapsing back into bed again.
    My sub plans, by the way, do have some detail and academic relevance to them, usually including worksheets or textbook lessons that review recent concepts. I don't know how Tom Winter became convinced that my sub plans basically consist of "Walk into the classroom at 8, stare long and hard at the kids, and say, 'You know what to do' – then leave and don't come back until lunch."
    Also, I promise I have never written a lesson plan that includes the phrase, "Brainstorm ways to survive in prison."
    I stayed in bed for most of Monday. Anytime I tried to sit up to read or to eat, I felt like monkeys were scrambling my brains with an egg beater. Even just getting to the bathroom and back was like running a marathon.
    Jill considered taking the day off to stay home with me but then thought it might be best if she was out of the house, just in case I was contagious. So I alternated sleeping, lying awake, and weakly munching on Saltine crackers for most of the day. My fever broke sometime in the early hours of Tuesday, but I was in absolutely no shape to go back to school. Especially after being haunted throughout the night by fitful dreams of a class full of Braxtons, each twice as big as me.
    It was a little bit of a tougher sell to convince Mrs. Forest I couldn't make it in again because yesterday was the day of the 4th grade Writing STAAR (the extra A is for Abdominal_cramping!). As much as I would have loved to stand around all day monitoring kids who don't want to write (and finally been able to wear my

"Save the comma for yo mama!" tie), I probably wouldn't have lasted an hour.

And Heaven forbid if I had blown chunks and desecrated a test booklet! I've actually seen cases where a student threw up during a standardized test. The teacher had to carefully wipe down the test booklet, seal it in a plastic bag, and send it to Austin along with all of the completed, puke-free test booklets!

They take their tests VERY seriously!

Thankfully, however, Mrs. Forest relented and assigned one of the teacher assistants to monitor my homeroom during testing. Meanwhile, I was still supine for most of the day, but I could at least keep food down, and I regained some of my appetite. I didn't feel like I was carrying a school bus on my head every time I walked from one room to the next, but I still tired easily. I moved from the bed to the couch and dozed through several dopey movies on TBS. This time, there were no school related nightmares. Just hiding out with Han Solo, fighting COBRA – a sure sign the fantasy world in my brain was returning to normal. Mateo would be pleased.

I could very easily have taken today off as well, but I sucked it up and soldiered through. I was a little tired of lying around anyway, and I was definitely getting tired of hearing Jill tell me, "You think you feel bad? Try being pregnant."

Whatever I had, there's been a lot of it going around. I was not the only one out this week, and I wasn't even the only teacher out. Three of my homeroom kids were out yesterday, plus Kirstie from my afternoon class. Two of them were still out today, along with Mr. Utoobay and Mrs. Del Torro. That's not even counting Tyrellvius, who hasn't been absent, but who spent the day making loud, over-the-top retching sounds before I finally convinced him to go to the bathroom.

I can't say it's surprising the germs are flying around like confetti on New Year's Eve. My kids don't exactly practice the best – or even average – personal hygiene. Every time I look at him, Greyson has his pinky either in his nose or his mouth (I'm always reminded of Dr. Evil), and Lewith can't ever be bothered to cover his mouth when coughing up a lung. Several kids continue to put markers and crayons in their mouths whenever we grade homework, and since these come from the community bucket, I have no doubt the germs are setting up camp in the kids' bodies and planning to stay for a while.

I'm tempted to fill the buckets with Purell and have the kids reinsert the markers each time like grapes suspended in Jello. But I'm 100% positive someone would try to drink the Purell before a day had passed.

Of course, there were the usual things waiting for me when I came back. The missing pencils. The desks in new positions. The note about how the sub was worried that Ja'Kendrick had fallen into a coma. And of course the endless, "Where were you?" from the kids. As if I had taken two days off to go wild down at Teacher-Con.

While I was out Monday, I had the sub reviewing capacity, and we continued today. One of the problems the kids looked at asked them to estimate the amount of lemonade in a jug. Julio was not familiar with the word "jug," and Blanca and Landon were trying to explain it to him, but neither their words nor their pictures were getting through to him. When I walked closer, Landon asked, "Mr. Woodson, can we get on the computer and look up a picture of jugs?"

With internal warning lights and a voice inside my head shouting, "DANGER, WILL ROBINSON!" I politely refused his request and carefully looked up a sterile picture of "lemonade container" on my phone to show Julio.

I don't think I've addressed anything from your email yet. Don't worry, buddy, I promise you, no babies (or animals) were harmed in the making of last week's note card quiz. And now that I've had a day to give my patented "When we spend class discussing how something works, don't ignore it all at test time and put whatever you used to think" talk, perhaps the kids have a slightly better grasp on gravity.

The kids must really love that talk, by the way, because they never seem to get tired of hearing it!

When I said we couldn't drop items off the side of the school roof, I'm so glad nobody made your suggestion to start chucking things out the second floor window. I'm not sure the "It's for science!" rationale would hold on that one. If we ever did that experiment, though, I'd make sure Ms. Butler's bullhorn was one of the first items being dropped.

I'm still not feeling 100%, so I'm off to bed now. Hopefully to dream of large jugs. Of lemonade.
Later,

Germit the Frog

Date: Monday, April 6, 2015
To: Fred Bommerson
From: Jack Woodson
Subject: Everything is different, but the same

What's up, dude?

I have fully recovered from last week's stomach bug, thanks for asking. Please tell everyone I appreciate their well wishes, and to answer Tiffany's question, Tommy was actually one of the kids who was out all week, so I didn't have to deal with questions of quarantine and super flu from his dad.

I'm sorry you had to sit through Larry's lengthy and disturbingly graphic story about the time he got sick in Brazil. But hey, that's the risk you take when you agree to go out to lunch with him.

Speaking of health and sickness, last week's double shot of forced fruit and veggies led to a couple of interesting developments. First, a rumor went around the school that blueberries cure and/or prevent cancer, so my kids were scarfing those little things down like there was no tomorrow. Except for RT, who took one bite, decided he didn't like it, and spit the whole mouthful back into the bag.

I guess no one passed on the cancer-curing news to the 5th grade, because a whole slew of them wound up in trouble for taking blueberries onto the bus after school and making the interior look like a post-paintball wasteland.

In addition, Rajiv and Rodrigo were inspired to start a cartoon strip during recess called "Stealth Fruit Ninjas." They explained to me that the fruits were the good guys and the vegetables were the villains. Their first strip involved Strawberry Ninja slicing and dicing several evil onions – and then of course crying over it.

I'm hoping in their next strip, they send a fruit ninja after a family of brussels sprouts, with the punch line – "It's nothing personal, but nobody likes brussels sprouts." If their audience picks up, I may suggest a recurring enemy – Captain Asparagus, whose sinister and vile plans involve making everyone's pee smell funny.

But hey, enough bodily fluid jokes. This week, we started a unit on rapid and long-term changes to the earth. Rapid changes include forest fires, avalanches, and earthquakes. Long-term changes include glacier movement, mountains forming, and Arianna's bathroom breaks. Seriously, that girl takes FOREVER!

Before we started the unit today, I wanted to see what the kids already knew, so I wrote two statements on the board:

Claim 1: The surface of the earth IS always changing.
Claim 2: The surface of the earth IS NOT always changing.

I then asked the kids to choose one of those claims and support it by writing thoughts, evidence, and examples. I know that reasoning and justification have historically not been among my students' strong suits, but I figure they'll never be any good if they don't get a chance to practice.

Before I turned them loose, we had a discussion about what "surface" meant and how that applied to the earth. I put emphasis on the fact that the earth is a sphere (not a circle, as a few kids wanted to argue), and the surface we were making a claim about was the outside of the planet – the ground, the part we walk on and can see. Kiara looked down at the floor when I said that, so I added, "We're on the second story of a building right now; the classroom floor is not the surface of the earth."

At that moment, I realized I probably sound just like Will Ferrell playing an exasperated Alex Trebek on Saturday Night Live's Celebrity Jeopardy! half the time when I'm teaching.

Anyway, the exercise was valid in that it showed me what the kids knew about landform changes. Unfortunately, they didn't know much.

Here are a few supporting statements from kids who chose Claim 2, aka the wrong claim – surface is NOT changing:

Olivia wrote, "The earth is a sphere and is not going to change to another shape, like cube, rectangular prism, triangle prism, cylinder, cone, pyramid."

She might not know about landforms, but I guess she showed she knows all about 3-dimensional figures!

Jeauxsifeen's entry said, "Because it is not moving, it is not changing colors, and the earth is not going up and down."

So the earth is not a Tilt-a-Whirl, in other words.

And then we have Lewith, who wins the "If you're going to be wrong, go big" award – "The earth is not changing because it just stays in the same place, it never does something different. It doesn't spin around the sun, the sun is the one spinning around the earth because the earth doesn't move."

Um... Copernicus would like a word...

On the other side, there were plenty of kids who chose Claim 1 (surface IS changing), but for all the wrong reasons.

Enrique said, "The surface of the earth is changing by the different people that are coming to the United States of America."

Maybe some of his ancestors moved mountains to travel to the US?

Phil Collins said, "Yes, because the grass is green and it changes to brown sometimes."

Getting closer to the right answer but not quite there yet.

Omar said, "The earth is changing because they're building a lot of new apartments."

Facepalm

Akasha was the only one who actually explained it properly. "New plants form and the ground cracks when there is an earthquake. When an ocean dries up, it turns into a desert. Lava pushes up from under the ground and makes mountains and sometimes volcanoes."

Right on!

We clearly have a lot of work to do this week. The good news is that I will hopefully be able to implement some rapid changes to the surface of their brains. Meanwhile, I'm going to go invest in blueberry stock. I heard it can work miracles.
Talk to you later,

Sue Nahmy

Date: Friday, April 10, 2015
To: Fred Bommerson
From: Jack Woodson
Subject: What's in YOUR wallet?

Hey buddy,

I think Lewith was just confused about our planet's place in the solar system. I don't think he's a "Flat Earther" as you called him. And I DEFINITELY don't believe Latya is a Flat Earther. You totally made that up! But just in case, you might want to have him ask one of Carmine's famous scientist friends on YouTube to set him straight.

This morning, I heard a bizarre boast. Andres and Omar had compared homework answers, and after several grunts of disbelief, Andres turned to Chloe and proclaimed, "I didn't do it the right way, and I STILL got it wrong!"

Chloe kindly comforted him with the words, "It's probably just because you didn't do it the right way."

Can't argue with logic like that!

When it comes to 4th grade math concepts, there are money issues and then there are money issues. I know I've lamented in the past about kids having trouble adding, subtracting, or sometimes even identifying money, and it often seems making change is a futile endeavor. But on top of those skills, a recent standards change has added a Personal Financial Literacy aspect to the math curriculum. At this level, there are standards on fixed and variable expenses, recognizing the role of banks and credit unions, and advantages and disadvantages between various methods of payment.

I think the idea in and of itself is great. We want these kids to know how to use, save, and assess their money responsibly and wisely in the future, and there are not often ways to learn how outside of school. There are new words and terms, though, and that always presents issues. I've kind of interspersed the financial literacy lessons throughout the past few months, sometimes spending a couple of days on a concept, sometimes just introducing a term and then coming back to it later. One of the first things we talked about was the difference between an income and an expense.

As a class, we discussed some sample incomes and expenses that might be reasonable for a typical 4th grader. Incomes might be $10 for walking their pet turtle or five dollars for polishing Grandma's dentures. Expenses might be a weekly 6-pack purchase (juice boxes) or going to the movies. Unless your name is Graciella, who proudly bragged about sneaking into movies for free, specifically Night at the Museum 3, which she claims to have seen 27 times now.

Once I turned the kids loose, I asked them to brainstorm some other incomes and expenses with their table groups. No fewer than three kids immediately ran up to me to ask, "Does it have to be legal?"

Should I be worried? I'm not sure if they had buying pharmaceutical grade codeine in mind as an expense or playing in an underground poker game as an income. At any rate, I asked them to stick to legal activities.

Recognizing the difference between fixed and variable expenses has presented a few problems. Actually, not so much the difference between the two but the definitions of the two. Electricity bills, water bills, and grocery bills are all pretty easy to identify as variable expenses, while rent, car payments, and gym memberships are good examples of fixed expenses. However, too many kids are convinced fixed expenses NEVER change while variable expenses ALWAYS change. That's an oversimplified (and not entirely correct) way to look at things, so I've been trying to correct that viewpoint. I brought up my two most recent water bills as an example, showing the kids that they were for exactly the same amount. I left out my personal opinion that this was a case of the utility company being lazy and shady and not actually reading my meter each month.

During our class discussion, Landon asked what type of expense a library card would be, to which several kids shouted, "A FREE expense!"

Curtiss just shook his head and grumbled, "If it's free, it's not an expense!"

We have also gone over how a budget works. In our perfect-world math class examples, we are usually trying to make total income equal total expenses for the month, even though people ideally want income to be greater than expenses. Much like milk shouldn't contain chunks, total monthly expenses should never be greater than total monthly income!

For the past couple of days, we've been talking about the advantages and disadvantages of cash, checks, credit cards, and debit cards. My emphasis has been on the fact that credit cards do not equal free money; rather, they do have to be paid off.

If only this lesson had been taught when my wife was in school!

I had signs hanging in four areas around the room, each with one form of payment written on it. I read a scenario card that described a person and a purchase they wanted to make, and the kids moved to the area of the room labeled with the form of payment best for that person. We then discussed the choices.

One scenario had Esteban, a college student with $75 in his bank account, wanting to go to a movie with friends. When I asked the kids to move to the part of the room labeled with Esteban's best purchasing option, most of the kids congregated towards "Cash."

As they meandered over there, I ad libbed, "Maybe he's going to see Avengers 2!"

As soon as I said that, Eld'Ridge gasped and ran from "Cash" to "Credit Card."

I guess cash is good enough for Furious 7, but The Avengers requires plastic?

The exercise was especially good for distinguishing between debit cards and credit cards. Slowly but surely, the kids started to realize that you could only buy something with a debit card if you actually had enough money in the bank, whereas a credit card could buy things that you don't have the money for yet.

Some kids also realized that "debit" is a strange word. Most notably Gavin, who kept hopping around the room shouting, "Look at me, I'm a rich frog! DEBIT! DEBIT!"

I have to give him credit, that's pretty funny.
Talk to you later,

Professor X Pence

Date: Tuesday, April 14, 2015
To: Fred Bommerson
From: Jack Woodson
Subject: Time to do a science

Hey buddy,

    I suppose Nancy's frequent trips to Winstar could be considered income AND expense, though from what I've heard, it's more often an expense. And congrats on finally selling your old "Kiss me down under" belt buckle on eBay! Consider it an Aussie income!

    Changing gears now, I had a bit of a problem today. My nose started bleeding this afternoon during class. Strangely, none of the kids even noticed. I suppose that's a good thing, as there weren't any silly questions – "You have blood in your NOSE?!?" – but it does make me wonder if the kids would notice if I was writhing on the floor, being eaten by a cheetah.

    It might make for a decent science project, though, and I would welcome a decent science project with open arms right about now.

    The rush to complete projects has begun, with our science fair coming up next Friday. Despite my insistence that a project has to be based on a testable question, I have a class full of kids who still believe that merely saying the word, "VOLCANO!" will fit the bill and give them an A.

    Personally, I'm thinking "What Are the Negative Effects of Holding a Science Fair Less than Two Weeks before the Major Standardized Tests?" should prove to be quite testable.

    Sometimes the kids come up with their own ideas, and sometimes they need prompting. A couple of Fridays ago, Tommy came running up to me urgently, asking, "Is it OK if you get hand sanitizer on your face?"

    I almost said, "Worst science project ever!" but then I saw he really had hand sanitizer on his face. And that he was acting as though he had been wandering around Chernobyl for three days.

    Tommy does tend to blow things out of proportion – see the Ebola Incident of 2014 – and I really didn't want to receive another frantic email from his father.

    "Is the school in lock-down mode? Have the kids been fitted for bio-hazard suits yet?"

I handed Tommy a paper towel and told him to wipe off his face. I added the advice, "Remember, it's called HAND sanitizer, not FACE sanitizer."

Last week, I set aside some time specifically designated for the discussion of project ideas. The kids sorted themselves into groups and began to brainstorm ideas. As I walked around the room offering tips and taking notes, I noticed Siddiq had sketched out a little sign that said, "Pluto – where did you go?"

Veena saw the sign and said, "Pluto didn't go anywhere. It's still out there. It's just not a planet anymore."

Siddiq nodded his head excitedly and said, "I know! So when the judges come by and ask us where Pluto went, we say, 'SPACE!' Boom! We're done!"

He then did what appeared to be a mic drop with his pencil to emphasize his point. Veena just shook her head in disgust.

Late last week, I did the usual group example project with the kids so they would remember all the necessary steps. You may recall this Jack Woodson Greatest Hit – "Will a Paper Airplane Fly Farther with or without a Paper Clip on its Nose?" I had a few kids in the morning class who for some reason left off words at the end, and "Will a Paper Airplane Fly?" would be setting the bar pretty darn low for a grade school science fair.

The hypotheses were split in my morning class, with just a slight edge to the paper clip fitted planes. Conversely, in my afternoon class, Tyrellvius was the only student who said he thought the plane with no paper clip would fly farther. It didn't take too much investigating on my part to learn that RT and Dodd had told everyone the results of the first class experiment during recess. Tyrellvius really doesn't like Dodd much, so I think his hypothesis was more of a "screw you" than a legitimate educated guess.

The procedure for our example project involved standing behind a line on the floor, tossing the paper airplane, and then measuring the distance from the line where it was thrown to the spot where it landed. Of course, much like their large steel counterparts, paper airplanes tend to skid along the floor after they land. Since we wanted the distance the airplane actually flew, it was necessary to quickly mark the spot where it first hit the ground.

Everybody was involved in the project. The kids rotated through the jobs of throwing the airplane, marking the spot where it landed, and using a tape measure to find the distance flown. As the kids took turns wildly jumping to mark where the plane landed, I found myself doing my own science experiment inside my head –

"What is the Average Distance between the Spot Where the Paper Airplane Actually Landed and Where the Child Put His/Her Foot?"

I concluded it was around 18 inches.

Still, the group project served its purpose of putting the kids in the proper mindset for science experiments and reminding them of the proper procedure. Most notably, it reminded them that they needed to repeat their experiment several times for it to be valid.

Today, the kids in my afternoon class helped out with one group project. Greyson, Landon, and Kirstie were the experimenters, and their project was titled, "Can You Tell Where Sound is Coming from When You Are Blindfolded?"

Their original title was, "Can You Hear a Sound When You Are Blindfolded?" but I convinced them that trying to pinpoint the direction might be a better idea.

Their experiment involved having one person stand in the center of the room, wearing a blindfold, while one member of the experimenting group moved somewhere else in the room and tapped on a book cover with a pencil. The blindfolded person was then supposed to point in the direction he thought the sound was coming from.

The kids asked me to go first. When I put the blindfold on (an old headband, really), I suddenly had a suspicion this was the culmination of a months-long scheme and that when I took the blindfold off, I'd be standing in the center of a completely empty room, the kids having stolen everything. Instead, I heard a tapping and dutifully pointed. I was relieved to hear Landon say, "Yes," and even more relieved to take the smelly headband off and see everything as it was before.

One at a time, the other 14 kids not performing the experiment were blindfolded and subjected to the same rigor. The performing group decided that Kirstie would have to be the one who moved around the room and tapped, because Greyson and Landon stomped around the room like elephants, making it easy to tell where they were. One at a time, all of the kids pointed in the correct direction. Then the three kids who were doing the project took their turn. One by one, they each pointed in the wrong direction when the tapping began. I'm not sure if they were just really disappointed that no one had erred so far and they wanted to spice up the data, or if their hearing is really that atrocious. Either way, Daredevil would not be impressed.

The science fair is next Friday, but I'm hoping to have the projects all finished up by the end of this week. Several groups –

including the sound-tappers – have finished their experiments and just need to finalize their write-ups and project boards.

My class has a pretty good mix of projects this year. One group is doing "Which Soda Will Dissolve a Hamburger Fastest?" (Hint: The results will not deter me from enjoying my favorite soft drink), and even "Which Toothpaste Cleans Best?" has promise.

At least our projects all seem to be better than the second grade class project – "Which Tastes Better, Dog Food or Cat Food?"
Later,

Science Ferris Bueller

Date: Thursday, April 16, 2015
To: Fred Bommerson
From: Jack Woodson
Subject: Praise Anatomy

Hey bud,

    You know, I find it very interesting that out of all the kids who have asked me, "Did you get a haircut?" over the past few days, not one of them has followed up with, "It looks good!"

    And no, it doesn't surprise me at all that the instant you mentioned science fair to Larry, he regaled you with stories of the foam volcanoes and solar system models he made as a kid in school. I guess that's what passed for an acceptable project way back then.

    One year when I was in school, I did a science fair project where I tested the strength of concrete reinforced with various materials. Pretty advanced for 5th grade, yet I only managed 3rd place. The next year, I used a store-bought circuit board kit to make a radio that played when someone touched both ends of the circuit. The radio was pretty much already built into the board, and midway through the science fair the battery ran out, so it didn't even work. I managed to win 3rd place again. It seemed really weird at the time, but that coincidence makes so much more sense now that I'm on the other side of the judging process.

    On a different subject, I want to get your opinion on a new term I'm trying out for a subset of kids. I call them "BSers," but don't worry, the BS doesn't mean what you might first think. These are the "Blissful Shouters" – kids who are wonderfully happy to be energetically participating without coming anywhere near meaningful participation.

    We had a perfect example in class today during a science review, and it went a little something like this:

Me:	"What are the four types of energy we talked about yesterday?"
Blanca:	"Light!"
Me:	"Yes!"
Lewith:	"Energy?"
Me:	"I'm asking for TYPES of energy."
Misaki:	"Sound?"
Me:	"Good one!"
Lewith:	"Energy!"
Rajiv:	"Heat!"

Me:	"Heat is number three!"
Lewith:	"ENERGY!!!"
Me:	"Lewith, are you really trying to answer, or are you just cheering on everybody else?"

Every time Lewith shouted out the word "Energy," he looked at me like he was waiting to be sublimely praised for his groundbreaking answer. An answer which was so very obviously NOT what I was looking for.

So many kids nowadays value the quantity of praise over the quality. I could ask Lewith what 2 + 2 was and he could answer, "Burnt sienna!" If I said, "Excellent!" he'd be just as happy as if he had just won the Olympic decathlon.

I fear that we are raising these kids to feel they should be bestowed with accolades for every little thing. Today it's, "You threw your trash in the trashcan! Way to go!" or, "None of the answers made any sense, but you turned in your homework! Super job!"

Tomorrow it'll be, "Hey, you didn't spill scalding hot coffee on your own crotch – you rock!" or, "You didn't hit too many pedestrians on your way to work today! Gold star!"

If Lewith was the one example of a BSer in my class this year, I wouldn't mind so much, but he's not alone. Not by a long shot. Yesterday, I took my class to the library, and we saw a jar filled with Reese's Pieces. Mrs. Drogz was running a contest where the kids guessed the number of candies in the jar.

Raina cemented her membership in the BSers Club by gleefully shouting, "One million!"

This was AFTER other, more reasonable, guesses in the low thousands had been given by her classmates.

Obviously, this is not a new phenomenon. I've had plenty of BSers, all the way back to good ol' Esteban from my first year. I called him the Flip-Flopper, though, because he never stuck with the same answer twice.

Esteban was perhaps the most extreme case I've encountered, but over the years, there have been countless other BSers. The thing that makes this year different is that some kids don't even attempt to answer with actual math or science words; they just throw out things I say or things I like!

Me:	"What do we call the top number on a fraction?"
Wrong Student 1:	"Show your work!"
Wronger Student 2:	"Use the fourths, Luke!"
Wrongest Student 3:	"Ketchup!"

Last week, we happened upon a problem that involved adding 26 and 26. I asked the kids what we call it when we add the same number twice, having seen kids in Ms. Phelps' 2nd grade class demonstrate a firm grasp on the concept of doubles.

Alvaro raised his hand triumphantly and shouted, "Regroup!"

Alvaro is definitely a member of the BS club.

The next day, I wrote the number 837,248,619 on the board and had the kids write it in word form. When I asked what form the original number was in – standard form – several hands went up, including Alvaro's.

I added, "And please don't say 'Total' or 'Sum.'"

Alvaro's hand slowly went down as the most dejected look formed on his face.

Back on the topic of unwarranted praise, in a few weeks, I'm going to have to assign at least two awards to every child in my homeroom, regardless of how many they actually deserve. This is a struggle every year with some kids, because I can't be TOO specific – "Opened his math book the first time I asked on February 11, 2015" – yet there are no subject-related awards I can in good conscience give them.

I'm seriously contemplating going the completely out-of-context generic praise route.

This Award is Presented to
<u>Fred Bommerson</u>
For Outstanding Achievement in the Area of
<u>You are totally awesome! Way to go, champ! Keep on rockin'!</u>

Talk to you later,

Spurious George

Date: Tuesday, April 21, 2015
To: Fred Bommerson
From: Jack Woodson
Subject: I must've taken a wrong turn at Albuquerque

Hey dude,

Yes, I'm very aware you consider Ron Philby and Dick Lorenzo to be founding members of the BS club there at HPU, but like I said, it has a different meaning with my kids. Though I'm sure both of those guys would be just as happy as Lewith with generic praise like, "Fantastic work, my man!"

When tutoring began this afternoon, I looked around and noticed Raina wasn't in the room. When I asked the kids if anybody knew where she was, D'Qayla shouted, "She had to drive her mom to the airport!"

I squinted at her and deadpanned, "Well, THAT'S impressive for a 4th grader."

D'Qayla's eyes grew wide, and she exclaimed, "No, wait! That's not what I meant!"

Driving a car is definitely one skill I would not want to teach my students. Given the way they don't pay attention when walking in line, crashing into each other and walls, I don't relish the thought of them ever getting behind the wheel. So driver's ed is out, but there are so many other areas of knowledge I wish I could improve in my students.

The big one is geography. These children know they live in Dallas and that Dallas is a city. Well, most of them know that. I'm pretty sure Clara thinks Dallas is a state. Beyond that, though, there is a very dark gray area, with lots of them not knowing the difference between a city, a state, and a country. I've asked the kids, just in passing conversation, to name other states besides Texas, and I've heard answers of San Antonio, Mexico, and Asia.

Their understanding of the layout of our great nation is nothing less than wonky, as well. This afternoon, one of the kids asked where I was born. When I told him I was from Washington, DC, Ja'Kendrick blurted, "Oh, I've heard of that! It's right by Florida!"

Only if you're thinking of the Hall of Presidents, buddy.

Admittedly there are times when I do my share of adding to the geographic confusion. Like last week when Rodrigo asked if Hollywood was in Nebraska, and I told him, "No, that would be Huskerwood."

History is another subject in which they are sorely lacking. Texas history is the focus of the social studies curriculum in 4th grade, so Mrs. Bird has plenty on her plate, trying to make sure the kids are up to speed on the Alamo, the Galveston hurricane, and who shot JR. But U.S. history, world history, or anything that happened outside of Texas? Total crapshoot.

Take the presidency for example. It's one thing to hear Dodd telling the kids at recess, "My dad says Obama is the worst president ever!" (I always feel like asking how Dodd's dad has never heard of James Buchanan, Millard Fillmore, or Frank J Underwood. Now THOSE were some bad presidents!)

But you'd think a 4th grader would know Barack Obama was not the FIRST president! Not the case, judging by my group. Some of them do know George Washington came first – he's on the one dollar bill after all. And by that logic, they believe Abe Lincoln was our fifth president and Benjamin Franklin was our one hundredth president. (It's all about the Benjamins, baby.)

Alas, I can't spend too much time delving into subjects beyond the scope and sequence of 4th grade. It's already a Herculean effort just trying to impress upon the kids the skills within the curriculum. Since we are now within a few weeks of the Math STAAR (the extra A is for Apocalypse!), we have begun our "lock-down" routines. All of us go over language arts for the first hour then math for the second hour. Today, my assigned topic was Fact and Opinion. I've always thought this was such an easy concept, but apparently that's just my opinion.

First my group and I had a discussion about facts and opinions which I peppered with examples. We talked about a fact being a statement that could be proven right or wrong, while an opinion is merely how someone feels or what they think – feelings or thoughts everyone in the world might not agree with. I used a student's shirt as an example.

"Rajiv's shirt is gray. Can we prove this?"

Everyone affirmed that yes, we could look at the shirt to prove it was, in fact, gray. Excellent. Gold stars all around. Moving on.

"Rajiv's shirt is awesome. Can we prove this?"

Everyone affirmed that yes, we could look at the shirt to prove that it was, in fact, awesome. Tommy emphasized this by pointing out that there were over 13 Lego characters featured on Rajiv's shirt.

I realized that wasn't working, so I tried a different tack.

"Spaghetti tastes delicious. Fact or opinion?"

"FACT!" the kids shouted, really warming to the academic discussion. "We can prove it's delicious by tasting it!"

After a boatload more examples and plenty more discussion, many of the kids started to see the light. By the end of the hour, however, there were still several who had not. At one point, I asked, "I am sitting in a chair – is that fact or opinion?"

At least five kids shouted, "OPINION!"

One or two BSers may even have shouted, "CONGRUENT!" just to feel like they were part of the experience.

At lunch, I told Mrs. Bird, "In my opinion, we absolutely need to spend another day on this topic, and that's a fact."

You know what else is a fact? It's a fact that when you have a practice test to prepare the kids for the big day, you can call it "a simulation," but not "assimilation." Mrs. Butler has been mispronouncing that word for two weeks now. I keep expecting to hear her shouting at the kids through her bullhorn, "Resistance is futile!" Talk to you later,

Factswell Smart

Date: Friday, April 24, 2015
To: Fred Bommerson
From: Jack Woodson
Subject: Dopey's choice

Hey bud,

Your question is a valid one, and yes, I actually have had kids who thought Lincoln was the first president because he's on the penny. I've never had any of them ask if Sacajawea was our 100th president, though.

Yesterday afternoon was unseasonably warm, and recess was far sweatier than usual. When the kids were lining up to come back inside, Tyrellvius looked at the tumbler of water in my hand and said, "You're so lucky! You get ice!"

All I could reply was, "Yep, it's pretty much the main reason I went into teaching!"

I most certainly did NOT go into teaching for the snotty attitudes and the troublemakers. Unfortunately, they come with the job. This year, I've had my hands full with Braxton and RT, and, to a smaller degree, Dodd and Tyrellvius. But none of them hold a candle to Macharkus.

Thankfully, Macharkus is not one of my students and never has been. He's a 5th grader in Mrs. Jones' class, but he's spent more than enough time in my classroom, since Mrs. Jones likes to send him to me as a punishment. It's not really clear which of us she's punishing.

Macharkus's antics are well known throughout the faculty. If he's not mouthing off to a teacher, he's threatening to kill a classmate. If he's not throwing a chair across the room ala Bobby Knight, he's mysteriously discovering that "someone" has placed a turd in the hallway.

Apparently, the last few times Mrs. Jones tried to send Macharkus my way, he flat out refused. I guess maybe she let him get away with it once or twice, but today when he refused, she had a teacher's aide come and take him down to the principal's office.

For some reason, Mrs. Forest tends to coddle the really poorly behaved kids, so I wouldn't have been at all surprised to hear that Macharkus returned to Mrs. Jones' class five minutes later with a cupcake and a comic book. But it was shortly before lunch, so he was probably down there for a while, waiting while Mrs. Forest and Ms. Butler ordered their lunch. No discipline issue is ever going to come before fast food!

Who knows, maybe Macharkus even had his lunch catered, just by virtue of being there at the right time.

5th grade lunch comes right before ours, and since today was rainy, we didn't go outside for recess. When I picked my kids up from the cafeteria and started to head back towards the classroom, Ms. Whitney came out and asked me to step into Mrs. Forest's office, while she took my kids upstairs. I entered to find Macharkus in his natural state – sullen – and Mrs. Forest sitting at her desk finishing a piece of fried chicken. She didn't invite me to sit down, which I took as a good sign, but she did launch into a little "bad cop" routine that was obviously designed for my benefit.

"Macharkus," she started, "were you supposed to go to Mr. Woodson's room?"

Macharkus did not answer. Mrs. Forest repeated the question twice before he finally muttered, "Yeah."

"So then why didn't you go to Mr. Woodson's room?"

Thoughts of Sartre flooded my mind while Macharkus glared and said nothing and Mrs. Forest repeated her question. Finally, she moved on. "Listen. I have the Dallas School Police Department on speed dial, and I can call them right now and ask them to come and pick you up. Then your poor mama will have to go pick her little baby up from the police station!"

At this, she paused for effect, but the only effect I saw was Macharkus rolling his eyes (as I tried hard to keep from doing the same).

"So tell me, do you want to go to Mr. Woodson's room now, or do you want me to call the police?"

Macharkus finally spoke up. "I want to go home."

"That isn't one of the choices," Mrs. Forest replied. "Do you want to go to Mr. Woodson's room, or do you want me to call the police?"

"I want to go home," was the reply again. I stood in the doorway while this exact interchange went on four more times. Finally, I couldn't stand it anymore, so I interjected.

"Mrs. Forest, I think he's made his choice. He is choosing not to come to my room."

Then things turned from merely annoying to downright bizarre/surreal/moronic. Mrs. Forest picked up the phone and "dialed" a number. Really, I'm surprised she didn't make "BEEP BOOP BEEP BOOP" sound effects as she did it, it was so painfully obvious she wasn't really calling anyone. Thinking back on it, I'm almost positive she never actually pushed a button on the keypad, and I'm pretty sure she only stabbed at the numbers eight times.

The fake conversation was just as horrendous.

"Yes, Dallas Police Office? This is Mrs. Forest down at the elementary school. I have a student here who has been making some very bad choices on this morning. Can you please come pick him up and take him downtown to talk to him? OK, thank you."

She then hung up and, I kid you not, winked at me before telling Macharkus to wait out in the hall.

As soon as Macharkus was out of earshot, I said, "You know, he's smart enough to know you didn't really call the police."

She looked at me and replied, "Oh, I DID call the police."

Here's where I should've just backed out of the room slowly without making eye contact. Instead, I answered, "Um, you know I'M smart enough to know you didn't really call the police, right?"

She looked at me sourly, and I could practically feel my next spot observation writing itself. So I did leave at that point.

As I walked back down the hallway towards my classroom, I noticed Macharkus was following me at a distance. Within a couple of minutes of me reentering my room, he appeared in the doorway and then took a spot in the corner. I had the pleasure of teaching under his hateful glare for the next half hour or so until I finally sent him back to Mrs. Jones' class.

Shockingly, no police officers ever came to our hallway to lead Macharkus away in cuffs, lending further proof to the illegitimacy of the phone call. I'm sure if I asked Mrs. Forest about it, she would tell me they showed up in her office right after I left, but seeing Macharkus repent and follow me down the hall, she sent them back to the station.

No doubt with a hearty, "Well done!" and a side of green beans.

Oh well, we may not get administrative support when it comes to student discipline, but there's always free ice!

Talk to you later,

Star 69

Date: Tuesday, April 28, 2015
To: Fred Bommerson
From: Jack Woodson
Subject: This is not a drill!

Hey bud,

What a crazy day! I have a feeling this is one of the few times when you and I may have very similar stories from the day. We never had a daytime tornado scare when I was with HPU, so you'll have to tell me all about the procedure you guys followed and how quickly Larry locked himself into the women's restroom. All kidding aside, I know none of the tornadoes came close to your office, but I hope everyone's families are all right as well.

Ironically enough, we just had a scheduled tornado drill last Friday, something we do twice a year. Since 4th grade is upstairs, we had to go downstairs and duck and cover with the 3rd graders on the ground floor. Picture about 250 kids being asked to put their noses on the floor and their butts in the air and not to talk. Very few kids take these drills seriously, instead seeing the opportunity to yell anonymously, giggle uncontrollably over how close their head is to someone else's rear end, and act like prairie dogs, popping up and looking around until a teacher tells them to duck back down.

Steven Spielberg needs to remake the movie Twister, but this time I want him to add a scene at a school where the class nitwit tries to make everybody laugh by making a huge farting sound – and then gets taken out by a flying cow.

The drill seemed like torture on Friday, but I suppose it was good practice since we had ACTUAL tornadoes today. It started to rain around 1:30 (you guys were still at lunch, I'm sure), so our recess was cut short. I didn't see anything out of the ordinary in the way the sky looked. About ten minutes after being inside, though, Mrs. Karras went from room to room showing us a text she had received from a friend saying that three tornadoes had been spotted in the Dallas area. Shortly after that, the siren came over the PA, and the "drill" began in earnest.

We hustled downstairs, and of course, the kids were their usual silly selves, laughing and making sounds. Proving that great minds think alike, Mrs. Fitzgerald and I simultaneously decided to jump on each other's class. I barked, "There really ARE tornadoes in the area, so keep your heads down!" at her 3rd graders while she shouted, "Stop talking! This is for real!" at my class. Either our words or the fact that another teacher was reprimanding them seemed to have an effect, as the hallway went suddenly silent.

Throughout the whole ordeal, I kept wondering where we teachers would duck and cover if the need arose, since there was hardly a square inch of uncovered floor in the hallway. The 3rd graders lined the walls, each with a 4th grader right behind them. I spent a few minutes weighing the pros and cons of remaining upright vs belly flopping on a couple of 3rd graders, should it come to that.

Ms. Butler showed up at the far end of the hallway with her damn bullhorn, using it to remind the teachers how important it was that we keep our grade books with us at all times.

Let me revise that scene I want in the Twister remake.

I hid my cell phone behind Mr. Redd as I texted Jill to make sure she was ok. She teaches on the 3rd floor of her school, and they broke protocol to let her ride downstairs in the elevator so the kids wouldn't be held up by the large pregnant woman slowly creeping down the stairs. She was able to sit down in the library, a large central room with no windows.

My kids were in the duck and cover position for nearly an hour while we heard the rain and thunder cracking outside. At around 2:45, we were allowed to go back upstairs to our window-heavy classrooms but told not to dismiss until we heard the signal. We all figured the worst was over.

A little after 3, Mrs. Forest came on the PA and announced, "Teachers, keep the students away from all windows, but have them assume the duck and cover position in your classroom."

I didn't understand the point of this at all, as it flew against everything we had ever practiced and drilled. Still, I had the kids help me push some desks together on the far side of the room to make a barrier for potentially fatal shattering glass then duck down opposite the wall of windows. I checked the weather radar on my phone. Nothing seemed to be in our area, so that eased a bit of my concern over the stupidity of what we were doing.

After about 20 minutes, when even the rain had subsided and it seemed like any imminent threat had passed, I let the kids grab their books and read, still staying away from the windows. It was after 3:00 at that point, well past the usual dismissal time, and we had received several announcements about not leaving our rooms.

Around 4:00, Susana asked if we were all going to have to sleep at the school. I told her, "I sure hope not, because this floor is very uncomfortable, and I didn't bring my pajamas!"

As I said this, I noticed Cesar was still in the duck and cover position, because he HAD fallen asleep.

Around 4:30, there began a mind-numbing litany of kids being called over the loudspeaker one at a time to go to the front office to go home with their parents. It would have been almost amusing to hear Mrs. Forest butcher so many kids' names if the situation hadn't been so tense and frustrating. She wouldn't let teachers take kids out to the buses until all of the onsite parents had their kids.

We were finally able to put the kids on buses around 5:15. As we were walking out of the building, I kid you not, Olivia looked at me and asked, "Is today tutoring?"

When I arrived home, I found out that Jill's school had dismissed as normal and then sent all of the faculty home immediately.

Oh, and to answer your question from last time, the name "Macharkus" HAD been on our Top Five list. But now, unfortunately, that name is forever ruined for us due to negative student associations. It's a real bummer, and we're scrambling to find a suitable replacement name in time for the birth.

Talk to you later,

Auntie Em

Date: Friday, May 1, 2015
To: Fred Bommerson
From: Jack Woodson
Subject: A waste (can) is a terrible thing to mind

Hey dude,

    I'm glad to hear no one was hurt by the storms earlier this week. Sending everyone home is certainly a simpler procedure than the one we had to follow. Of course, I'm not at all surprised to hear Latya just stayed in his office, oblivious to anything going on around him.

    Jill is fine, thanks for asking. The events of Tuesday were certainly stressful, but she's a trooper. Her kids all did their part to make sure she was ok. With the due date only three weeks away, all of her kids have been on their best behavior around her, or so she says. I'm just glad she doesn't have a Macharkus or a Braxton in her class (or a Butler as an administrator).

    We just had another impromptu after-school meeting, this time reminding us that we have to cover up anything that is instructional in our classrooms before the big tests next week.

    So I guess I'll be wearing a burqa come Tuesday morning.

    There was really no need for a Friday afternoon meeting. We all know the drill by now. I've had my concept wall, math posters, and signed portrait of Dolly Madison covered up since Monday. And since next Monday will be a stress-free day of review games and fun activities, I had the kids help me clean out the desks this afternoon.

    We switched back to homeroom twenty minutes early today to make use of some unpaid child labor, since the desks have to be completely empty during the STAAR (the extra A is for Abyss!). I guess the state thinks if there are closed math textbooks deep inside a covered desk, the students will undoubtedly pull them out, look up the concepts being utilized on the test, and pore over a few examples to review the correct strategies to use when solving these sorts of problems.

    If only that sort of "cheating" had been going on all year long!

    At least they've stopped treating us teachers like cheaters (and yes, I realize that "teacher" and "cheater" contain exactly the same letters) – we will once again be allowed to test our own kids. This is great for two reasons. One is that I really didn't want to have to spend all day corralling Macharkus and trying to keep him in the classroom. The other is that I believe our students really benefit from having their own teacher in the room with them. Nothing against any of my colleagues, but I've spent most of a year developing a relationship with these kids, and we know and understand each other. When a kid looks nervous or depressed during the test, a pat on the shoulder or a whispered, "You're doing great!" from me can turn the tide. By the same token, there are kids who would most likely slack off and not care in the slightest if another teacher was trying to coax some work out of them. But if those same kids hear my low growl and see my penetrating glare, you'd better believe they'll get my meaning – "I swear, I will follow you home and destroy your stash of Pokemon cards if you yawn one more time. Just try me!"

Back to the spring cleaning. The first thing I had the kids do was pull out all of the textbooks, workbooks, math journals, and white boards. After that, theoretically, the desks should have been empty.

They most definitely were not.

The kids found library books, busted crayons, old homework papers, pages full of doodles, and a myriad other pieces of garbage. Frankly, I'm shocked they didn't find evidence of Amelia Earhart's fate. In the desk shared by Eld'Ridge and Olivia, there were at least ten snack-sized Ziploc bags containing potato chip crumbs. I'd lay down big money that Olivia wasn't the one responsible for those bags. I can't believe they didn't find a bajillion ants in that desk as well.

In another desk, the kids found a school supply list from the first week of class, and you would have thought they had discovered a priceless copy of Action Comics #1. Kiara kept exclaiming, "I REMEMBER that!" as if it had happened shortly after her birth, while Andres asked if I would autograph it, and Rodrigo and Anita argued over who would be allowed to take it home.

Thankfully, they didn't argue over anything else, and in no time at all, both of my under-sized classroom waste baskets were overflowing. One of my oft-repeated mantras throughout the year has been, "Throw it IN the trash can, not NEAR the trash can!" but today, there just wasn't enough room.

Until Kiara decided to try and make some more room, that is. Her idea wasn't bad in theory – compact the trash so it frees up some space – but her execution was sloppy. Instead of using her foot and stomping down the trash, she decided to use her ample derriere.

She SAT in the trashcan, and you can certainly guess what happened next. Sure, she pushed the trash down (WAY down), but she also got stuck. I was stacking all of the math books away in a cabinet when I heard a peal of laughter by the door and turned to see what all the fuss was about. Kiara looked like a turtle that had flipped upside down and couldn't right itself. She didn't seem to be in pain or majorly upset, but no part of her was touching the floor.

Naturally, the other kids found this hilarious, but when a few of the laughs seemed to turn mean and pointed, I stepped in to help.

I took Kiara's hand and helped her to her feet, but the trashcan remained firmly stuck on her rear end. This caused even more laughter, but at least Kiara was laughing, too. Veena and Chloe rushed forward to pull the trashcan off of her, but it wouldn't come off easily.

I considered turning this into a science lesson on force – push and pull – but it was almost 3:00, and the bell would be ringing soon. Eventually, the can came off with a big pop and trash went flying. With a little hectic prompting from me, the kids all helped pick it up and put it back in the trashcan. When it started nearing the top again, Tommy shouted, "Hey Kiara, you want to come sit on the trash again?"

Seeing her actually consider it, I quickly intervened and put my foot down, literally, showing Kiara how she should have done it in the first place.

It wasn't until the kids had gone home that I showed Mrs. Bird the photograph I had surreptitiously snapped when Veena and Chloe were trying to help Kiara out of the waste basket. That one's a keeper.

Talk to you later,

Trash Gordon

Date: Tuesday, May 5, 2015
To: Fred Bommerson
From: Jack Woodson
Subject: STAAR-Mageddon

Hey buddy,

    Somehow, I don't think Ron Philby would ever willingly sit on top of a pile of garbage, and picking him up and throwing him into the dumpster out back would probably get you fired. But maybe the next time the temperature drops below freezing, you can triple dog dare him to lick the flag pole.

    Happy Nurse Appreciation Week! Last week, Mrs. Bird asked the kids to make cards for Nurse McCaffrey to say thanks for everything she does for them and the school. I especially enjoyed Gavin's card which featured the title in big bold letters – "THE TIME I WAS BLEEDING FROM THE HEAD."

    I'd certainly rather read that story than "The Time the Monkey Peed on My Leg."

    Mrs. Fitzgerald later shared that one of her 3rd graders had written a card that said, "Thank you for all of my asthma problems."

    Sadly, I'm not sure Nurse McCaffrey had much of a chance to relax and enjoy her appreciation today, as this was also the math day for the STAAR (the extra A is for Antibacterial!). I'm sure she had her hands full with headaches, nausea, stomach cramps, and yes, quite possibly, some bleeding from the head.

    Thankfully, the closest thing to injury that occurred in my classroom was me slapping my own face a little too hard while trying to stay awake. It is not easy to keep from drowsing in a warm classroom while doing absolutely nothing more exciting than glaring at kids. I was wide awake when the day started, though, and I greeted each student with a fistbump and a hearty, "Good morning, sir or madam, and welcome to Room 214. My name is Mr. Woodson, and I'll be your tester today."

    We had asked the kids not to bring their backpacks today unless absolutely necessary. They could bring a couple of books from home to read after the test or they could borrow from my classroom library. Siddiq walked in with a Nancy Drew book in his hand and a Nancy Drew ditty on his lips.

"Nancy Drew, you're the best!
Everyone loves you, Nancy Drew!"

I feel like this kid would really like Ziggy, Beetle Bailey, and the Katzenjammer Kids.

I placed all of the books over on a side counter so they'd be easy to pass out when the kids turned in their tests. As I looked over the stories the kids had brought, I had to suppress a sudden urge to shout out spoilers.

"Hey, Omar! Snape kills Dumbledore!"
"Akasha, it's so sad – they shoot Old Yeller at the end!"
"Cesar, Waldo is in the lower left hand corner, near the bottom of the staircase!"

I fielded a couple of last minute questions, including Eld'Ridge's "Do we need to show our work?"

"YES! That's like asking if you need to breathe! The answer is always yes!"

After I passed out all of the materials and got the test underway, I slowly paced around the classroom, monitoring as best I could. Technically, we are not supposed to look at the test questions, because technically, we've been told that would be cheating. How exactly that constitutes cheating, I have no idea. My theory is they tell us it's cheating in the hopes we won't look and then get upset if some of the questions are in German, Elvish, or binary. Either way, our job value hinges on these mystery test questions that we're not supposed to read.

Here is what I IMAGINE most of the questions to be like:

Talukadiah arrived home at 4:55, after a long day of planting rutabagas on his family's 449 square-foot plot of property in Northern Gnome, Alaska. He read that there would be 13 inches of snowfall that night, nearly twice as much as the week before! His 3 brothers and five sisters each had planted 38 magic beans, with one of those sisters, Groznzk, then planting 12 more. After a nice 5-course meal, Talukadiah and his family, minus one brother, compared their earnings. In all, they had made $450 total. The oldest brother kept 1/9 of this, while the oldest sister claimed 1/10 of the remaining money. Talukadiah normally put away all but $5 of his earnings in a bag under his mattress, but only on weeks ending in an even numbered day. Other weeks, he used a debit card to buy between 4 and 15 mice. He looked at the calendar and saw that it was Wednesday, December 4, that it was 14°F outside, and that 25 minutes had passed since dinner. If Talukadiah is 8 inches taller than his youngest sister, how much money is in the bag underneath his mattress? Also, symmetry.

I can honestly say I did not read any of the questions on today's test. However, glancing at the kids' pencils to check for tip sharpness and eraser consistency allowed me to see large blocks of text and full-page graphical questions out of the corner of my eye. Here's hoping all our practice paid off. And man, did we practice.
Starting early in the year, I gave the kids lots of opportunities to experience ludicrously long and overcomplicated word problems addled with unnecessary extra information. I wanted the kids to start recognizing which pieces were needed to solve the problem and which pieces they could ignore. During the second week of class, I gave the kids this problem:

Billy and his four friends caught 18 worms on Saturday. Two days later, they went to a restaurant and bought nine hamburgers for a total of $23.28. Each boy ate 12 french fries and used 3 napkins. 20 minutes later, they saw six of their friends. How many french fries did Billy and his friends eat in all?

The answers were all over the map. A few kids were correct, but most were way off. I didn't go over the correct solution with them that day, but I let the kids talk with each other about their answers. Some of them very proudly declared they had just added all of the numbers in the story. Some randomly cherry-picked a few numbers and used them, ignoring the rest. A couple even focused in on the french fries at the end but only multiplied by four, forgetting Billy had eaten some too. I gave the kids the same problem about a month later, after we had practiced hard on focusing on the question first and only looking for needed information. The results were much better. Only a handful still added all the numbers together, and those are the kids who would probably do that even if they had a magical Frankenstein mashup of Mr. Chips, Ms. Frizzle, and Mr. Miyagi teaching them every day.
We've also had long hard discussions about names in math problems. Most of my kids are classified as English as a Second Language, and even the ones who aren't tend to get completely bogged down by an unfamiliar name. They also get ridiculously overexcited when they see their own name or the name of someone they know in a math problem.
"Tommy?!? OMG, I KNOW HIM!!!"

We've talked about the unimportance of names in math problems many times throughout the year. My initial Patton-esque speech went something like this:

Names do not matter at all in a math problem! Does it matter whether it's Jimmy John eating the M&Ms or whether it's Skylar Clydesworth Yooombi the Fourteenth eating the M&Ms? NO! It's going to be the same number of M&Ms eaten no matter what the name is! So when you do a math problem, you put your OWN name in place of the name in the story! And if you can't remember your own name for some reason, you put BATMAN in place of the name in the story!

I suspect Siddiq substituted "Nancy Drew" into his word problems today, and I'm ok with that.

I turned the tests in a little before 2:00, then a while later we all went outside for some much needed recess. The playground was crowded, with all three testing grades out there at once. I tried to warn people what would surely happen if 3rd, 4th, and 5th grades were all at recess at the same time. Sure enough, it happened. Spontaneous conga line!

I'd love to say the tedium of testing is now over for the year, but unfortunately, we have the reading test tomorrow. So I'm off to dream of sealed booklets, broken pencils, and never-ending requests to go to the bathroom.

Talk to you later,

STAARsky and Hutch

Date: Friday, May 8, 2015
To: Fred Bommerson
From: Jack Woodson
Subject: One Angry Man

Hey brother,
    You're welcome to celebrate Nurse Appreciation Week any way you see fit, but try to do it in a way that doesn't result in a restraining order. Let's not forget what happened six years ago.
    I have to deal with standardized testing every year around this time; it's clear that you go through a period of being annoyed with Dick Lorenzo every year around this time. What's my favorite Quality Reduction Engineer's reasoning for delaying your shipment THIS time?
    If you'd like to press charges against him, let me know, because I have contacts within the court system now. Just when it seemed like my life couldn't get any more trying, I found myself invited to an actual trial! Actually, I received the jury summons back in November, but I went online and postponed it a couple of times, wanting to wait until I was free and clear of the STAAR (the extra A is for Arbitration!). I couldn't put it off any longer, though, and I figured the day after testing would offer a nice break away from the kids. Still, I really did not want to be selected for a lengthy trial. I figured I had a pretty good reason to be excused – "My wife could pop any minute!" – so I didn't have to resort to lowbrow tricks like loudly proclaiming the death penalty for jaywalkers, answering the lawyers' questions in Elmo's voice, or dressing as Princess Leia in a gold bikini.
    I arrived at the courthouse first thing yesterday morning and was sworn in with several hundred of my peers. Then we were all split up into groups of 50 or so and sent to the individual courtrooms. Once we were seated on the hard uncomfortable benches, I expected the lawyers to start asking us questions and making their selections for the jury. Instead, the judge talked to us for a bit and made me realize I REALLY did not want to be on this jury.
    First, she told us that we wouldn't be there long that morning, because she was going to send us home with the questionnaire to bring back today. Then she told us the trial would be a case of murder (most foul) and would likely last six to eight weeks. After a few more bits of information, she dismissed us, asking anyone who felt they had a valid excuse not to be on the jury to stay behind.

Easily 30 people, myself included, remained seated. We were then asked to wait out in the hallway while the judge and attorneys heard excuses one at a time. When I was called in, the judge and attorneys were laughing like they had just heard a real whopper. The phrase, "Nice try!" was practically hanging in the air.

I presented my case, telling them Jill's due date was fast approaching, and that it could happen anytime now. The judge asked (somewhat jokingly, I think), "And you feel like you need to be there for the birth?"

I replied (again, somewhat jokingly), "Your Honor, if I'm not there, you'll be presiding over MY murder trial within the month."

That seemed to satisfy her, and I was let off the hook, though I was prepared to make "Wapner" my son's middle name in exchange for my freedom.

Needless to say, Jill was pleased to hear the news, though she confirmed that what I told the judge was not actually a joke.

Back at school today, I was greeted with the usual shouts of, "Where were you yesterday?" as if I had wandered down the wrong aisle at the Super Target. I was not at all surprised to find a note from my substitute telling me that Kiara hit someone at recess, RT was disrespectful, and Eld'Ridge kept trying to leave the room.

Seriously, I do not understand that kid. A large percentage of the time, he doesn't seem to be in control of his own body. He'll stand up and wander around the room in the middle of a lesson, and when I tell him to stop it and sit down, he has the look of someone who has been sleepwalking and has no idea how they woke up on the airport runway.

One day, after Eld'Ridge ambled out of Mrs. Bird's classroom – for about the 20th time this year – she asked me if we should look into fitting him with one of those invisible dog fence collars. Knowing that would be neither practical nor legal, she instead chose to post a sign at her door that says, "Eld'Ridge! Don't leave this classroom!"

Surprisingly, she says this has kept him from leaving several times.

Regrettably, I never had the opportunity to stand up and shout, "YOU CAN'T HANDLE THE TRUTH!" as a result of jury duty. However, I could very easily have justified telling my students, "You can't handle the TOOTH!" upon my return.

In addition to the page of notes the sub left for me, I also found four nurse's notes detailing lost teeth. This was just from yesterday! Enrique and Graciella each lost a tooth, and I couldn't help wondering if they had both been natural losses or if one had been forcibly self-extracted, just to keep up with the other. The trend continued today when Veena came running up to me at recess, holding a tooth out in front of herself and wailing, "I have bleeding in my mouth!"

Truth be told, the cafeteria rice DID look severely undercooked today.

Whenever a student has a tooth fall out, Nurse McCaffrey sends them back with the tooth inside a little plastic treasure chest. I assume this is to make it easier for the child to hold onto the tooth and put it under their pillow for the Tooth Fairy. I've heard the kids discussing what they've received for lost teeth, and the payouts seem to range from a quarter to five dollars to a Buy One Get One Free coupon at Arby's.

Whatever the value, 4C is poised for quite a haul this week. Myself, I'll just stick to the dreams of teeth falling out and keep my real ones.

There was also one nice surprise awaiting me upon today's return. During my planning period, Mrs. Bird and I stopped by the office to check our mailboxes, and Mrs. O Riley told us that Braxton's mother had filled out withdrawal papers this morning. Mrs. Bird had marked Braxton absent this morning and was supremely enjoying the lack of bullying and back talking going on. At recess, I learned more. Olivia and Blanca live in the same apartment complex as Braxton, and they said his family had been evicted from their apartment because he destroyed the weight room. Apparently, they have a strict "No one under 18 allowed" policy and an even stricter "No throwing dumbbells at the mirror" policy.

Braxton and I never really saw eye to eye during his time here. I hope a move closer to his grandparents will settle him down and he'll be able to make a fresh start at a new school. I just hope I am never called downtown for jury duty and find out it's this former student who's on trial.

Have a good weekend! I plan on sleeping in and being a bum, recovering from this VERY long week!
Talk to you later,

The Manjuryan Candidate

Date: Monday, May 11, 2015
To: Fred Bommerson
From: Jack Woodson
Subject: HE'S HERE!!!

Fred (and entire world),

It gives me great pleasure to announce the birth of Latya "Larry" Bommerson Woodson XVII!

Wait, I'm running low on sleep, and I'm a little delirious. Let me try that again.

It gives me great pleasure to announce the birth of Benjamin Montgomery Woodson, who arrived into the world at 6:30 this morning.

Benjamin weighed in at 8.6 lbs, so it's probably a good thing he came almost two weeks early, because he may very well have been a ten pound baby like his daddy if he had stayed inside until the due date.

Jill went into labor last night around eight, and we set foot in the hospital around ten – not because the hospital is that far away, but because Jill insisted I finish dinner, repack the bags, and water all of our outside plants before we could leave the house. No major complications, mother and child are doing well, father is about to crash and burn. Aside from a small doze in the waiting room last night, I have been awake for over 30 hours. Take THAT, Jack Bauer!

My parents and brother stopped by earlier today to see how everyone was and to take some pictures. Zack was kind enough to bring me a 2-liter bottle of Mountain Dew, and that's about all that's keeping me conscious right now.

We took some great pictures, and I'll attach some here. At one point – I don't remember if it was when I was holding Ben up like Simba from the Lion King, tucking him under my arm and striking a Heisman pose, or holding him in front of my head like a face-hugger from Alien – Jill groaned and said, "Great, I haven't given you a son, I've given you a prop!"

Feel free to stop by tomorrow to meet the little guy. Oh, and bring a tape measure. I don't believe for a second that any son of mine is only 19 inches long.

More after sleep.

Later,

Father Goose

Date: Monday, May 18, 2015
To: Fred Bommerson
From: Jack Woodson
Subject: Welcome Back, Woodson

Hey buddy,

Thanks again for all the fun baby gifts. I will have hours and hours of fun with them, and perhaps I'll even let Ben play with them someday soon!

It was nice of Nancy and Tiffany to stop by the house last week and deliver hot dinners. I don't get to see them nearly as often as I see you, and it was great to catch up. Plus, Benny really seemed enamored with Nancy. Larry sent me an email last Wednesday that supposedly linked to a video of him saying, "Coochie coo" over and over, but I never opened it because Larry's links have been known to lead to viruses. I don't need any more soup cans, pantyhose, Wahoos, OR coochie coos in my life.

Jill is doing great, and please tell everyone thanks for asking. Her favorite thing is having Benny nap on her chest. Her least favorite thing is changing his diaper, which would explain why she never did it before today. Actually, neither one of us had ever changed a diaper in our lives a week ago. I changed my first 500 last Monday and about 2,000 since.

I originally thought I would only take a couple of days off, just enough to stay with Jill until we left the hospital, but a couple of days morphed into a whole week. So today was my first day back to school since Ben was born. Mr. Utoobay graciously stepped up and handled the lesson planning and substitutes while I was out. I am very thankful for that, and the school should be too, because if I had been required to do it in my state of exhaustion last week, the plans would have been nothing but five full days of Thumbs Up, Seven Up.

While I was out, the kids worked on their money skills as well as their creative abilities. First they played Monopoly for a day, then they spent a couple of days designing their own Monopoly boards, and lastly, they played each other's versions. When I read the plans, I fully expected to see squares on the boards labeled "Park Playground," "Poor Reading Railroad," and "Marvin's Fouking Gardens." Instead, most of the properties were named after friends or siblings, though I did like Akasha's clever "Time Out Corner" in the space usually marked "Jail."

I've loved every minute I've spent with Benjamin, but I was ready to leave the house for a few hours and return to work. The kids seemed very happy to see me today, though it's possible that one week of fatherhood has aged me severely. I guess Phil Collins had never noticed my school ID badge before today. Most kids look at it and are astounded to discover I have a first name. Not Phil Collins. He looked at it and asked, "Is that a picture of you when you were younger?"

The photo was taken in August.

Most of the kids were a bit kinder. I received several nice handmade cards and posters. Enrique's said, "Happy Father's Day, Mr. Woodson!" It may be a little early for the official holiday, but I'll certainly accept it. Misaki, Chloe, and Akasha teamed up to draw a banner that said, "You're like a weird older brother to us, but now you're a daddy to your little boy!"

A weird older brother who rocks at math, thank you very much!

At recess, a bunch of kids crowded around me wanting to see pictures and asking questions. D'Qayla asked, "Does your son like numbers?"

Yes, he especially loves two, four, five, and six, because those are the hours in the a.m. he always wakes up crying!

Mateo seemed very interested in Benny's health, and he asked if I had taken him to see the vet yet. I told him we just brought him home from the hospital, so he's free of distemper and mad cow disease, and we hope he can avoid the cone of shame for a few more months at least.

Chloe asked for the baby's full name. When I said, "Benjamin Montgomery Woodson," I heard several responses simultaneously.

Chloe said, "I like that name!"

Rajiv asked, "Will you call him Ben?"

Alvaro wondered, "Woodson???"

Yes, you little muppet, we opted to go with the nontraditional practice of giving our child OUR last name.

Veena asked what the baby likes to eat. I told her all he eats or drinks is baby formula right now, but if you looked at his diapers, you'd think we were feeding the kid a steady diet of Toblerone.

My day ended on a high note. Outside at dismissal, a little 1st grader walked up to me and asked, "Can I have a hug from the tallest man in the building?"

A few weeks ago, I passed by this girl's class in the hallway, and she asked, "Are you the tallest man?"

This seemed like a bit of an open question, so I specified, "In the building, yes."

She must have a really good memory. Now I'm off to the house to see how good Jill's memory is and if she remembered which end of the diaper goes up.

Talk to you later,

Papa Smurf

Date: Wednesday, May 20, 2015
To: Fred Bommerson
From: Jack Woodson
Subject: STAART spreading the news

Hey bud,

You're missing out if you're not playing board games, man. Sure, Monopoly takes forever, but it gets the kids dealing with money. I applaud your idea to start a lunchtime games club at HPU, but maybe you should start with quicker games like Risk, Clue, or Civilization.

Just when I thought I was done with state-mandated standardized testing for the year, they pull me back in. Thankfully, my 4th graders are entirely done, but I was asked to monitor a small group of 5th graders who did not pass the math STAAR (the extra A is for Apathy!) back in April.

As you probably know, 5th grade is one of those years where the kids MUST pass the reading and math STAAR in order to be promoted to the next grade level. Because of that, 5th graders take their math and reading tests earlier than the other grades so they can fit in another testing date closer to the end of the year. If a student doesn't pass on the first attempt, he has to try again before school ends. If he still doesn't pass, he must go to summer school and try one more time. If he STILL doesn't pass after that, he is sent to the salt mines of Zambookistan to apprentice under a one-eyed man named Chansorkus.

Just kidding! If a child doesn't pass the third time, the state of Texas mandates retention for that child. And holding a child back in the same grade level for another year is a binding decision that is almost impossible to overturn. Unless a principal, teacher, parent, baby sister, wandering vagrant, or family pet votes to deny retention, in which case – 6th grade, here I come!

There were 20 kids who did not pass the math test back in April, so their teacher, Mrs. Jones, took half of them today, and I monitored the other half. Mrs. Forest told me yesterday I would be proctoring today's exam. She mentioned this as I walked out the door to go home.

So first thing this morning, I ventured into the Valley of the Shadow of Death (AKA the 5th grade hallway). When I entered the classroom where I would be giving the test, I saw that four of the kids were former students of mine from two years ago. One of them smiled at me, one didn't seem to recognize me, and the other two rolled their eyes as if they had just been asked to take their younger brother to a birthday party. Thankfully, Mrs. Jones kept Macharkus with her.

Once we started the test, it didn't take long to see that some of these kids actually did care that they hadn't passed the first time around and were working hard. Mrs. Jones had told me the kids were supposed to begin by writing out all of the multiplication tables on scratch paper so they'd have them readily available to use throughout the test. Four of the kids were doing that.

On the other end of the spectrum, three kids had filled in ten bubbles on the answer sheet before I had even made one walking circuit around the room. Of course I couldn't read the questions – because that would be CHEATING! And cheaters never win!! But it was apparent that absolutely nothing had been written on their scratch paper. No notes, no computation, no diagrams. Nothing.

Well, that's not entirely true. One of these kids, a boy named Roger, had written something on the measurement page. He had written, nice and large, "I hate math! I hate STAAR! I hate Burger King!"

There's clearly a story there, but I wasn't going to draw it out of him today.

One of the slackers kept falling asleep. When I woke him up for the third time (before 10am!), I asked what time he had gone to bed the night before. He had no earthly idea. Here's hoping there weren't too many clock-related questions on the test.

One of the eye rollers broke four pencils in the first two hours – including one before I passed out the test! I finally had to threaten her that she'd be using a crayon if she broke another.

Tara was in my group this morning, and I taught her and her twin sister Dara two years ago. Both are sweet but extremely quiet girls who paid attention in class but who always struggled with math. Tara asked to use the restroom once this morning, and right as she was leaving the room, Dara walked by, headed to the restroom as well. SPOOOOOOOKY psychic twin connection!

Speaking of bathroom breaks, when Roger the Burger King hater asked to use the restroom, I told him he could go but he needed to be back in his seat in three minutes. I've found this helps curb the wandering and dawdling. Roger was able to meet this deadline. 15 minutes later, though, he asked to use the restroom again. I said, "No, you just went 15 minutes ago!"

He calmly replied, "Yeah, but I gotta do something different this time."

I still said no, and he spent the next 20 minutes bent over in his chair, grabbing his ankles, and loudly moaning.

Before lunch, I picked up all the tests and testing materials to lock them in the cabinet. When I passed the tests back out after lunch, one child's test had barely touched her desk before she had her hand raised to tell me that she was done. Mrs. Jones had clearly told them not to turn the test in before lunch, and this girl was taking that advice to the absolute letter. Unfortunately for her, she had forgotten to fill in one answer on her bubble sheet. I didn't point out which one she had left blank – because that would be CHEATING! – I just told her that she hadn't completed all of her answers. It took her an hour – and three more attempts to turn in the test – before she finally found her mistake.

After Roger turned his test in, he zipped his jacket up over his head and began swaying and rocking back and forth, slapping himself in the face several times. He looked like the Headless Horseman on meth. I didn't stop him because he was doing it quietly, though I desperately wanted to ask him if he was having Whopper-induced flashbacks.

Today was one of those few times I allowed myself to go home immediately after dismissal. After such a long, tedious day, it was absolute bliss to walk in the door and hold my baby boy for a while.

Then I went back out to pick up some carryout from Burger King. I just had a craving.
Talk to you later,

The Last STAAR Fighter

Date: Wednesday, May 27, 2015
To: Fred Bommerson
From: Jack Woodson
Subject: Throw the book at 'em!

Hey buddy,

No, I never did learn why Roger hates Burger King so much. I mentioned the note to Mrs. Jones, and she said he's a very odd little man. He's only been with her since February, and he apparently reads like a champ but can't (or won't) do a lick of math.

His behavior, however, was bad enough in that short time period to warrant him losing the chance to go on the 5th grade field trip today. Mrs. Jones left Roger and another student in my class with some work to keep them busy. She gave me a break from Macharkus, placing him downstairs in Mr. Redd's room.

Roger chose not to do his work, instead staring at my kids, sleeping, and tapping a pencil on his desk. Finally, I had enough and put a note in front of him that said, "If you sit here and do NOTHING all day long, you will stay with me this Friday while the rest of the 5th grade has their Field Day."

I drew a smiley face at the bottom of the note to add a touch of class. It seemed to do the trick, as it motivated Roger to begrudgingly open his work packet and start writing. Thank goodness, since I'm not sure we'll even have Field Day this week because of all the rain.

Since it's rained so much, we've had plenty of inside recess. Curtiss and Gavin have spent most of their recess time writing short stories, which I've found very entertaining. While a few of their stories are about aliens and vampires, the vast majority of their writing centers around Justin Bieber. More specifically, Justin Bieber being pushed off of progressively higher cliffs. I feel there could be a large audience for these stories.

It's great to see the kids writing for pleasure, and I often get a kick out of what they are reading as well. Mrs. Bird has the kids keep a reading log, and the weekly chart is kept in the homework folder we share. Yesterday, I saw that Tracy Jane had logged a book called "Solomon Grundy" – AND it was in the Monday slot! That made me giggle for some reason.

Even though he's not even three weeks old, I think Ben is going to be a book lover. Jill and I have both seen the effects of parents not reading at home with their kids, so we've been reading to him every night since we brought him home. His favorites so far seem to be The Very Hungry Caterpillar, The Very Busy Spider, and The Very Gassy Grasshopper.

Actually, the ones we read the most are Five Little Monkeys Jumping on the Bed and Goodnight Moon. These are both classics of children's literature, though they each annoy me for their own reasons.

Five Little Monkeys reminds me way too much of many students I've had over the years, kids who seem unable or unwilling to learn from past mistakes. In the story, the monkeys jump on the bed until one falls off and gets a career-ending concussion. Much like my kids, instead of learning a valuable lesson in safety and furniture respect, the other monkeys choose to do the exact same thing that just landed their colleague in the monkey hospital! Inevitably, one at a time, the monkeys face plant on the floor, doomed to experience history repeating itself.

I earned stern looks from Jill one night when I veered from the story, ad libbing, "The mama called the doctor, and the doctor said – You're a terrible parent, and I'm calling CPS!"

Goodnight Moon, on the other hand, involves a child rabbit saying good night to every conceivable thing in his room, his city, and his universe. I find it confusing that the rabbit has kittens for pets and that a little mouse lives in his room. The rabbits can talk, but apparently the pets and the rat cannot. Is this evidence of slavery in the animal kingdom? Or just poor vermin control?

Also, there appears to be a stranger in the room with this rabbit as he's preparing to sleep. He doesn't say, "Good night, Grandma," or, "Good night, Aunt Fluffy," or even, "Good night, babysitter with personal space issues."

Instead, it's a very generic shout out to an unnamed "Old lady whispering 'Hush!'"

Is he sleeping in a public library?

But hey, despite any issues I may have with these stories, Ben seems to enjoy them. He especially enjoys the taste of them, and it's hard to keep the big board pages out of his mouth. He also seems to appreciate the repetitiveness of Goodnight Moon, so I often calm him before sleep by walking around his bedroom, rocking him while following a Goodnight Moon course of action.

"Good night, humidifier."
"Good night, stinky diaper genie."
"Good night, Darth Vader helmet."

Speaking of the Dark Lord of the Sith and kids, I was talking with some kids this morning about Star Wars, and I mentioned that Darth Vader was Luke's Skywalker's father. Rajiv immediately shouted, "Spoiler alert!" in a wounded tone of voice that seemed to imply I should keep that little "secret" to myself.

I really don't think the spoiler tag can be used on movies almost 40 years old. Or by people who were born decades after the movie was released! I'm not yelling at anyone who tells me Rosebud is the name of the sled or that the Titanic sinks!
I doubt I ruined the surprise for these kids anyway, since Olivia immediately asked, "Who's Luke Skywalker?"
Talk to you later,

Drools Verne

Date: Friday, May 29, 2015
To: Fred Bommerson
From: Jack Woodson
Subject: Playing the field

Hey buddy,

What have you been smoking, man? Of course we're not going to read The Exorcist, Flowers in the Attic, or Mein Kampf to Ben! We don't want to give him nightmares so early in his life!

Jill, though, insists on using a baby monitor in his room that might give ME nightmares. Everything shows up in spooky photo-negative like something out of Paranormal Activity. Eyes are sinister pools of black and everything has an eerie greenish-white glow to it. No thank you!

No nightmares at school today, as it was actually one of our designated fun days. We've worked hard all year, and today it was time to play! The weather cooperated, so today was our Field Day – or as I like to call it, Field Hour-and-a-Half. That's about how long each grade level had out on the field, and with the temperature and humidity we had today, that's about all the time we needed to be outside.

Field Day always makes me think of Battle of the Network Stars, only without the Z-List celebrities and colorful unitards. It's a lot of fun for the kids and teachers alike, except maybe for the specials teachers who have to be outside running the stations all day long. By the time we went out there for our turn in the afternoon, Mrs. Holloran, the music teacher, looked like she was about to melt, and Mr. Vann, the art teacher, was a lovely shade of lobster.

It's fun for the kids, but it's most fun for those kids who didn't lose out on any of the stations. Since Spring Break, Mrs. Bird and I have been holding Field Day events over the kids' heads as a reward for good behavior. We've been keeping a record of kids' strikes, with three strikes equaling the loss of one event. A strike was given for things like not turning in homework, fighting, bouncing checks, etc.

I made it perfectly clear to the kids that lost events would not necessarily come in chronological order. In other words, they might not lose the very first station we went to on Field Day; rather, the lost events would be of MY choosing, and I always take away water events and bouncy house events first. At this announcement, several kids' looks changed from "Whatever, dude," to "Holy crap, this guy means business!"

I could easily have given Omar a strike or two this morning for being blunt. As soon as I walked into the gym to pick up the kids, Omar shouted, "Whoa, Mr. Woodson, you do NOT look good in shorts!"

Thanks, Omar, but save those compliments for next year's Teacher Appreciation Week!

Fortunately, we only had a small handful of kids who had to miss any events, and only one who lost out on more than one event. Over in the bilingual 4th grade classes, though, there were six kids who missed Field Day entirely. These six stole some items from the library last week. This is upsetting and disappointing on so many levels. For one thing, we shouldn't have to be dealing with theft at this age. They stole tiny items, but everyone knows pencil sharpeners and bookmarks are gateway thefts, with wallets, cars, and the Hope Diamond not far behind. For another thing, some of those kids, from what I was told, don't seem to feel the slightest bit of remorse. In fact, Mrs. Del Torro told me that one of them seemed happy that she was being suspended.

However, the biggest reason I find Bilingual-gate so depressing is that two of the little girls involved are the most adorable little munchkins in the whole school. I've known them for the past three years, and they've always been very friendly to me, often speaking to me in Spanish at recess. I had heard the rumors that they were not as innocent as they appeared, but I hated to believe it. Several months ago, when I heard they were calling kids names, I asked them in the lunch line if it was true that they had called a classmate "la phantasma gorda" (The Fat Ghost), and they actually seemed upset. They promised they would not get into any more trouble, even going so far as to pinky swear with me.

Now that trust has been completely violated. And if you can't count on the sanctity of a pinky swear, then what's the point of life?

Back to the fun of Field Day, my class's first station was the Tug o' War. We started with the mandatory boys vs girls showdown. It was totally unbalanced and unfair, and the boys won easily. You would have thought they had just won the Superbowl with the way they were strutting around and celebrating. Next came the obligatory boys vs girls + Mr. Woodson. The boys still won – there are just so many of them! – but not nearly as easily.

After that we mixed up the class and went through several much more evenly matched iterations. Lastly, Andres insisted that he was so strong, he could take on all of the girls by himself. He posed and postured and huffed and puffed – and then was promptly yanked onto his face like a first-time water skier. I'm thinking about making it the screen saver on my phone.

The centerpiece of this year's Field Day was a bouncy house water slide, and it was our fourth station. The kids were loving this one – except for the few who had lost an event, because of course this was the one I took away first – until things came to a screeching halt. Literally. Becky had climbed up to the top of the slide, decided she didn't want to go down after all, and started screeching in terror.

Becky is a little girl in Miss Knox's special education class. She has Down Syndrome, and while she occasionally joins my class for science or social studies, it's pretty rare. Miss Knox usually teaches Becky all day. Since she's in the 4th grade, though, Becky joins my class for specials, lunch, and recess. All of the kids know her and have played with her, and most really like her. She's a sweet girl. She and Miss Knox went from station to station with my group today.

Nobody else could use the water slide with Becky up there, and since I didn't trust the tact or diplomacy of most of my students – Exhibit A, Omar – I figured I should climb up and handle the situation myself. Plus, I really wanted to go down that water slide.

Long story short, I was up at the top of that slide for about twenty minutes, trying to coax Becky down. The first four or five of those minutes were spent with her screeching in my face in an attempt to make me go away. The kids below started chanting her name, in what I thought was a very touching gesture of support for their sometimes classmate. Unfortunately, that just upset her even more, so I had to shout down at them to stop.

I could easily have pushed her down the slide, but I didn't want to scar the poor girl for life, so I had to get creative.

I tried encouragement – "It's going to be so much fun, and Miss Knox will be so proud!"

I tried lecturing – "You're keeping everyone else from being able to enjoy this!"

I tried pleading – "Please give it a try, for me and for all your friends!"

I think eventually she just grew tired of hearing my voice. She finally dropped down the slide and I followed right behind her. After splashing down into the pool below, I looked around, but before I could even get to Becky to thank her/see if she liked it/see if she was traumatized for eternity, she had jumped out of the landing pool and was climbing up the bouncy stairs again. Miss Knox and I exchanged an "Oh crap, here we go again" look, but there was no hesitation this time. Becky flew down the slide, laughing.

When my class rotated to the next station, Becky refused to leave, so Miss Knox just let her stay. She told me later that Becky must have gone down the slide fifty times.

Our final event of the day was the racing event. The entire year, kids have been challenging me to race or boasting they are faster than me. I've answered every comment with, "We'll see."

Mr. Vann organized several races with groups of kids while I waited to run in the last one. Mrs. Bird even brought her class over since so many of her kids wanted to race me as well. She had no interest in running against the kids, but she suggested the last race be the seventy-five yards down to the end of the field and back. I squashed the "and back" part. At almost 40 years old, I'm fast, but it doesn't last long. I also didn't give the kids a head start this time like I have in years past.

Standing at the starting line, I felt a little sluggish. I hadn't sprinted since last year's Field Day. It might have been nerves, it might have been the heat, it might have been the barbecue lunch from a few hours beforehand. But when Mr. Vann blew the whistle and I had those first couple of strides out of the way, it all came back to me, like riding a bike or gutting a shark. My competition was 25 nine- and ten-year-olds, and I beat one of them by only about three steps, but it still felt really good. My legacy is safe for yet another year.

Now if you'll excuse me, I'm going to take the ice off my knees and go reapply the Ben Gay liberally to my back and calves. Talk to you later,

Sore-Kneed Racer

Date: Tuesday, June 2, 2015
To: Fred Bommerson
From: Jack Woodson
Subject: Classroom supply giveaway – FREE (or best offer)

Hey Fred,

Listen, you and Omar are entitled to your shared opinion about me in shorts, but Jill happens to feel differently. And if he could speak, I'm sure Ben would disagree with you as well.

It's the last week of school! The finish line is finally in sight, and while a few of us may not be completely upright on two feet anymore, we are going to cross that line!

In keeping with tradition, I will be sending the kids home with full backpacks every day of this last week. Yesterday, it was leftover homework and worksheets, today it was workbooks, tomorrow it will be folders and notebooks. Thursday, I'll fill their backpacks with joy and the prospect of summer vacation.

At the beginning of the year, we received way too many consumable math workbooks. I don't know if the district was secretly planning to add another section of 4th grade or if the publisher was having a buy one get one free sale, but I've had roughly thirty unused workbooks sitting on my back counter all year long. There is no reason to keep them, because we will be receiving a brand new shipment next year. So I pawned them all off on the kids today, and some were far more interested than others. All of the kids took their own workbooks home, and many of them were happy to take a second. Even then, I still had six left. Four kids insisted they could find a good home for a third workbook, and then one of those four – Kirstie – practically begged me for the final two. She was more excited about those workbooks than inmates in prison are about free cigarettes.

Yesterday, I chose three or four kids in each class to pass out the extra worksheets I've accumulated throughout the year. I usually made a few extra copies of anything we did in class and kept the leftovers in a big pile on the shelf. I'd pull out a few sheets any time a kid got in trouble and needed extra work or if a parent asked for review work. With just a couple of copies of each item in the pile today, everybody didn't receive the same papers, but everyone was given enough to fill their packs.

While passing out a stack of challenge question homework sheets, Blanca decided to channel her inner Oprah. As she handed them out, she shouted, "YOU get a word problem! And YOU get a word problem! You ALL get word problems!"

Cleaning out the classroom is not the only thing we've done this week, though. Mrs. Bird and I joked about ways to fill our lesson plans this last week. I suggested a science experiment – How many pieces of blank white paper can you completely darken using a single crayon? Do different colors give different results?

She suggested turning the tables and letting the kids teach us about something they love. She added that we would need to appear to grasp the concept perfectly on Tuesday but then forget it completely by Wednesday.

I settled on having the kids working in groups of three on planetary research projects. They loved it in 3rd grade, and I figured they'd love it in 4th. We checked all of the relevant books out of the library, a few kids brought their own books from home, and some kids even found things online. Each group made a big poster to highlight and share interesting pictures and facts they found, and we began the presentations today.

As usual, I asked the kids to cover up Uranus while the other planets were discussed.

Tracy Jane, Landon, and Kirstie presented a poster about Venus. Their picture of the planet looked fiery and cloudy at the same time, which was accurate, but there was a giant satellite on a dotted line around the planet. It wasn't a moon or other natural satellite, this looked more like a NASA product, complete with dishes and solar panels.

When I asked why they had included a picture of a satellite, they replied, "It's to show that there is no satellite around Venus."

I then asked why they had not drawn a picture of a unicorn, or a circus clown, or veteran character actor Robert Loggia to show that Venus does not have any of those things orbiting around it, but I think the irony was lost on them.

Arianna's group compared Jupiter's Great Red Spot to "a big zit on an ugly teenager's face." I'm guessing they got straight A's during the metaphor writing unit in Mrs. Bird's class.

Ja'Kendrick made the bold claim that scientists think there may be water on earth. Yeah, but not intelligent life, apparently.

In honor of our science theme, I made this week's Challenge Question – the last of the year! – all about the planets. It said, "Jupiter has 14 known moons and Saturn has 22. If we sent 13 probes to each moon, how many probes would be sent in all?"

Akasha's paper showed a drawing of three aliens holding a banner that read, "Welcome, earthlings!" – along with the correct answer and proper work, of course.

Chloe drew borders made of stars and planets around each of the major portions of her work.

Greyson's had a note on the back that read, "Actually, Mr. Woodson, scientists have discovered more than 60 moons around Saturn, so you are a little off. But I did your math problem anyway."

Sadly, Tracy Jane and Raina only added the moons, and even worse, Susana added Saturn's moons and the 13 probes. These kids clearly fell into a black hole.

Maybe the computation would have been easier if I had included Uranus in the problem.
Talk to you later,

The Trouble Space Telescope

Date: Thursday, June 4, 2015
To: Fred Bommerson
From: Jack Woodson
Subject: Papa don't teach

Hey buddy!

I'm typing quietly here, with only a desk lamp on, because little man is dozing in here with me. He's set up like a pampered king in his comfy little baby chair. For some reason, this kid cannot stand to be lying down on his back. Our fancy bassinet has been utterly worthless, at least when it comes to its intended purpose. On the other hand, it's been a fantastic tool for when we need Ben wide awake and screaming and crying. He does love sleeping on this inclined chair, though.

Jill and I discussed our summer schedule, and we decided that she will go to bed early and feed Ben in the mornings while I stay up late and feed him after midnight then sleep in the next morning. We may not be rich, but there are definite child raising benefits to having a two teacher household!

I'm so sorry I didn't save a math workbook for you. If you really need to practice your 4th grade computation skills, I can direct you to some great resources. I can also direct you to YouShouldNotBeAnEngineer.com.

Yesterday, we sent home the results of the STAAR (the extra A is for AAAAAAAARRRRRRRGGGGGGGGGHHHHHH!!!). We took the tests a little later than usual this year, and I wasn't sure we were going to learn how the kids did before the last day of school. But the results came in yesterday, and thankfully, most of my kids passed both tests.

It took just a smidge of my pride away when I learned the passing score for the math test was a 55 this year. But, as they say in the sporting world, a W is a W, so I'll accept Carmine passing with a 58, Susana passing with a 60, and Raina and Clara skirting the razor's edge right at 55.

Ja'Kendrick and Cesar were the only two who didn't pass the math test. They didn't pass the reading or writing tests either, but there were a couple of other kids who joined them there. I'm disappointed but not surprised in the least. If I could combine their scores, then, well, they still wouldn't have passed.

Today was a nice easy day, with shortened class periods, so my lesson plans were quite simple – "Give each student one volume of the Encyclopedia Britannica and several sheets of notebook paper. Students will copy each page verbatim, including illustrations."

I'm kidding, of course. We played games, signed autographs, and had pizza brought in after lunch. I gave the kids a memory book which had pages for collecting signatures and comments, so the kids didn't have to write on their nice uniform shirts. The kids wrote notes like, "Have a great summer!" and, "I'll miss you!" and, "Vote Andres for Mayor of Pizza Town!"

The memory books also had a couple of pages with prompts for favorite things, such as favorite book, favorite movie, etc. I enjoyed walking around and looking over the kids' shoulders to read what they were writing as their favorites. Whether or not they were trying to suck up to me, I did like seeing "Favorite subject – math" several times. Still, nothing could beat Rodrigo's "Favorite subject – spelung."

One category was "Favorite thing that happened this year." Kirstie wrote, "All of the things that we did, and lots of school." I was afraid for a moment she was going to be vague. Ja'Kendrick filled in his favorite moment with "Recess."

I bit my tongue and kept the sarcastic comments to myself whenever I heard Tommy say, "I wish we had one more day of school!" or, "I wish school lasted all year long!"

Dodd kept asking when the party would be.

"This IS the party, Dodd! Enjoy it!"

A few kids made comic books, and I was featured in two of them. In one, I was King Pig fighting the Angry Birds. In another, titled "Three Heroes Versus the Slob," I was – well, not one of the heroes.

A few of the girls brought out a deck of cards, and they called me over to ask if I wanted to join them in a game of Bluff. I asked them to explain the rules of the game. As they told me, I recognized the rules and wryly told the girls, "Oh, OK. I know this game under a different name."

Akasha laughed shyly and said, "Yeah, we know that name too, but we have to use the clean one."

"Good idea," I told them. I played a few hands with them, then Misaki came over and asked if she could play. The girls started to explain the rules to her, and she interrupted with, "Oh yeah! I know how to play BS!"

At least she didn't use the full name.

I received several cards and notes today. Veena seemed genuinely sad to be leaving, and she gave Mrs. Bird and me thank you cards. Mine said, "You were the best teacher ever! You always push me to my best and you make me enjoy math. I will never forget you and your sense of humour."

Notice the British spelling in that last word? Veena always was sophisticated that way.

And speaking of sophisticated, Misaki gave me a piece of paper torn out from her spiral notebook where she had written, "I will miss you," and drawn what appeared to be a crying cow's head. I shall cherish it always.

Carmine gave me a card that said, "You're the only teacher who didn't give up on me this year."

I thought that was a nice sentiment, but I did mention to him that none of his other teachers ever gave up on him either. He replied, "I know, but I mean you're the MATH teacher who didn't give up on me."

In your FACE, Neil deGrasse Tyson and other YouTube luminaries!

Raina gave me a note that said, "I still like you from my bottom of my heart to the top of my head. Just like a piece of cake, just a big cake!"

This is odd as far as similes go, but Raina's intent seemed genuine.

As the school buses pulled away for the last time in the 2014-2015 school year, all the teachers started to do the robot dance out on the sidewalk, focusing primarily on the "broken arm." And when I say all the teachers, I mean just me, while the others gave me strange looks.

I had my end of year checklist completed, so I didn't linger long after the kids left. I turned out the lights in my classroom, turned in my key, thumbed my nose at Crazy Voyeur Lady, and zoomed out of there. Another great year is in the books, and now comes three months of learning how to be a daddy! I've already got my "Father of the Month" parking spot staked out (center cushion of the living room couch), and I'm ready for some one-on-one time. I'm expecting to have Ben up to at least a 1st grade reading level with a working knowledge of all 2- and 3-dimensional shapes by the time August rolls around. Or, if that proves impossible, he'll at least know the difference between Green Arrow and Green Lantern. See you later,

Justin Time

Made in the USA
Coppell, TX
12 February 2023